GET READY FOR BATTLE

RUTH PRAWER JHABVALA

A FIRESIDE BOOK
Published by Simon & Schuster Inc.
NEW YORK • LONDON • TORONTO • SYDNEY • TOKYO

Fireside
Simon & Schuster Building
Rockefeller Center
1230 Avenue of the Americas
New York, New York 10020

Copyright © 1962 by Ruth Prawer Jhabvala
All rights reserved
including the right of reproduction
in whole or in part in any form.
First Fireside Edition, 1989
Published by arrangement with the author.
FIRESIDE and colophon are registered trademarks of
Simon & Schuster Inc.
Manufactured in the United States of America

1   3   5   7   9   10   8   6   4   2   Pbk.

Library of Congress Cataloging in Publication Data

Jhabvala, Ruth Prawer, 1927–
Get ready for battle/Ruth Prawer Jhabvala.—1st Fireside ed.
p.   cm.
"A Fireside book."
I. Title.
PR9499.3.J5G4   1989   89-1569
823—dc19   CIP

ISBN 0-671-68340-3 Pbk.

For
C.S.H.J.
again

Treating alike pleasure and pain, gain and loss, victory and defeat, then get ready for battle.

1

Everyone knew the party was for someone, but no one quite knew for whom. Almost everyone in the room could have been useful to Gulzari Lal, so it was difficult to pick on anyone in particular. As a matter of fact, it was for a very insignificant guest indeed – for a municipal engineer who had some time in the future to pass some rather tricky plans of Gulzari Lal's; he stood around in his best suit and was dazzled by the superior company. To dazzle him had been exactly Gulzari Lal's purpose, and now that it was accomplished he had lost sight of it and was enjoying the party for itself. He always enjoyed his own parties: he liked assembling influential people in his house and he liked being a host and seeing people grow satisfied and expansive on his drinks and his food.

And no one in the room was more unmistakably the host than Gulzari Lal. A tall man, festive in white leggings and a long white coat buttoned up to the neck, he stood beaming on his guests and, smiling from beneath his moustache, he urged them with gentle insistence, a glass always in his own hand, to drink more of the whisky which cost him Rs 65 a bottle. He made the most of whatever conversation there was, which was sometimes difficult for the guests did not, on the whole, have much to say to one another.

However, no one was bored, for almost everyone in the room could be of use to someone else and this was stimulating. There was a Commissioner who was stimulating to a number of fairly high-ranking civil servants, who were in their turn stimulating to a number of middle-ranking civil servants, and so on, down to the municipal engineer for whom the party was made by the presence of the vice-chairman of his Board. An overall stimulus was provided by a Maharaja, an imposing figure who, now that his kingdom and a good deal of his income were gone, was taking an interest in business affairs; he was really of no importance to anyone, but his presence made everyone feel they had got into good company and had come a long way from where they had started.

These being modern times, many people had brought their wives, who sat in a semicircle at one end of the room and sipped pineapple juice. Most of them were strangers to one another, but even those who had met before did not feel easy enough, in these overwhelmingly social circumstances, to make any kind of conversation. So they only sat, stiff in their best saris and jewellery, and patiently waited for their husbands to say it was time to go home. They accepted their boredom without resentment, for they understood it comprised the social life which, as modern women, it was their duty to take part in. Only one of their number had joined the throng of men at the other end of the room: an English girl who, after desperately trying to engage the ladies around her in lively small-talk and as desperately failing, had used the prerogative of her earlier and more ingrained emancipation to join her father, who was Gulzari Lal's bank manager. The two of them provided the European element which gave a party like this a little spice and variety; they vaguely realized their special position and tried to live up to it by being lively and interested. The girl exchanged a few words with the Maharaja, which thrilled her, and then she was taken up by Gulzari Lal's son Vishnu, whom she entertained with her impressions of India while he looked down at her with much charm and gallantry and wondered to himself at her flat-chestedness.

Perhaps the best time of all was being had by Kusum, Gulzari Lal's mistress, who was supervising the preparation of the dinner. She bullied the servants with exuberance, from time to time snatching the cooking-spoon from the cook's hand and giving an energetic stir herself in one of the vast stainless-steel vessels. Then she flitted to the dining-room, where under her instructions dozens of plates and damask napkins were piled up at one end of the long Burma-teak table and all the silver cutlery, superbly polished for the occasion, was laid out in splendid array for the buffet dinner which was to follow. The widow of a not very well-to-do army officer, Kusum loved to see things done in style and she was proud of Gulzari Lal because he could so do them. She peeped into the drawing-room and caught a glimpse of him, tall and distinguished in elegant white among his guests, and though she had two grown-up married daughters and a grandson, she felt herself as full of passionate love as any young wife. And like a young wife, she swished in silk between kitchen and dining-room, spry, alert, goading and exhorting the servants to their highest efforts. She arranged the dishes with her own hands, placing silver foil on the meat preparations and gold on the vegetarian ones, smiling to herself, her pretty little mouth pursed with pleasure.

When the party was over, Gulzari Lal felt happy and fulfilled but very tired. He was not as young as he had been. He lay, with a sigh of satisfaction, on his bed while Kusum took off his shoes and soothingly

8

pressed his feet. But if he was tired, she was not, and she had yet to hear all about the party. So, after making sufficient cooing noises at his fatigue, she began to ask him questions. Had everyone liked the food? And the municipal engineer, had he been sufficiently impressed? And the Maharaja (such a charming man)? How many bottles of whisky had been drunk? What had the Commissioner said to the Deputy Secretary? Gulzari Lal answered at first in monosyllables and then merely in grunts; she found this extremely unsatisfactory and tickled the soles of his feet to make him more responsive. He drew them away indignantly: 'Please,' he said, 'I am tired.'

'And I? Who has been cooking all day and making the arrangements?'

'The food was excellent,' he murmured. 'Everyone said so.'

'At least you can let me hear about the party,' she said, in no way mollified, 'since I was too busy looking after the comfort of your guests to be there.'

He yawned, in real tiredness but with some degree of ostentation too. 'I think I am falling asleep.'

'I am going home,' she said in a threatening tone.

'Tell the driver to take the car out,' he said thickly, as one already the other side of sleep. But it did not do him any good. She began to shout, stamping her foot and bringing up all her grievances. It ended in tears, and he had to soothe her and promise her all sorts of things without actually committing himself: which was a difficult enough feat at any time, even when he was not as tired as he was now.

Kusum did not live in the house but she came almost every day and was in full charge of the household. This in spite of the fact that, five years ago, Gulzari Lal had married off his son Vishnu and there was now a daughter-in-law who had every right to dispute Kusum's position. But Mala made no attempt to do so, which was fortunate for everyone. She might in any case have been no match for Kusum; and she did not try to be. She liked Kusum and missed her when she was not there.

For Mala was lonely in the house. She sat all day in a little room off the main drawing-room, a cool little room with nothing in it but a few chairs, a rug, a plaster bust of Byron bought at an auction, a stag's head on the wall and a picture entitled 'Houseboat in Kashmir'. Mala sat there and did needlework. She did exquisite needlework: it was the only thing the nuns in the convent she had attended had succeeded in teaching her to any real degree of proficiency. She often sighed and sometimes a tear ran down and stained her fine work. She was not happy in Delhi. Her family, though originally from the Punjab, had settled in Bombay and she had grown up there; now she missed everyone – her grandmother and her mother and father and brothers and aunts – and the sea and all the places she was used to. She also missed her girl friends, with whom she had had such pleasant times. They had been lively Maharasthian and Gujerati girls, whose high spirits had swept her along and who had got used to her and to her slow laughter and slow heavy ways. She had not succeeded in making any friends in Delhi. True, she had a little daughter now to whom she was passionately attached; but Pritti was not yet old enough to be very satisfactory company and she made a lot of noise which gave Mala headaches. So there was only Kusum.

But Kusum had lately curtailed her visits to the house. It was a deliberate change of tactics. She wanted to bring Gulzari Lal to a certain point and saw that she could not do so without some degree of coercion. She made an attempt to explain herself to Mala and to Vishnu, both of whom she needed on her side. They were all three having tea in the drawing-room, and Mala and Vishnu were quarrelling.

'Why don't you want to go to Bombay?' Mala said, and Vishnu shrugged: 'Because I don't want.'

'And I? I am nothing! When you know how much I want to go.'

'Children!' said Kusum. 'Why do you quarrel and make life bitter? You are such a fortunate young couple, you have one another and our darling Pritti and you live here in this beautiful home' – she indicated the drawing-room (the huge settees and armchairs covered in black and gold brocade, the waist-high vases of a vaguely Japanese character, the chandelier, the vast brass Buddha which had been sold to Gulzari Lal as a valuable antique). 'Not everyone,' she said, 'is as fortunate as you are. There are others for whom there is no home like this, nor any loving heart.' She looked tearful and drew her handkerchief out of her handbag.

'When we were first married,' Mala told Vishnu, 'you promised, as soon as you could, you said, you would take me to live in – '

'When my dear husband was still with us, then it was different for me, then I still had my place in the world. And now – no, sometimes when I wake in the nights I cry in my bed, all by myself.' She dabbed her handkerchief daintily against her eyes and nose. 'My darling daughters are both married, God be thanked, and they don't need me any more. Of course, they are always first with me . . . But your father too has a place in my heart.'

10

Vishnu moved a little nervously in his chair – he knew about his father and Kusum, everybody knew, but nobody had ever spoken to him about it openly like that; and it did not seem a thing to talk openly about, not to someone his age about someone theirs.

Kusum realized his embarrassment so she said, simply and with feeling: 'I am your mother, Vishnu, and you are my son, I can say, no, it is my duty to say everything before you.' But then she got a bad conscience which made her add: 'Of course, you have your own mother also, I know no one can take the place of the real mother.'

'What real mother?' asked Mala pointedly, which made Vishnu get angry, as perhaps it was meant to do.

Kusum said hastily: 'No one understands your mother's heart better than I do.' She spoke with conviction though she had never met Sarla Devi, who now lived with her brother and did not come to Gulzari Lal's house. 'But perhaps it is better as it is. Dear children, we are all modern now, we have a Hindu Code Bill, we have divorce,' and here she stopped, for this was what she had in mind.

Vishnu understood perfectly, but was too embarrassed to take her up and continue the discussion as she wanted.

'Yes,' Mala said, 'we have divorce,' and she gave a loaded look at Vishnu.

'Any time,' he said. 'I am ready.'

'No, no!' cried Kusum, putting her plump little hands over her ears. 'Two beautiful young people who love one another so much! You must not even think like this, something evil will happen. No, divorce is only when people don't live together any more, and perhaps one of them has found someone else to be happy with ... I am old now, perhaps it is no longer fitting to speak of happiness. It is only that your father needs me so and he doesn't understand that my position here is very bad.'

It was in an effort to make him understand that Kusum stayed away from the house. She wanted to be missed and she was; and not only by Gulzari Lal. Every day Mala telephoned her: 'Please come,' she said always. But Kusum, while protesting her love over the telephone for Mala and Pritti and Vishnu and, yes, for all of them, nevertheless stayed away.

It was a whole week before she came again. And then the first thing she did was get after the servants, check the stores, look at accounts, discover door-knobs that had not been sufficiently polished and stains on the marble floors; and when she had roundly abused everyone and sent them scuttling off in all directions to devote themselves vigorously to their allotted tasks, then still red from her exertions and glowing with achievement, she sat on the veranda and rocked herself to and fro in Gulzari Lal's rocking-chair.

'Why do you stay away?' Mala asked her plaintively.

'Sweetheart, you know I want to be with you, but please understand my position – '

'But you have been here for so many years, and nobody has ever said anything about your position!'

'It is quite different now,' Kusum said; and then she fished for news about Gulzari Lal. 'Does he talk about me? Does he miss me? Who looks after his clothes? Does anyone give him massage?' She asked questions rapidly, but Mala was slow in response; Kusum, impatient, asked more questions and then cried: 'But say something, why don't you answer! Oh,' she said, leaning back in her rocking-chair when Mala hesitated for an answer: 'I see he never talks about me, he never thinks of me even – '

Mala began to protest, but Kusum was by this time rapidly rocking to and fro in agitation and talking apparently to herself: 'Why did I come here? He doesn't care for me, when I am not here he doesn't think of me – '

'If you don't come,' Mala interrupted her with some spirit, 'then I too shall go away.'

Kusum was touched. She affectionately pressed Mala's hand and said: 'Don't talk like that, child. You belong here, with Vishnu, you are the daughter of the house. It is different for me.' She sighed deeply. 'I have no place here.'

'If you have no place, then who has? His mother perhaps?' Mala demanded scornfully.

'She is still the wife,' Kusum pointed out with meek good grace.

'She has never cared for anyone, only herself.'

'She is a very clever woman, so I have heard from all sides,' Kusum offered as a stimulus.

'Thank you, such clever women it is nice to read about in the newspapers, but when they are your mother or your wife, it is different. Ask Papa what he thinks – '

'He doesn't like to speak about her much.' She had often tried to draw Gulzari Lal out on the subject of his wife; but though he was

ready to confide in her – or at least be drawn out – about most subjects, he was tantalizingly reticent about this one.

'Because he doesn't like to think about her – '

'Sh!'

'What?'

'Here he is.'

'I don't hear anything,' Mala said, and indeed it was some time before she did. Gulzari Lal was calling to the servant to help him change into his home-clothes. By that time Kusum had seized her handbag, gathered her sari about her and skipped out into the garden where she hid behind a neem-tree.

Mala was surprised. She followed Kusum into the garden but could not find her. Suddenly a hand came out from behind a tree and seized hers. 'Oh!' cried Mala, in fright.

'Did he ask for me?' Kusum urgently whispered.

'He is still in his room. How you frightened me.'

Kusum whispered: 'Perhaps it is better if I don't meet him now for a time.' She fondled Mala's hand and made her sit with her on a bench which stood by a little stone fountain. The fountain represented a nymph growing out of a lotus, but it was not playing now and there were a few dead leaves lying in its basin. 'You see, child, sometimes it is necessary to be a little bit strict with men. It is not good always to say yes to them, it spoils them. Sweetheart, men are like children in this, one can spoil them with too much kindness.'

'My husband is very much spoilt. It is nothing to him if I am happy or unhappy, and sometimes,' and Mala's mouth trembled a little, 'I am so unhappy.'

'Who is not unhappy sometimes,' Kusum said – a little absent-mindedly, for her senses were all strained towards the house for any sign of Gulzari Lal. 'Listen, child, if your father-in-law should ask after me, please don't tell him I was here.'

'If he would take me to live in Bombay, I could be much happier. All my family are there and my friends.'

'A woman's happiness can only be where her husband and children are. Where is Pritti?'

'Ayah has taken her for a walk.'

'How late she brings her.' But just then the ayah and the child entered through the rear gates. Pritti came running up to them and Kusum kissed her very tenderly: 'Our darling, our little joy, our pride.' To the ayah she said: 'Have you no sense in your head, bringing the child home at this hour.'

The ayah began to defend herself with spirit, but suddenly Kusum jumped up and next thing she was only a flutter of pale blue silk disappearing out of the rear gates. For there was Gulzari Lal, descending through the french windows and peering towards the group by the fountain.

'What happened to Auntie?' Pritti cried.

The ayah, still in the midst of her own defence, broke off to remark shrewdly: 'Some quarrel must have taken place between her and the Bara Sahib.'

Gulzari Lal had seen something – and maybe he had been meant to – disappear out of the rear gates. He cleared his throat and said: 'Was Mrs Mehra here?' for this was how he still referred to her, after all these years, before others.

'No,' Mala said, too promptly.

'Did you see how Auntie ran away?' cried Pritti. The ayah gave triumphant looks all round which made Gulzari Lal – curious and on edge though he was – realize it was not the moment to probe any further.

Gulzari Lal Properties (Private) Ltd was a prosperous concern. This was reflected in the expensive fittings of its Senior Director's office which was fully air-conditioned, with a pile carpet and concealed lighting of a slightly orange tint. There was a large, shiny desk with a presentation inkstand on it, and behind this sat Gulzari Lal. He had the Bombay file open before him; facing him sat Vishnu, whom he had called in from the adjoining Junior Director's office.

Gulzari Lal fluttered through the Bombay file and said: 'They have taken premises on Hornby Road.'

'Mehta can carry on very well without me.'

'But I want you there,' Gulzari Lal said. 'I want someone to build things up, the way I have built them here – ' He waved his hand, meaning this room and beyond that the other rooms, full of agents and draughtsmen and typists, and beyond that again all the properties and estates he controlled throughout the city and its outskirts. 'There are some very interesting possibilities. For instance, that fishing village Mehta wrote about – '

'I think I can be more useful here,' Vishnu lied. He did not feel useful at all and never had done.

'Of course,' Gulzari Lal said, 'you are very useful to me here. I shall miss you, the whole office will miss you.' He said this rather hastily, for fear he had offended Vishnu; he was always very tender of his son's feelings.

And Vishnu was equally tender of his father's feelings; so he too fenced: 'I don't think – forgive me – I can do any good there without you.'

'No, no, you must learn to stand on your own feet,' Gulzari Lal rallied him in a hearty voice.

Vishnu looked bashful; standing on his own feet was exactly what he wanted to do, but not for anything would he say so before his father.

'Remember you come from a race of sturdy warrior landowners who have always tilled their own soil and shot their own tigers, ha-ha.' But Vishnu had grown up in the city: maybe that was the trouble, the boy did not have that love of land, land and more land that he himself had. 'And your wife,' he said, 'wants to go.'

'She wants something every day.'

'It is important for a man's happiness that his wife also should be contented and happy.' But as soon as he had delivered himself of this maxim, Gulzari Lal realized that he was not quite the man to propound it. His own wife had been so little contented and happy that she had left his house; and last night his mistress, also apparently not contented and happy, had run away from him out of the rear gate . . . He sighed and looked worried, so that Vishnu felt sorry for him and would have liked to do something to please him.

But there was nothing he could do. He certainly had no intention of going to Bombay to the new branch of his father's business. Perhaps he should have welcomed the opportunity of being more or less on his own – but he knew he never would be on his own. Not only would his father be constantly corresponding, telephoning and taking flights to Bombay, but all the time Vishnu himself would be thinking of his father and what he would do in his place. It would not be any different from what it was now.

He left the office early – he left earlier and earlier nowadays, he got so bored – and drove around in his car for a while. He wondered whom he should go and see. He had many friends – his old college friends and others whom he had met at the club or at dinners or in the course of business – all of them, like himself, comfortably settled and socially acceptable young men. They were doing well in their father's or uncle's business, or – helped by their nice manners and their influential relatives – were making good progress in one of the professions; or they had entered Government service and were smoothly on their way to a Deputy Secretaryship. But Vishnu did not want to see any of these. He was tired of comfortable and prosperous people.

So he drove straight to Gautam's. Gautam was neither comfortable nor prosperous, but kept himself by giving a little private tuition here and there, by selling books which he strapped on the back of a borrowed bicycle and by living with whatever relative would put him up. At the moment he had installed himself with a patient elder cousin called Shankar, who was something not very high up in some Ministry

15

and lived in a small tumbledown house with damp rooms provided for him by the Government.

Gautam was out in the garden, sprawled in the overgrown grass, with one hand beating out a rhythm on a small drum. A girl with naked feet and ankle-bells was practising her dance steps: this was Sumi, Mrs Shankar's younger sister. Gautam kept saying: 'Not like this – ta-*ta*-ta, ta-*ta*-ta – like that!' Sumi shook back her plaits and started again. She was so thin, she was really no more than a child, with pathetic ankles and wrists. Vishnu sat next to Gautam on the grass, swaying his head and humming in time to drum and ringing ankle-bells.

'Sumi!' shrilled Mrs Shankar from within. Sumi danced her way into the house and Gautam stopped playing. 'Whenever I make her practise,' he grumbled, 'her sister calls her on some pretext.'

Mrs Shankar could be heard scolding Sumi inside, for idling away her time with idle Gautam and failing to help with the housework and bathing of children. Gautam sighed and said: 'You see, she is a very close-spirited sort of woman, she can think only of housework and money and all little things.'

'Most women are like that,' Vishnu said.

'Sumi isn't. But I am afraid her sister will make her so, she will take poor Sumi's spirit and make it small like her own with household cares.' He lay down flat on the grass, his arms behind his head. 'Of course, I know it is often difficult for people to keep their spirit free – for instance, they marry and they have children and then they have to look after the children and earn money to keep them. So they get all tangled in worldly things. It is wrong.'

Vishnu said yes, he knew it was wrong, and thought of himself and Mala and their car and their clothes and all their fine habits.

'To have nothing, to want nothing,' said Gautam, luxuriantly stretching his arms to the sky for he had nothing and, for the moment, wanted nothing, 'this is the ideal.' Vishnu thought how he too would like to want nothing, but how difficult it was for him because he had always been used to so much.

'How I admire your mother,' Gautam said suddenly. 'She has shaken off everything, all the things that due to her station in life had been piled on to her.' He got up and strolled over to a mulberry tree at the bottom of the garden and began to pick the fruits which hung down from its branches like fat worms. 'I am worried about Sumi,' he said. 'They will marry her and then she will become her sister.' He offered some mulberries to Vishnu from the palm of his hand: they were purple and ripe and melted sweetly in the mouth. 'I want her to become like your mother. Your mother is for me the ideal of all women.'

Vishnu began to pick mulberries on his own account, selecting, like Gautam, the fattest and ripest.

'Even though she was married to your father, yet she retained a pure spirit.' Vishnu was used to Gautam's free ways so, coming from him, he did not resent this open discussion of his parents; he listened with as much detachment as if it were two other people.

'You know my opinion of your father,' Gautam said cheerfully. 'He is to me the worst type of man, attached to money and money-making and existing not as a man but only through the things he possesses, like his car, his house, his mistress. Women and gold, as Sri Ramakrishna has said, these are the worst temptations in the life of man, and your father has not only tasted of them but has swallowed them whole. Don't take that one, it is too green.' They were already cloyed and sated with mulberries and their mouths and hands were stained purple with the juice, but they kept on picking them.

Suddenly Gautam said: 'I want to start a school – to teach, to guide little children, what better work can there be than that?'

'What about the theatrical troupe you were going to start?'

'I was on the wrong track.'

'How often you have been on the wrong track.'

'And you?' Gautam cried. 'From birth you have been on the one track your father put you on, the key has been turned and you run round and round.'

Vishnu shrugged and went on eating mulberries. In between he said: 'My father wants me to go to Bombay.'

'You leave your father and come with me. We will start a school, somewhere in some little town or village – it doesn't matter where, all we need is a little land and a tree and some children. We shall lead a very simple life. Perhaps there will be a river also and every day we shall take the children to bathe in it. And there will be fruit-trees in our garden and we shall grow vegetables and eat them – '

Just then Mrs Shankar appeared arms akimbo in the doorway: birds she had to guard against, she shouted, and children who knew no better, but now two grown men stood and ate the mulberries off her tree . . . Vishnu felt very much ashamed, he drew out his handkerchief and hastily wiped his stained mouth and hands. 'Sister,' said Gautam, calm and righteous, 'God has given them to be eaten.'

'I think it is better if I go,' Vishnu murmured. He felt very bad.

'There is no need to let yourself be put to flight by an ill-tempered woman,' Gautam said. She had now withdrawn into the house, from where she could be heard shouting about good-for-nothing cousins and their loafer friends.

Sumi came out and said: 'She is very angry.' She put her hand before her mouth and giggled. Gautam too began to laugh, and after a while Vishnu joined them. He no longer felt bad; on the contrary, it was rather delightful to be scolded for stealing mulberries.

Vishnu climbed up the stairs to his mother's room. She lived with her brother Brij Mohan in a crumbling old yellow house which stood in an acre of neglected land. The house belonged to Brij Mohan, but he had long since lost the means and the initiative to keep it up to any degree of respectability. Sarla Devi occupied a room on the roof which had a tiny shed of a bathroom attached; both room and bathroom had been a later addition and not quite in keeping with the rest of the house, but since the whole property was by now in an equal state of neglect, it no longer mattered.

Sarla Devi was busy reading in some fat old tome and all she said was: 'Why have you come today?'

Vishnu lay down on the low seat made of wooden boards and covered with a plain cloth and a bolster. He leant his head against the bolster and smoked a cigarette. The room had whitewashed walls and almost no furniture. There was a tin trunk in which Sarla Devi kept her belongings, and a tiny table with a plaster image and an incense-holder and a rosary on it. On the wall hung a picture of Sri Rama-krishna and the Holy Mother. Everything was very clean and there was a faint smell of soap and incense.

After a while he felt his mother looking at him over the top of her book, but he pretended not to notice.

'It is bad for you to smoke,' she said at last. She glowered at him: 'You do so many things that are bad for you.'

'I know,' he said, sliding down so that now only his head was supported by the bolster and he looked very much at his ease. He liked visiting his mother; he had always liked her company better than anyone else's.

'Your whole life,' she cried, shutting her fat book with a snap, 'is bad!' She was a skinny ageing woman, with her skin wrinkled and darkened by the sun and her short hair almost quite grey; but she still had her quick gestures, her passionate tones. 'You are becoming like your father. In everything you are like him. You care for nothing but money and clothes and business – oh, Vishnu, Vishnu!'

'It is terrible.'

'No, it is no laughing matter!' Looking at him, she began to laugh herself, but checked herself at once and was annoyed: 'For you everything nowadays is a joke. That is not the way to live.'

'You are like Gautam,' he said. 'He is always trying to lead me into a better, purer life.' He got up and strolled out on to the roof. From here he had a magnificent view of the tops of vast old trees and, quite near, of the river and its banks.

'Then I am thankful to Gautam,' she cried, coming out after him 'that there is someone else to try and open your eyes – '

He peered down into the neighbouring garden, where three girls sat shelling peas under a tree.

'Everything I tried to teach you, everything I showed you, you have forgotten.'

He did not contradict, but it was not true. He remembered very well, all the places she had taken him to when he was small and how he had hung on to her sari and had been happy. They had gone to political meetings and to religious ones, they had taken part in demonstrations, processions, hymn-singing and communal spinning. There had been mass meetings addressed by white-capped Congress leaders, and then the quiet, sweet evenings in some garden where people sat cross-legged on the ground and a swami in an orange robe spoke of holy matters.

'Now you follow only your father's ways, and your wife's'; and when she mentioned Mala, she frowned and looked displeased.

Vishnu smiled: 'I think she doesn't like you very much either.' He looked down at the three girls shelling peas, trying to make out which of them was the prettiest.

'Of course not,' Sarla Devi said scornfully. 'I can't sit and talk with her about her saris and her embroidery.' But a moment later she was clutching his arm: 'No, no, forgive me, it is wrong to speak of her like that.'

He strolled up and down the roof, which was pocked with chimney-pots and bathroom pipes. Kites glided spread out and slow motion against the hot blue sky, crows cawed quite close in the tops of the trees and the Jumna was dry and grey like a desert of sand.

'But it is your fault,' she said, repentant no longer. 'You have just let her live the life she is used to and never shown her that there is anything else.'

'You could make it look so nice up here – you could grow creepers to hide the pipes, and there could be garden chairs and flower-pots – '

'Leave me alone! That is all you can think of, how to make things look nice – garden chairs and flower-pots!'

'Then I could sit here and be happy and look down at your neighbours' daughters.'

'No, I won't be angry. You can't make me angry.' She spun round and walked with a quick swagger, a toss of the head, back into her room. By the time he joined her she was already sitting on the floor with her legs crossed and the large book resting on them, reading with furious concentration.

'Nobody is satisfied with me,' Vishnu said in mock self-pity. She never looked up. 'Papa is not satisfied either. He wants me to go away to Bombay.' She ostentatiously turned a page. 'And Gautam wants me to start a school with him. And you – '

'I don't want anything from you. Nothing, nothing.'

'Is he up there?' cried a voice from below.

Sarla Devi gave a sound of exasperation: 'He must have seen your car.'

'I parked it round the corner.' He always did this and then he came climbing stealthily up to the roof, so that his uncle would not see him.

'I thought,' said Brij Mohan, wheezing up the stairs, 'I saw him standing up there – ' He arrived at the top and saw Vishnu: 'There he is!' he cried joyfully.

He embraced Vishnu, clapped him on the back and on the chest, held him at arm's length to look at him: he always loved seeing his nephew, it made his own youth come back again.

'So, you are having a fine time, hm?' he said; and he chucked him under the chin and laughed. 'Don't be shy with me, son, there is nothing new you can tell me, I know it all!'

It was true, he had, in his day, had a fine time. The son of rich landowners, he had been abroad for a few years, had travelled in Europe on a generous allowance and returned home with a very fine English accent and a trunkful of handsome suits. He professed great admiration for western culture but had succumbed, after a while, back again to the pleasures of eastern culture, for which he had a more deeply ingrained taste. He drank his whisky not sitting up like an English gentleman but lying down like an Indian one, he chewed betel-leaf, cried when he heard a beautiful poem and had a predilection for the company of dancing girls. He had been married once, but had soon tired of his wife and sent her back to her parents.

'Tell me of your conquests, son,' he said with a big wink.

'Mama says I must conquer myself,' Vishnu said. Though he tried to sound jovial, he was not really easy. He could never fall into the right tone of youth and gaiety that his uncle expected of him.

'Don't listen to your mother!' Brij Mohan cried, stretching out his arm in her direction and shaking his hand at the end of it. 'She is mad, quite mad, everybody knows it. Come down with me, son, we will have a good time.' He bent forward and whispered in a loud whisper: 'Tara is down there with me.' Tara was a plump young dancing girl who frequently came to visit him.

'I hope you pay her properly,' Sarla Devi said. 'The poor girl doesn't come here for her pleasure.'

'Listen to her! Madam Social Service, her heart is always with the oppressed. Your mother is a wonderful woman, Vishnu: the sufferings of the whole world she makes her own.'

'If you have nothing more to say, then please go,' Sarla Devi told him. 'I wish to speak with my son.'

'Why do you come here?' Brij Mohan asked Vishnu. 'All she will do is to try and improve you and tell you what a bad life you are leading.'

This was too near the truth for Sarla Devi not to get angry. Vishnu said quickly: 'He is only joking.'

'I am always joking,' Brij Mohan said. 'My whole life is a joke.'

'Now he will begin to feel sorry for himself,' Sarla Devi said, 'and tell us how sad his life is.'

'Sad!' cried Brij Mohan. 'How is it sad? I am still a man and can enjoy a man's pleasures.' He bulged out his chest and tried to look proud, but the effect was ruined by the onset of a cough. 'Just wait,' he said with difficulty and before his cough had properly finished, 'till I get my full compensation, then you will see what sort of a life I am still capable of.' He had had some measure of official compensation for his properties lost through Partition, but he still hoped for more. It was a futile hope, as he well knew, but it did him good to indulge in it. 'Scoundrels,' he said, 'I will teach them yet who they are dealing with, I am not so easy to fool.'

Sarla Devi laughed out loud: 'The milkman, the washer-woman, your servant – who cannot fool you?'

'Because I am not higgling-niggling' – and he rubbed the fingers of one hand together to demonstrate the mean miserliness he himself eschewed – 'that doesn't mean I am fooled. I think in lakhs,' he cried, 'in crores of rupees, not in your one-two anna pieces!'

Sarla Devi said: 'Will you go now?'

He stroked Vishnu's smooth, olive cheek: 'When I am with this boy, I don't know how it is with me – I am young again, my blood wells up, I am happy, I want to laugh.' And he did laugh. Vishnu was embarrassed, he tried to turn away, but suddenly Brij Mohan came a step closer still and he said urgently: 'Don't ever listen to your mother, son. You see what she has made of her life, what a sad wreck she is' – he pointed at her – 'look, just look at her – '

'Enough now!' cried Sarla Devi, but she was half laughing.

'With her politics, her religion, her social work – what has it brought her? But look at your father now: there is a man. Yes, yes, I am going!' he cried, backing towards the door as Sarla Devi jumped up and stood with her hands on her hips. From out on the roof he called: 'Always take your father for example! Don't look at me, don't look at that mother of yours! Only follow on your father's golden road!'

Gulzari Lal had been used to finding Kusum when he came home in the evenings, and it was hard for him to have to do without her. For eight years now she had been always there: she would have his bath ready for him, serve him with drinks, massage his legs; and at the same time she entertained him with accounts of all she had been doing during the day, whom she had seen and what gossip she had heard. She was always lively and entertaining. Now there was only Mala, sitting with her sewing. He was fond of Mala, but she lacked that womanly sparkle he felt he needed after a day at the office.

He perfectly understood the purpose and meaning of Kusum's new tactics. He had, as it happened, no objection at all to marrying her – on the contrary, he would have welcomed this guarantee of having her always with him. But what he did object to was getting a divorce from Sarla Devi: that seemed to him a step definitely unsuitable for someone in his position in life and one that would undermine his status in circles where he wished to appear beyond reproach.

But he missed her terribly. He wandered from room to room and through his garden, tried to make conversation with Mala, played with Pritti: but nothing satisfied. Finally he had his car taken out and let himself be driven to his club, where he sat in the bar and had several drinks. He met acquaintances – prosperous businessmen like himself, with a taste for westernized good living – and spent what seemed like a pleasant social evening, but which only left him, when it was over, with a greater sense of desolation.

One evening, half-way to the club, he told the driver to change direction. They drove straight to Kusum's house. She lived in one of the new colonies, in a tiny downstairs flat which she had made very attractive with window-boxes and a scarlet-painted door. Her little sitting-room was hung with crisp flowered curtains and all the chairs and footstools were in dust-covers of the same material, ending in ruffled fringes. There were flowers in pretty vases and a fruit-bowl filled with mangoes and oranges and everywhere little painted toys, gay gods and peacocks and yellow tigers. She had also surrounded herself with all her family in photographs. In the place of honour over the mantelpiece hung the late Major Mehra, dignified in full uniform; her two daughters in various stages of growth were distributed over window-sills and occasional tables, and a charming picture of her grandson, fat and naked on a tiger-skin, hung above the flowered sofa.

Reclining on this sofa was Kusum herself, plump and powdered and in a crisp white sari with a design of red cherries on it. She greeted him with a pout and a plaintive 'I am not well.'

He at once looked concerned and placed his hand on what proved to be a perfectly cool forehead. She pushed his hand away, saying weakly: 'Please don't touch me, I am too unwell.'

'What is the matter?' But he had to say it several times, in ever more pleading tones, before she would answer.

At last she said: 'What can be the matter? I am an old woman, a widow, people like me no longer have the right to have anything the matter with them.'

He began to protest, but she would not heed him. 'In my prayers today I asked the Mother to show me the way. Should I go, Mother, I asked, to some hut on the banks of the Ganges and give over the little life I have left to Your worship? Why are you laughing?' she sharply asked Gulzari Lal, who at once looked very sober and innocent. Nevertheless she relapsed into a dignified silence, which she ultimately broke to say: 'Please don't have your car parked outside my house. It creates a very bad impression.'

He forebore to mention that she had not previously objected to his car, and indeed frequently called for it to take her to and fro.

'A woman in my position must live modestly and quietly. I am sorry I cannot offer you tea, there is no milk.'

'Come home, we will drink tea there.'

Suddenly she sat up on the sofa and, all indisposition shaken off, was very energetic. 'I am not entering your house again. I know now it was wrong for me to come to you so often, it will make people think ill of me.'

'Chuchu,' he said pleadingly using their mutual pet-name for one another and laying his hand in her lap.

'No, please don't try to change me, my mind is quite firm.'

'My little blossom,' he whispered and leant forward till his moustache tickled her ear.

'All is finished. I am a mother of grown-up married daughters, a grandmother even – '

'And I a grandfather,' he murmured into her ear. She began to giggle: 'Grandfather,' she giggled, and 'Grandmother,' he replied, and they laughed together and she let him be affectionate with her.

It seemed there was milk after all, and soon they were having tea, sitting lovingly side by side. She had her shoes off and rested her feet on his while he rocked them playfully up and down. He was relaxed and content. She gave him her news, listened with sympathy to his; tickled his palm, made him laugh; and then with a look at his glowing face said in a sweet low voice: 'But, really, my life must be different from now on.'

'A queen's life,' he said, spreading his arms.

'Please speak seriously.' She took her feet off his, and was prim and withdrawn, her hands in her lap. 'I think I will go and live with one of my darlings, my sons-in-law are always saying Mama, why won't you come and stay with us?'

'Chuchu, why can't we – '

'No, we can't. What do you think of me, what sort of woman do you take me for?'

He drank the last of his tea, all contentment gone.

'Why can't you take divorce!' she suddenly shouted. She jumped up and began to pace up and down the room, her stiffly starched sari rustling, her bangles furiously jingling. 'My God, all the world is taking divorce, but he – oh no' – and she swayed her head pompously – 'his position will be very bad, think of what people will say of him. And what they will say of *me*,' she cried 'that is of no importance, *my* position, what does that matter – '

'Sh,' he said, nervously looking round to where the servant was already standing in the doorway, with a shovelful of coal and an interested expression.

'Let everybody hear! Let everybody hear how you treat me, let them know what advantage you take of a Major's widow.' She halted before her husband's picture and began to stroke it. 'Ah, with what honour he used to treat me, what love, what respect, what care. He was a real gentleman. And that one' – her eyes blazed as she swung round to him. 'What am I to you? A moment's pleasure, a two-anna toy to be played with and broken and thrown aside.'

Gulzari Lal had jumped up and he bellowed like a bull: 'You insult me!'

'I insult you!' she repeated derisively.

'Everything is finished!'

'Finished!' she cried triumphantly.

24

His head swollen with rage, he made for the door. 'Bibiji,' said the servant anxiously, 'he is going.'

'Let him go,' she said, proudly watching with her arms folded over her bosom.

The scarlet front-door banged. Kusum ran to the window, then said to the servant. 'Quick, tell him I am calling.'

The servant ran. She watched from the window and saw Gulzari Lal, already with one leg in the car, reluctantly withdraw this leg and return to the house. She darted to the sofa and lay down with her eyes shut. Even when she knew he was standing before her, she did not open them.

'What do you want?' he said.

Then she turned her head slowly towards him and he saw there were tears running down her nose. 'Forgive me,' she said in a broken voice.

He said: 'It is all finished.'

She was up and then down at his feet, incredibly agile. 'Forgive me,' she said, clutching them.

He tried to raise her. 'Kusum,' he said, 'get up. Get up, Kusum.'

'Say you forgive me,' she said, beating her forehead on his toes.

He sat down on the floor with her and stroked her hair and her tear-wet face. He was touched but all the same he could not help feeling somewhat undignified. She rested her head on his chest and said: 'I am like this only for love of you, for love only.'

Gautam arrived with Sumi early in the morning when only Gulzari Lal was up, pacing slowly in his garden and inspecting his trees. There was something regal about Gulzari Lal in his own house. Tall, stately, dressed in white leggings with a loose knee-length white shirt over them, he moved with the grace and command of a hereditary over-lord. Gulzari Lal had come to the city as a young man to set up in business and make his own way: but he still retained the manners of his forefathers, who had lived stately lives in large country houses and dispensed charity and justice to their villages.

So it was with an inbred courtesy, a dignity and sweet con-descension that he welcomed Gautam and Sumi, though they were obviously of no importance and indeed he could not quite remember who they were. Since Vishnu was not up yet – he was, as a matter of fact, having a quarrel with his wife in their room – Gautam settled down to have a talk with Gulzari Lal. He joined him in his pacing up and down the garden, while Sumi followed behind, looking right and left at the well-tended trees and lawns and flower-beds and back at the large white house with its verandas and pillars and porticos.

Gautam said: 'I came to speak very particularly with Vishnu. I have a scheme in which I wish him to join.'

When he heard the word scheme, Gulzari Lal was somewhat on his guard. People were always coming to him with schemes and they usually involved some disbursement of money on his part.

'Look, a fountain!' cried Sumi behind them. Gautam turned round to frown at her, but Gulzari Lal smiled the pleased smile of ownership and began to explain the mechanism of his fountain and how sorry he was that nowadays there was not enough water to make it play.

'Naturally,' Gautam said severely, 'when there are whole colonies with many families and only one water-tap, you cannot expect to play fountains in your garden.'

'Ah, perhaps you will join me for breakfast,' said Gulzari Lal, making determined strides towards the veranda where the servants stood ready to serve him. Gautam made no objection, so all three sat cross-legged on a rush-mat spread out on the veranda. Gulzari Lal had furnished his house in western style and had indeed largely adopted a western manner of life: but when he was alone, he still liked to sit on the floor and eat his food from little bowls with his fingers. And he still adhered to the breakfasts of his youth, to lentils and fried puris and hot pickles in little dishes.

Gautam said: 'I am starting a school, and Vishnu wishes to come in with me.'

Gulzari Lal nodded; he gave no indication that this was news to him but only that he was prepared to give it all possible consideration.

'Vishnu is not meant for business. I have seen for myself how it is corrupting him. He must have some creative work, such as I am offering him, and also he must give up all this' – he swept his hand towards the house, the garden, the servants – 'and take up a simple life.'

'He has always been used to this kind of life,' Gulzari Lal tendered respectfully, 'it may be difficult for him to change.'

'This is exactly why he must change,' Gautam said. 'He will sink into sloth and luxury if he carries on in this way and all higher life will be lost to him.'

Gulzari Lal pretended to be listening with serious interest. He could afford to be tolerant: he had lived longer in the world than Gautam and had learnt that, in spite of fine words, the end, the goal of life, towards which all men strove, was to be rich and comfortable.

'I am offering him a chance to escape,' Gautam said. 'Probably

26

you don't want him to escape, but you must consider what is best for him.

Sumi said maturely: 'Every father wants only what is best for his son.' Gulzari Lal smiled encouragingly in her direction: he was full of goodwill towards her too.

'We haven't come here,' said Gautam, 'to talk platitudes. I don't want to waste time on such things; I have a great aversion to wasting my time.'

So, as a matter of fact, had Gulzari Lal, but he forbore to mention that Gautam was wasting his. He had a busy morning in front of him, an interview with the Chief Commissioner, a new site to be looked at, a member of the electricity board to be treated to lunch. He looked at his watch and murmured: 'I am sorry he is keeping you waiting.'

'It is very bad to get up at such a late hour,' Gautam said.

But Vishnu was up and dressed and was being detained only by Mala, who sat on their bed brushing her hair with vicious strokes. 'You promised,' she accused him.

'But I must go and see my mother some time.'

'Why yesterday? When you had promised you would take me out – '

'We can go out some other evening.'

'And I sat and waited and waited.' The hand brushing her hair became slower, glided slowly down that dark expanse and then rested, holding the hairbrush; hopelessly in her lap, as she recalled how she had sat and waited.

'Has it done you physical harm?' Vishnu said, and she rose to it at once: 'Yes, I know – what do you care, if I sit here for ever, all alone with nothing to do and no one to speak with, what is it to you?'

'You have everything a woman can want.'

'I have nothing!' She flung the hairbrush from her and stood up and faced him, her bosom rising and her eyes burning. He liked to see her like that, with all her lethargy shaken off, strong, vital and angry; and so it gave him pleasure to provoke her further. He opened her wardrobe, indicated the saris stacked shelf upon shelf right up to the top. 'Nothing?' he said; and then he swept his hand over her dressing-table, where rows of scent-bottles and oils and creams and nail-lacquers and gold lipsticks stood splendidly mirrored; and he opened the drawers, tapped on her locked jewel-boxes: 'Nothing?'

'Don't touch my things!' she cried.

He laughed. 'But there is nothing to touch. You have nothing.'

She began to pull her saris out of the wardrobe; she flung them on the bed, the floor, wherever they happened to fall. 'Take them then, what do I care for such things, what good are they to me? I would rather be poorer than any sweeper woman than be the way I am here, with all these things! Is there any love to be got out of them, do they care what I feel, are they sweet to me like friends?'

Vishnu passed into his dressing-room where he stood in front of the mirror and absentmindedly stroked his chin. He could no longer play at being amused, he felt troubled and was beginning to get angry. Mala followed him, she leant in the doorway. 'For you it is easy,' she said. 'You have the office, you have your friends. You drive off in your car and do what you like, while I sit here only and wait for the day to be finished.'

'It is not my fault that you don't know what to do with your time. What do other women do? They don't sit on their husbands' heads – take me here, take me there, don't go here, don't go there' – he made a sound of disgust and swung away from the mirror, to find himself facing her as she leant there in the doorway, with her long hair still hanging loose and her angry eyes. 'You are living in modern times,' he cried at her, 'go and be modern!'

She shrugged contemptuously and went back into the bedroom, and over her shoulder she said at him: 'I am not modern. Such things must be left to your mother.'

'Yes,' he said, following her, 'there is a lot you could learn from my mother.'

'How to neglect my child and leave my husband?' He was behind her and looked at her splendid back, at the crumpled thin cotton sari clinging round her small waist and over her large hips. 'That is easy, that I can do tomorrow.' She tossed back her head and her heavy hair with it. 'I need only take a ticket to Bombay, my family will be very happy to see me home again.'

'Should I book it for you?' But then suddenly he began tc kick at the piles of saris she had thrown on the floor; he shouted: 'Why can't you leave me alone? Why must you start on me from early morning?'

Mala was never tuned to prompt reaction, so it took her some time to decide how to counter his sudden anger. And by then Vishnu – always the quicker of the two – was already out of the door and hurrying through the adjoining rooms and passages to join his father on the veranda. He knew he was safe out there: not for anything would Mala appeal in front of her father-in-law before she was bathed and properly dressed.

He was not pleased to see his visitors. He felt it was too early in the morning for Gautam. Besides, he began at once to wonder what

Gautam could have been saying to Gulzari Lal. He was sure it had not been tactful and it annoyed him to think of his father treated with anything but that same tact and courtesy which Vishnu himself always showed him.

Gulzari Lal noticed his son's cool reception of his guests, and to make up for it said at once with double heartiness: 'We have been having a very interesting discussion while waiting for you.'

'Gautam talked a lot,' said Sumi. She and Vishnu looked at one another and smiled; and at once Vishnu felt better pleased. He liked Sumi. There was something gay and free about her which was refreshing to him after his scene with brooding Mala.

'Yes, it has been very interesting,' Gulzari Lal said. He looked at his watch, for now that Vishnu had come, his own obligations were over and he could go to his office.

'I told him about our school,' Gautam said, when Gulzari Lal had gone. 'He seemed quite interested. Your father is an intelligent man: he will realize, if it is explained to him, that it is better for you to start something on your own than to remain in his office.'

Vishnu laughed wryly: 'I think he knows how much I am worth in his office.'

Mala had heard Gulzari Lal's car leave and now came in pursuit of Vishnu. She had in the meantime thought up one or two forceful things to say to him. But when she saw the visitors, she stopped short and looked startled. She was still wearing her crumpled night-sari and had been too engrossed in thoughts of what to say to Vishnu to have had time to braid the hair she had begun to brush. She stood there and lowered her eyes and put her arm up against her bosom as if to hide as much of herself as possible.

Gautam greeted her as if they were old friends; which they were not, for they had only met a few times before. She had not taken to him then; nor did she do so now, for Gautam – in his coarse homespun clothes and with his feet cracked and a little dirty from walking round the town in his wooden-soled sandals – was not the sort of person she was accustomed to see in the house. She had always mistrusted him: she did not know what sort of a life he led and suspected that he took Vishnu to strange places and among strange people. Nor was she reassured by Sumi, who looked as shabby and poor as Gautam. Mala had nothing against people being shabby and poor – on the contrary, she understood that it was necessary for most people to be so and she felt sorry for them – but she did not want them to come to the house and be friends with Vishnu.

These reflections made her greeting very cool; and she gave a covert look at Vishnu to say, first, why are they here, and second, there is still much I have to say to you.

It was a look Vishnu perfectly understood and it made him turn to Gautam with more cordiality than he had shown up till now: 'Come along to the office with me.'

'She insisted on coming here with me,' Gautam said, indicating Sumi, 'even though I told her she will be only in our way. So in the end I said all right, come. It is as well for women to go out more and see what sort of things go on in the world, it will prevent them from growing only into household shrews.'

'This is exactly my opinion,' Vishnu said, elaborately not looking at his wife.

'Yes yes, we know,' cried Sumi, 'you all have opinions what is good for us and what is not.' She turned to Mala: 'There is only one way, and that is never to listen to what they say, but do just what you like.' Mala smiled a little, and she began to soften towards Sumi who talked to her in such a friendly way.

Suddenly Sumi stepped close to her and drew her hand down Mala's long loose hair: 'How beautiful,' she said, wondering and admiring, like a child, like Pritti; and then she said: 'May I braid it for you?' and she lifted the heavy strands, quite reverently, and began to plait them. Mala flushed with pleasure. It was years since anyone had done anything so sweet and spontaneous to her – in fact, not since her Bombay days, when she had been unmarried and had had friends as lively and young as Sumi.

'Come on now,' Gautam said impatiently, 'we are going to Vishnu's office.'

'Wait,' said Sumi, ardently plaiting, her tongue protruding between her teeth. Mala glanced at her over her shoulder and then said shyly: 'Perhaps you would like to stay with me and let them go?'

Sumi stayed; she stayed all day. And it was the first day that Mala never once phoned Kusum.

After that Sumi and Mala were friends. Sumi came as often as she could – as often, that is, as her sister would let her – and spent the day. It was always the same: always a lot of eating and talking and dressing up in Mala's best saris and playing with Pritti, and sometimes Sumi sang and danced.

But mostly she talked; she had so much to say. She told Mala all about her family – her father was a Government official in Mathura, a gazetted officer, quite an important man in Mathura; but he did not draw a very high salary and he had six daughters for all of whom dowries had to be found. The three eldest had already been married off, and that left Sumi and her two younger sisters at home in Mathura. It was dull in Mathura, Sumi sighed, very dull. Her parents were old-fashioned, they would not let their daughters go out on their own and so there was nothing for them to do but sit in the house and wait to have a marriage arranged. A few months every year Sumi stayed with one of her married sisters, but that was not very exciting either; none of the sisters had been married too well, they were all poor and had a lot of children and expected Sumi to work hard in the house.

Yes, said Sumi, sighing and looking at herself as she stood in front of the mirror in Mala's bedroom, for she had just tried on one of Mala's saris (a peacock-blue with a heavy gold border) looking and admiring herself and sighing – yes, she said, she wished a marriage could be arranged for her soon; she was tired of living at home, tired of going from one sister to the other. She wanted a husband of her own and to live in his home and have children and be grown-up and do what she liked. But, of course, she said, turning round to look at the peacock-blue sari from behind, it was difficult to find a husband for a girl like herself whose parents could not afford much dowry; and she would just have to wait and try and be patient while her family did the best they could. Mala, lying on the bed, with her elbows propped up and her chin on her hand, looked at Sumi's insufficient little figure overwhelmed by her own splendid sari, and she too sighed and said that one's troubles did not stop with marriage but, on the contrary, might even be said to begin.

Vishnu came home earlier in the evenings, hoping to find Sumi. He joked with her and was happy and good-humoured; and she joked back, cocking her little head at him, while Mala watched them and was proud of them both, of her friend and of her husband. Though she was of a jealous temperament, it did not occur to her to be jealous of Sumi. She knew her husband's tastes, and poor little Sumi was hardly the girl to appeal to them.

There was, however, one person who was not happy with Mala's new friend, and that was Kusum. She missed Mala's usual daily telephone calls, her plaintive 'Auntie, please come.' Now it was Kusum who telephoned, asking: 'What are you doing, child?' To which Mala would reply, with shy pride: 'I have a friend with me.'

'A friend, child?'

'She is called Sumi.' And Mala turned round to smile at Sumi who, at the sound of the telephone ringing, had come hurrying to listen to the conversation.

Kusum did not like it. She was used to Mala having only herself as friend and she missed being missed. Besides, who knew who this Sumi might be, what scheming outsider with designs of insinuating herself into that family, which was so dear to Kusum? Mala, dear child, was inexperienced, and trusting; anyone could impose on her. One morning when she had telephoned and been again informed that Mala had her friend Sumi with her, Kusum decided to go and see for herself.

She arrived at the house in a warlike mood, and the first thing she did was raid the kitchen and inspect the stores and take the cook to account for spending too much; and after the cook, it was the turn of the other servants, so that a hush descended on the house and they all went about their duties with grave preoccupied faces. After that, she went in search of Mala and found her in her bedroom, with Sumi sitting in front of the dressing-table, trying on Mala's earrings.

Kusum was very displeased and she showed it. Mala said weakly: 'This is Sumi.'

'What are you doing?' Kusum asked in an ominous voice. Sumi turned round from the dressing-table, a heavy gold earring ending in a little bejewelled pagoda weighting down her ear and dangling incongruously against her pinched little face. A jewel-box stood by her elbow, its lid wide open and its treasures poured out over the dressing-table. Kusum went straight up to it, swept everything back in and then held out an imperious hand for the earring Sumi was wearing. Sumi hastily unhooked it. 'These things,' said Kusum, firmly closing and locking the jewel-box, 'should never be exposed in the open.'

'But Auntie,' Mala protested, 'who is there to see?'

'Any moment one of the servants might come in, and you know how their minds will work once they see these things of yours. And also,' she added darkly, 'one can never trust – ' She did not look at Sumi at all. 'Child,' she said to Mala, sitting down on the bed with her, 'you know very little of the world.'

Mala was uneasy. She wanted Kusum and Sumi to be friends, but did not know how to effect this. And Kusum continued to talk as if there were no Sumi there. 'Even in your own household you don't know how to manage. Sweetheart, the servants are *robbing* you.'

'As long as you are here, Auntie,' Mala murmured obsequiously.

'You know I can't be always here. And soon perhaps,' she sighed, 'I shall not be able to come at all any more.' She looked into the distance with sad eyes, and Mala said, 'Oh, Auntie,' as sorrowfully as seemed expected of her.

At this point Pritti followed by her ayah came home from her kindergarten and made at once for Sumi, who tugged at her pony-tail and tickled her under the arms and in the stomach with quick playful motions. Pritti squirmed and squealed with delight, but Kusum cried out 'Stop!' and then she said: 'It is harmful to tickle a child.'

Everyone looked put out.

'Come here, my little darling,' Kusum said to Pritti. She kissed her lovingly on the forehead and then looked into her face; she turned to the ayah: 'The child is looking pale. You are not giving her milk properly.' The ayah began to protest, but Kusum would brook no interruption. 'Nothing,' she said, getting up from the bed with majesty, 'nothing is done, not even a child's meals are attended to, unless one runs after these people day and night.' She swept out of the bedroom, holding Pritti by the hand, and everyone felt constrained to follow her.

Sumi whispered to Mala: 'Is she your mother-in-law?'

'No,' Mala whispered back, 'she is Mrs Mehra.'

'She behaves like a mother-in-law,' whispered Sumi and began to giggle. 'Sh,' Mala warned, but her mouth-corner twitched, and she felt torn between two affections.

Kusum stayed a long time that day, though Sumi found it expedient to go home early. So it happened that when Gulzari Lal came back from the office in the evening, he was greeted by the sight of Kusum sitting straight and stern in an armchair on the veranda and checking the laundry, while the washerman squatted on his haunches in front of her and scratched his head with a guilty air. Gulzari Lal was delighted: this was how life should be, and he hoped Kusum had decided that from now on it would again be so.

But though she followed him to his bedroom and helped him change into his home-clothes, her face and attitude remained stern. 'Things are not right in your house,' she told him.

'Of course they are not,' he said affectionately. 'As long as you are not here – ' He attempted to kiss her, lips pursed lovingly under his moustache, but was foiled.

'You need a woman in the house to see to everything.'

'Of course, this is exactly – '

'Poor Mala is a child in these matters. She misses a mother or mother-in-law. Remember she comes from a large family and is not used to being left alone.'

'She needs you. You must come every day.'

'It is all very well to say one must be modern and do away with the old joint-family system, but it is not so easy. Our girls are used to living in the joint-family and to have many people about them and an older woman to direct them. This is how things are done in our country. We cannot be modern only because it is written in the news-papers.'

'You are right,' Gulzari Lal cheerfully agreed.

'Lie down, I will give you massage.' She pressed his legs skilfully while he lay on his bed, with his head turned in her direction and a loving look in his eye; which, however, she refused to meet. 'Nat-urally, the child feels lonely.'

'Naturally.'

'And then she forms friendships and brings people into the house who are not perhaps the sort of people who should enter a house like this.'

Gulzari Lal shook his head and clicked his tongue.

'Of course, you know nothing of what goes on in your house – you are busy all day in your office, only work work, money money; what goes on in the home is nothing to you. Lie still, how can I give you massage properly if you don't lie still. And the servants run helter-skelter; no one takes care of what is to be done and what is not to be done and our darling little Pritti also is looking pale.'

'Pritti?' He raised himself in anxiety, but she pushed him back. 'I am surprised,' she said, 'you cannot see it with your own eyes. But men are always blind in these matters.'

'Of course,' he said playfully, 'that is why every man needs at least one woman.'

'If that is a joke – '

'No no,' he said.

'The state of affairs in your house is no joking matter. You need a woman here who knows how to manage a household. I am telling you for your good.'

'I know it,' he said humbly.

'Well, you will have to make your arrangements.' She stopped massaging and got up from where she had been kneeling on the floor. She threw a look at the magazines on his bedside table – *Men Only* and *Gentleman's Relish* – and gave them a contemptuous little push. 'At your age you should not be reading such things. You should be concentrating your thoughts only on the holy books. Tell your chauffeur to take me home.'

'Chuchu!'

But she would not be detained.

She had succeeded, at any rate, in leaving him thoughtful. He tried to revise his ideas about divorce. His objections to it had always been social not moral; he considered that legal divorce was still too new-fangled an idea to be introduced into a family such as his. To keep a mistress was different: it was an old-established custom and one that he had every right to follow. Kusum, however, had now become modern and decided that mistresses were no longer socially feasible and that remarried widows were. Perhaps she was right, he did not know; all he knew was that he missed her and needed her. He decided on an important – and, for him, difficult – step. He decided to go and see his wife.

He came at a wrong time. He was hardly surprised for it seemed to him that it had always been so, that whenever he had approached her, it had always been the wrong time. All through their married life, whenever he had wanted her, she had been busy with something else; she had many interests and none of them had ever included him.

Now she was busy talking with two men; their shoes – big, cracked, broken, laceless shoes – stood outside the door, and they sat on the floor of Sarla Devi's little room and were having an earnest discussion with her. If she was surprised to see her husband, she did not show it. She even made it seem as if she had been expecting him, by turning to her two visitors and saying: 'He may be able to help you.'

They greeted him, respectfully enough, but without getting up. 'They live in Bundi Busti,' Sarla Devi said. 'They have lived there for fifteen years, and now the municipality want to acquire that land and turn them away.'

Gulzari Lal contrived to look interested and concerned.

'You know the Commissioner,' Sarla Devi said, 'you know so many people, it is just in your line. You can help them.'

The two men looked at him with a very guarded hopefulness and as if they were aware that they could not count on much disinterested help from someone like Gulzari Lal. And indeed, Gulzari Lal, who was used to parrying attempts to interest him in alien causes, had already assumed a faraway thoughtful look. 'There are large-scale plans for development in that area,' he said cautiously and in a way which made it clear to the two men which side he was on.

But Sarla Devi cried: 'How can large-scale plans be made when there are people living there?' and she looked at her husband with angry eyes, as if it were he who was threatening Bundi Busti.

'It is a question of over-all development,' Gulzari Lal said in a pompous and off-hand voice which suggested that this was something she could not be expected to understand.

'Don't try and frighten me with big words! The issue is clear: people are living there and you cannot evict them.' The two men nodded; they were leaning forward eagerly and Gulzari Lal felt as if it was himself he had to defend.

'Alternative accommodation will probably be offered,' he said, stiff and official.

'Sahib,' cried the two men, 'how can we go and live where they want to put us? It is out in the jungle, and how are we to get to our work?'

Gulzari Lal wished this could be stopped and the two men got rid of. But, of course, if he told his wife that he had particular business with her, she would tell not them but him to come another time.

'As usual, these Government people are being quite unrealistic,' Sarla Devi said. 'They can think only in files, and in files it is easy to transfer a colony from one place to another.'

To escape any further involvement, Gulzari Lal walked out on to the roof. He walked up and down and looked over the parapet at the rest of the property. He shook his head at the state of neglect it was in: he hated to see a good piece of property go to waste, and at once his mind idled with ideas of how it should be developed. He even wondered whether Brij Mohan would be interested to sell, and began rapidly to calculate how much (at Rs 60–70 a square yard) it would come to. He looked down at the ramshackle servants' quarters which – since Brij Mohan had only one servant, who slept on the floor of his kitchen, and Sarla Devi had none – had been given out to rent. They were a row of four yellow, dirty huts with iron-barred windows and tiled roofs from which many tiles were missing. Outside stood two string-cots, and some tattered bedding had been hung up to air on a piece of string. The quarters would have to go, Gulzari Lal reflected; and this house too, Brij Mohan's ill-kept crumbling old house, not much worth salvaging there. But it was a good piece of ground; if one were to sink a little capital and develop it, putting up one or two neat whitewashed bungalows, it would fetch a good rent.

His pleasant reflections – and any reflections involving the development of land were pleasant to him – were interrupted by the appearance of Sarla Devi's two visitors, who were thrusting their feet back into their shoes and taking leave with respectfully joined hands. Sarla Devi called after them 'I will do what I can!' and when Gulzari Lal rejoined her inside the room, she told him: 'I count on your help in this.'

He knew it was useless to protest his inability to give any. So he made no reply, but sat down on the hard little bench covered with a coloured cloth and stretched out his long legs. Sarla Devi walked up and down, thoughtfully. 'Please sit,' he said. 'I have come on some particular business.'

'For fifteen years they have been settled there!'

'If you will please listen to me.' But for the moment he was quite glad of her preoccupation. It was difficult to know how to say what he had come to say. He had not seen her for some years, and she had grown thinner, greyer, older.

'And now to be told – the land is wanted, get out!'

'If you will forget this for one moment – '

'Forget! I don't find it so easy to forget cruelty and wrong.' And she looked at him with a look he knew well. It was a look of condemnation, and though he was ready enough to admit that there was in him as much to condemn as in the next man, he had always been hurt by her wholesale condemnation, which included even his virtues: and perhaps especially his virtues – that is, his realism, his capacity for hard work, his shrewd business sense, his balanced view of life.

'It is all very well to say they will be resettled in other colonies. But you know where these other colonies are, how far from the city, how far from their work!'

It was as difficult to get to a point of one's own with her as it was with any wily business rival. But at least the latter knew what game he was playing, and there was some enjoyment to be got out of playing along with him. Sarla Devi's tactics, on the other hand, were more deadly because she was not conscious of employing any.

'I know,' Gulzari Lal spoke up bravely, 'that it is a great problem and that you are very much concerned. Perhaps we will talk about it some other day and I will see what can be done. But today I have come to talk with you about something else.'

'Is it about Vishnu?'

'No, not about Vishnu.'

'I have been very worried over him.' And now she came and sat beside him and he saw her face close to, and how wrinkled and dark it had become. 'Every time I see him he is more like – ' Perhaps she had wanted to say 'like you', but she stopped short at the end.

'There is no need to worry over Vishnu. He is doing well in the office, he has a good wife, a beautiful child, he lives at home with me – there is nothing more he can wish for.'

'You have left him nothing to wish for! You have given him everything you think he should have and now he no longer knows what else there is to wish for.'

'I don't understand you,' Gulzari Lal said, and he did not.

She turned her head away from him, and he saw the wrinkled flesh of her thin neck and, glancing down, how loose and flat her breasts had become. 'I know you don't understand,' she said. 'This has always been the trouble. You understand only how to make money, how to eat, how to dress, how to buy cars and furnish your house. All right; it is all right. I am not quarrelling with you. This is the way you are, this is the way you want to live. But my Vishnu – '

'He wants the same.'

'How wrong you are! How little you know my son!'

'Well, well,' said Gulzari Lal, 'it is not something to be argued about.' He was irritated, not so much with what she was saying – he had learnt long ago not to take offence at her unbalanced views – as with the way she was saying it. All this passion and fire of hers – her quick movements, her flashing eyes – had been very well when she was young and beautiful; but now, when there was no beauty left, they struck him as merely grotesque.

'I am not arguing with you. I don't ever want to argue with you again.' She put her hands to her head, as if remembering with anguish the years when she had argued with him. 'I am grateful that I am alone at last and can live the way I like.'

'Did you ever live any other way?' he asked, thinking of her hundreds of interests away from him, her swamis and politicians, her refusal ever to be a wife such as he wanted and thought he had a right to expect.

'Please don't start to quarrel with me now. It is all over, and where was your fault and where was my fault, *that* it is better not to discuss any more.'

Gulzari Lal thought silently to himself that his greatest fault had been in the first place to marry her. His family had wanted to arrange for him with her cousin, a placid Punjabi beauty, well versed in household duties and content to stay, like all the other girls in the women's side of the family house and marry anyone who was chosen for her. But Gulzari Lal had been a bold, original youth. He had gone to the city and had established himself there, independent of anyone; and now he wanted to be original in the choice of his wife too, and who was there to be original with but Sarla Devi, whom he had known and teased since childhood and against whom everyone laughingly warned him? 'It is cheaper to marry a horse,' his uncle had said; 'she will kick you just the same.' But he had been a much loved, much indulged elder son, and the marriage talks were transferred from the placid, uncomplaining cousin to Sarla Devi.

'We have a Hindu Code Bill now,' he began on his main topic.

'I want Vishnu to go away. Somewhere on his own, away from you, where he can start again from the beginning all by himself.'

38

'It is no longer necessary to remain married, if the marriage is not successful.'

'Why are you saying all this now? It is ten years since we have finished being married.'

'But by law – '

'By law! In my own eyes, in yours, I am no longer married, and I need no law to come and tell me what I am.'

'Yes yes,' he said in some exasperation, 'that is all very fine, but as always you forget that you are living in a society.'

'I forget! Who is it who cares only for himself, who never thinks of the millions who have nothing and live in hovels on a handful of rice –'

'I think it is better if we take a legal divorce.'

'Just now, when these two men were here,' she cried, 'who was it who didn't care, you or I? When I ask you, when I beg you, do something for them, speak to the Commissioner, you shrug your shoulders and speak of long-term plans. And then you come and say to me I forget I am living in a society!'

'We are not speaking of the same thing,' he said patiently.

'No, you are right, we are not speaking of the same thing! I know what you mean when you speak of society – you mean the people like yourself who have houses and cars and go to clubs, for you only these people are society, only they are human!' She had her eyes closed with passion; her fists were clenched, showing up blue veins, and her badly cut grey hair tumbled about her face. She looked, he thought, ugly and ridiculous; he was embarrassed to see her like that and out of delicacy kept his eyes fixed not on her but on the opposite wall, on the coloured picture of Sri Ramakrishna and the Holy Mother. He had known her when she was young and beautiful, and it did not seem decent to look at her the way she was now.

After a while he said, quite gently, 'If you will allow me, I will start proceedings for a legal divorce.'

She opened her eyes. She had got excited and now it was over, and she was quite calm. She said: 'I don't want to offend you – it is only, you know how it is, I feel so strongly about some things.'

'I know.'

'Why should I want to hurt you, why should I want to quarrel with you? All that is over.'

'That is why it is better we should have divorce.'

'If you like,' she said meekly. 'I am ready to sign anything you want.' He knew she meant it: was nothing to her, a kind of mild favour she did him out of contrition for having spoken too hotly.

*

Before Vishnu could climb the stairs up to his mother's room, Brij Mohan appeared from behind some tangled bushes and declared: 'Your mother is mad.'

'So you keep telling me,' Vishnu said.

Brij Mohan took his arm: 'You know what she has done now? Oh the fool!' he cried, striking his forehead dramatically. He drew Vishnu inside the house. Tara was sitting on the floor, applying red dye to the soles of her feet. She was a buxom young prostitute in a pink transparent sari. When she saw Vishnu, she covered her head with an exaggerated air of modesty. 'No need of that!' Brij Mohan cried at her. 'He has seen enough like you before!' He squeezed Vishnu's arm. 'How do you like her, eh? You don't think she is looking better? More – hm?' and he made suggestive rounded gestures with his hands.

'Yes, very nice,' Vishnu said politely. As a matter of fact, she looked far too clean for the room. She kept herself very carefully – her pink sari, gold ornaments in her ears, round her arm, round her neck, in the parting of her hair; powdered, scented, her tiny pursed lips painted scarlet, the red mark on her forehead, the nails of her plump hands pink-tinted, the palms dyed red. Whereas Brij Mohan's room was dusty and dirty, and almost completely empty of furniture except for a soiled armchair and a bed in the corner; some clothes were hung on hooks along one wall. Although he had the whole house to himself, Brij Mohan had got into the habit of using only this one room: it saved him, he thought, a lot of trouble.

'How would you like someone like him?' he asked her, patting his nephew proudly on the chest. 'You would like someone young and strong like that, eh? What? Doesn't he make you – ' And he became crude, describing the physiological symptoms that Vishnu's beauty must be calling forth in her.

'Leave her alone,' Vishnu said in embarrassment.

'Don't worry about her! She is used to such talk – see how she enjoys it, just look at her, look!' And indeed, Tara was simpering from behind her pink sari which she had drawn to cover her profile like a screen. 'Sing that new song for him, Tara – he would like to hear.'

'Shame!' giggled Tara, wriggling her plump body so that her ornaments jingled in a delicious little shudder.

'What a song! And how she sings it! She is a shameless little whore.' He bent down and, with a mischievous look on his face, tried to put his hand down her blouse. She warded him off with a practised movement.

'What did you want to tell me about Mama?' Vishnu said.

'Mad!' cried Brij Mohan.

'What has she done?'

'I will tell you.' But he needed to strengthen himself before he could do so. He fumbled under the bed and came out with a bottle which he held against the light; he did not trust anyone where his whisky was concerned. Tara got up at once and found two tumblers on the window-sill; she took the bottle from him and poured two drinks. The first she offered to Brij Mohan, the second to Vishnu. She moved softly on naked feet with a swing of plump buttocks and a manifold tinkling of ornaments. The tumblers were stained and cracked, but the gesture with which she offered them full of grace.

Brij Mohan took a refreshing draught and then he said: 'She has promised your father to give him divorce, that is what she has done.'

But Vishnu took it calmly. His parents had not been living together for the past ten years, and a legal divorce seemed logical to him. He did not have his father's social aversion to it; and anyway, Kusum had already prepared him. So he answered his uncle: 'What difference does it make?'

'You are as big a fool as she is. At all costs this must be prevented.'

'But why?'

Brij Mohan raised appalled hands to heaven: 'What have I come to, that he asks me such a question!' Tara had gone back to applying red dye to the soles of her feet; she sat on the floor and seemed as unconcerned with the conversation as a pet monkey.

'No, I must not blame this boy,' Brij Mohan said, changing his tone. He sank down in the soiled armchair and sat there despondently, holding his glass in a limp downward-hanging hand. 'How does he see me now? What am I now?' He looked round the bare, dirty room. 'Squalor, poverty' – his eyes rested on Tara; he sighed – 'sin. This is how my nephew sees me.' Then he drew himself up, his cheeks swelled, the very thighs in his crumpled trousers seemed to fill out. 'But you should have seen me in the old days, then you would have known. Then no one would have dared to come and threaten my sister with divorce.'

'You said she is quite willing – '

'Do you know who your great-grandfather was? His glory is still sung in the folk-songs of Punjab. Do you know what sort of family we were? Proud, noble, rich' – and with each word his voice became more resonant – 'kshatriyas – warriors, heroes, landowners, kings!' Tara delicately took the end of her sari and applied it to her nose in ladylike fashion; she had finished with her feet, and now sat cross-legged on the floor, staring in front of her and quite vacant till some-one should stake a claim to her attention.

'I know all that,' Vishnu said. He had heard it often enough – from his father's side as well, for his father came from the same group of proud Punjabi landowners. Certainly, he was glad he had such a good ancestry, but he did not feel it as a very active force in his life. What his grandfathers had been and done was one thing, what he himself another.

'Listen, son,' Brij Mohan said, and he drew closer to Vishnu and laid a compelling hand on his knee. 'You see me now in very bad shape. But I am not what I seem. That is a quotation, son; from English literature. I am a man of education, I have had expensive schooling and also I have travelled abroad. No, I don't wish to boast, a man from a family like mine has no need of boasting. Only I wish to say this: don't judge me from what I am now. Wait till I get my compensation, then you will see something. Then you will see what sort of man I am, what it is to be a gentleman born and bred and what style of living I shall show to the world.' He finished his drink and held the glass for Tara to refill.

'I think Mama may be waiting upstairs,' Vishnu murmured.

'I will send for her. No, don't move !' He called his servant, but had to do so several times before his summons was answered. Brij Mohan's servant was bedraggled, old and sleepy. He was always sleepy, and indeed spent a good deal of his time fast asleep on the back veranda. It was a habit he had got into and – since there was little work – not one of which there was any urgent need to break himself.

'No, I don't blame you,' Brij Mohan told Vishnu. 'On the contrary, I pity you. We have lost everything, but at least we know what it is we have lost. We remember all the old glory, but what have you, poor boy, to remember? Born in the city, brought up in the city, what do you know of your ancestral rights? In the city you are nothing, an insect' – he waggled two fingers to demonstrate insect – 'among a million other insects. But on your land now – ah! in your own an-cestral home, there you are a man: and not only a man but a mon-arch' – and he became one – 'monarch of all you survey.' His chest was thrust out, his eyes rolled proudly in large bloodshot sockets. It would have been unkind to remind him that in the days before Par-tition, when the family property was still intact, he had spent very little time on it, preferring to live amid the city-pleasures of Lahore.

Sarla Devi came in and said: 'Why are you keeping my son down here?'

'You have no right to call him son,' Brij Mohan answered her severely. 'You who are letting yourself be publicly deprived of the title of wife no longer have a right to the title of mother.'

She made an impatient sound with her tongue and turned to Vishnu: 'Have you ever heard of a colony called Bundi Busti?' She began to tell him about what was happening in Bundi Busti. 'I want you to help, Vishnu. If you could talk to someone to have the notice to quit suspended – '

'Revoked,' Brij Mohan said.

'Please don't try to correct me. I speak only to be understood by my son.'

'Why do you meddle in these things? These are legal matters and you don't even know the correct legal terms. It is no business for women.'

'I would like you to come with me to see these people,' she told Vishnu.

'Don't go son!' Brij Mohan cried. 'She is quite capable of making a fool of herself on her own, there is no need to aid and abet her in this.'

'I have spoken with your father also about it.' She bit her lip in recollection. 'Vishnu, I behaved so badly to your father.'

'For thirty years you have been behaving badly to him,' Brij Mohan said. 'It is late to be sorry now.'

'Come upstairs with me,' she told Vishnu.

'Leave him here! Today he has come to visit his uncle, he is tired of you. Tara,' he commanded and pointed to Vishnu's empty glass. She got up at once and, holding the bottle like an offering with both hands, minced over to Vishnu, her head covered, her eyes downcast, but her hips dancing and prancing on their own. Vishnu covered the top of his glass with his hand.

'I feel bad when I think of it now,' Sarla Devi said. 'What need was there for me to shout at him? He had not come to quarrel with me.'

'With you, shouting starts very quickly,' Brij Mohan said. 'I also don't come to quarrel with you, but always before very long you are quarrelling with me.'

Tara stood close to Vishnu. Her scent – attar of roses – was heavy and heady and mingled with her perspiration. She put out her hand and tried to remove his from the top of the glass; but so gently that her soft moist palm only just touched him.

'You see, these people from Bundi Busti were there, and when I asked your father to help them, he – no!' she cried, 'what right had I to ask him for any help?'

'Make him, make him drink,' Brij Mohan told Tara, giggling and rubbing his hands.

'It was wrong of me,' Sarla Devi said, now deep in repentance: which was a mood of hers Vishnu knew well. Even when he was a child, she had often come to him in such a mood, and knelt beside him with her hair hanging down over her face and tears flowing, and she had sobbed and accused herself, telling him things which he did not understand but which nevertheless made him cry with her.

'Just a little – a little drop,' whispered Tara, close and hot and scented. Vishnu put down his glass and harshly turned his back on her. She smiled, her head bowed in submission to his will. Brij Mohan gave a roar of laughter: 'You see, the young one is not so easy to coax as the old one'; he held out his glass to her and she filled it, still smiling and looking from under bashful lids.

'After he had gone I felt very sorry for the way I had spoken to him,' Sarla Devi said. She paced up and down the room, glancing absentmindedly at the clothes hung on hooks, the shoes and bottles pushed under the bed; and in passing she said to Brij Mohan: 'Why don't you clean and tidy in here?' to which he shrugged and said: 'My servant is too lazy.'

'You should make him, Tara,' she said.

But Tara chose to take offence. She pushed out her lip and swayed her head on her neck: 'Am I his servant?'

Sarla Devi at once became very anxious to appease her: 'No no, that is not what I meant.' Tara turned her face away sullenly: she mistrusted and disliked Sarla Devi. 'I only thought if you could tell the servant – '

'What harm is there in cleaning a room?' Vishnu cried suddenly, furious to see his mother apologizing to his uncle's prostitute.

'Why do you shout?' said Sarla Devi. 'Why are you angry?'

'He is right,' Brij Mohan said gloomily. 'It is horrible to live like this. When I think how it used to be – how I lived, what company I kept – '

'We were only talkng,' Vishnu said, 'of the dirt in the room, which you could have very easily cleaned.'

'You are young, son,' Brij Mohan said. 'What do you understand of the way a man feels when he has lost everything and knows he is old?'

Tara began to giggle. 'You are old?' she said slyly. 'Perhaps you should ask me about that.'

'Be quiet!' roared Brij Mohan, in a fury – though at any other time he might have greatly appreciated this little sally. 'How dare you open your lewd mouth when my sister is in the room!'

'This is new now,' said Sarla Devi. 'Tara, please forgive him, he is an old fool.'

'It is not my place to forgive,' said Tara, pert and on her dignity.

'At least she knows her place,' cried Brij Mohan. 'But you – what are you? When your husband says to you, you are no longer my wife: I shall publish everywhere in the bazaars and in the newspapers that I shall divorce – divorce! – you, you say' – and he clasped his hands in his lap and simpered, woman-like – 'please do just what you like, I am quite ready.'

Vishnu went out on to the veranda. He looked at the tangled overgrown bushes and a broken plaster pillar lying abandoned on the brown grass.

'Where are you going?' Brij Mohan called after him.

Vishnu walked out into the garden, into the hot sun, with his hands in his pockets and an angry frown on his face.

His mother followed him: 'If you will come with me to Bundi Busti, these people will feel new hope to think there is someone else willing to help them.'

He kicked the fallen pillar.

'Don't be angry,' she said. 'Your uncle is an old man and he misses so many things.'

Brij Mohan appeared on the veranda: 'Come in, son! We will send the old woman back again upstairs and have a good time!'

Vishnu freed himself from his mother and made for his car. She followed him, saying: 'You will come back again soon? You will come to Bundi Busti with me?'

2

Whenever Vishnu came to see Gautam, Sumi managed to be there. She sat with them in the garden and took a lively part in the conversation; she and Vishnu had a lot of jokes together. Her sister, Mrs Shankar, did not approve of this at all and often called her into the house. But Sumi was irrepressible and was always back again quite soon.

Later in the evening they were usually joined by Gautam's cousin, Shankar. He was a civil servant, an employee in one of the Ministries, who spent his days amid files in a hot and crowded office; when he came home in the evenings, he liked to sit quietly in his garden and think his own thoughts or listen to Gautam and Vishnu. Gautam

45

talked a lot about his school, and Shankar – though he seemed sceptical about Gautam's ability to start it – enjoyed hearing him talk about the principles on which it was to be established, all that freedom and gaiety. He nodded with appreciation and said: 'Youth is so short, it should be only happiness.' He sighed – a balding man with a sagging stomach and melancholy eyes. From inside the house came his wife's angry voice and the sound of slaps and a child crying.

Gautam said: 'We should retain youth throughout our life. We must not clog ourselves down with cares and possession, then the spirit will remain young and fresh even though the body grows old.'

But Shankar shook his head. 'Once you are married and the children come and there is never enough, though you spend your life in work – no,' he said, 'youth and happiness flee quickly.'

Vishnu quoted:

'In my father's house I laughed and there was sport;
I climbed trees.
Today in my own house I am heavy with care;
And my son laughs up in the mango tree.'

The words moved him (as all poetic sentiments moved him) but he did not feel that they concerned him closely. There was still plenty of youth in him and he was confident that, if only he knew where to look for it, there would be plenty of happiness too.

Mrs Shankar came out with a betel-leaf for her husband. He took it from her without a word, and she went back into the house without a word. She was a gaunt woman with a lined and unsmiling face. Vishnu had never heard her talk to her husband and Shankar communicated his wishes to her in low grunts which no one else could understand.

'For men,' said Shankar, 'life is labour and the cares of a family. And for women' – he sighed – 'yes, for women also it is difficult. Childbirth wears out her body, constant anxiety her spirit – ' He glanced towards the house and his face was full of sadness and compassion.

Vishnu lay on the grass, his head supported on one hand. He enjoyed a feeling of peace, with the sky high and dark above him and the still earth beneath him. The night was full of household noises (the house was in a busy colony of minor officials and radios played and women shouted in their kitchens) but they were no more than pinpricks in that tall silence.

'When we are first married,' said Shankar, 'ah! what beauty there is in one's wife, what spirit, what playfulness. Then she is to us a new world.'

Vishnu thought of Mala in the first year of their marriage, and all she had been to him then. They were strangers when they were married, but when their shyness had worn off, how they had loved and luxuriated in each other. Every day she had been a new discovery to him.

'But afterwards everything changes,' Shankar said. 'Life makes us weary and our delight is dead.'

Vishnu silently agreed that his delight was dead but he did not feel that life had made him weary. On the contrary, his complaint was that it had not made him weary enough and that he had such energy still with nothing to spend it on.

'The world is always the same,' Gautam said, 'always beautiful: why should we let our delight in it die? The answer to this problem lies in education. If we teach our children to love everything about them – the sky, the air, water, flowers, animals – then they will keep their youthful spirit for ever, whatever may happen to them in the trivial world of affairs. Vishnu, this must be the ideal we shall keep always before us. It is the life's task we must set ourselves in our school.'

But Vishnu failed to get enthusiastic. The school was too remote an ideal for him; besides, he did not think he would find fulfilment in leading children along what Gautam considered the right path. He wanted something much more for himself.

Suddenly he said: 'Why don't we start a new business together? A factory perhaps, for making spare parts.'

'Spare parts for what?'

'For anything: just to make something, start something new.' He sat up on the grass; he felt excited at the thought of doing something for himself, something vigorous and modern and industrial. 'There are new schemes all the time – you know, all these steel plants and dams and bridges – I don't know,' he said, unable to convey in words his sense of great wheels turning. 'If I could just set up something . . . For instance, a factory to make some special kind of screw for some special part for some special kind of machine.'

'Very good!' said Shankar. 'I like to hear a young man talk like that. Our India is now growing into a great industrial nation, it is like a giant waking up. What a fine thing it is to take part in his awakening, what opportunity and challenge for the spirit of youth.'

But Vishnu did not want to hear it put like that. He was tired of hearing of the spirit of youth, tired of words.

Sumi came out of the house and sat next to Vishnu on the grass: 'What are you talking about?'

47

'Have you helped your sister with her work?' Shankar asked.

'Oh,' groaned Sumi, 'all day and all night I am helping her.'

Gautam laughed: 'It is said that a woman's work is never ended.'

'But I am a girl, I am not a woman! I am not even married yet.'

Shankar smiled indulgently: 'Sit, child, sit in peace.'

Vishnu rolled over on the grass to face her. He forgot his longing and his dissatisfaction, and concentrated on teasing Sumi. 'When you are married, Sumi,' he said, 'what sort of a life will you lead your husband?' Gautam answered for her and Sumi pretended to be angry and Shankar smiled.

Gulzari Lal was happy. Ever since he had told Kusum about his visit to his wife, she had been very kind to him; and this evening she had with her own hands cooked his favourite dish (green spinach and maize bread) she had served him and complacently watched him eat. Vishnu was out, Mala and Pritti had gone to bed. There were only the two of them. They sat for a while in the drawing-room and then they strolled out into the garden. The night air was warm and soft and laden with the scent of flowers. Kusum tucked her arm in Gulzari Lal's and entertained him with the latest news. She knew all that was going on, for she got around a lot: she went on shopping tours, to coffee-parties, tea-parties, dropped in on life-long friends and had them dropping in on her. So she was well up on everything – on the marriages that were being arranged, the secret adulteries that were not secret enough, the sicknesses, servant troubles, deaths, births and family quarrels. And Gulzari Lal listened to her, indulgent and happy, and pressed the hand which she had tucked under his arm, close to his heart.

It was like this that Brij Mohan found them. He had swept the servants aside and walked straight through into the garden. Dressed in an old suit of beige silk, with a black tie, a solar topi on his head and a silver-topped malacca cane under his arm, he looked like an Indian gentleman under the British Raj: which may have been his intention, for the British Raj spelt for him those qualities of respectability and decorum he wished, for this particular interview, to represent.

Gulzari Lal's feelings, on seeing him, were wholly unmixed. He was ill-pleased enough at any time to meet Brij Mohan; and now to have his delightful evening with Kusum interrupted and, more, to suspect that Brij Mohan had come to discuss the divorce, was a really unfair test of his patience. It said much for him that his innate courtesy made his welcome appear almost a cordial one. And Brij Mohan acknowledged it with a ceremonial, a restrained, a gentlemanly bow; which he repeated – at the same time sweeping his solar topi from his head – when Kusum was introduced to him. He had, of course, heard of Kusum's existence, and, never having met her, was more than interested to do so now; but so firm was the dignity on which he stood that he betrayed nothing beyond that formal interest which must be accorded to any lady on first meeting.

They sat, all three of them, under the fans in the drawing-room, Brij Mohan on one high brocaded settee, with his hat and cane laid beside him, Gulzari Lal and Kusum side by side on another. Gulzari Lal wished Kusum would go away. There was nothing to be gained by her and Brij Mohan getting to know one another better; on the contrary, they seemed to him two people in his life to be kept very much apart. But Kusum had evidently no intention of going away. She was as interested in meeting Brij Mohan as he was in her: with this difference, that she saw no reason not to show it. She sat there, bright and alert, her back straight, her hands in her lap, looking from one to another and waiting for interesting things to be said.

Brij Mohan, still on his most correct behaviour, saw to it that first the formalities of a social visit were fulfilled. He commented on the weather, asked after everyone's health and discussed his own. Gulzari Lal helped him sustain this conversation, and Kusum too chimed in from time to time. The visit was going very nicely. Gulzari Lal, never failing in his duties as a host, instructed the bearer to bring whisky; and when it came, Brij Mohan took his glass with as damp and demure a good breeding as if it had been a cup of tea.

Yet still nothing was said. Kusum, having had her fill of seeing them behave like two perfectly bred gentlemen, was beginning to get impatient. It was time to bring the conversation to a point of some interest to her; and so, in her most winning manner, she arranged the sari over her lap and with a shy little downward glance said to Brij Mohan: 'I am sorry I have never had opportunity to meet your sister.'

Gulzari Lal's expression of social decorum froze on his face. So did Brij Mohan's: but he was taken aback less by Kusum's matter than by her manner. For the way she cast down her eyes and coquettishly fidgeted her sari reminded him – and it was a shock – of Tara.

'I have heard so much about your sister,' continued Kusum, addressing herself solely to Brij Mohan and not so much as a glance at Gulzari Lal whose reactions she could guess and was determined to ignore. 'I would like very much to meet her one day.'

'Certainly,' said Brij Mohan, still a little too distraught quite to know what he was saying or to whom, 'certainly you must meet.'

Gulzari Lal cleared his throat in a disapproving manner. However, he did not like to put his disapproval into words for fear of bringing things into the open which might, with luck, remain under decent cover.

'I have so long been wanting to meet her,' Kusum said. 'We shall have much to talk about. We shall be like sisters with one another.'

Gulzari Lal would have liked to get angry with her there and then and to call the car to take her home.

'It is strange with us women,' she told Brij Mohan. 'Often when we meet it is as if we have always known one another – we can read deep into one another's hearts and at once we love each other.' Then she cried, in a voice brimful with sincere feeling, 'Already I have so much love for her!' and she clapped her hands in her enthusiasm so that her golden bangles jingled, the way Tara's did.

Gulzari Lal said sternly: 'Sometimes it is wiser for people not to meet.'

'How can you say so?' But she did not have much time for him; she turned back again to Brij Mohan: 'Now you have promised me,' she said archly, 'you have promised to arrange a meeting,' and she smiled and shook her finger at him so that he at once became gallant and declared himself ready to arrange whatever she wished.

'You see!' she cried triumphantly to Gulzari Lal. 'He understands the position! He knows that it is necessary for us to meet and talk with each other quite freely.'

Brij Mohan looked nervously at his brother-in-law. He saw that Gulzari Lal was displeased; as a matter of fact, he was not too pleased himself, for it seemed to him that he had been manoeuvred into a position he had not meant to occupy. He had, after all, not come here to arrange peace and solidarity between his sister and Gulzari Lal's mistress. He decided it was time he spoke up and cleared his throat accordingly. 'I came today,' he began, slowly and weightily, wondering how to put it why he came today, when Kusum interrupted him:

'It is good that you have come today! Perhaps now some matters can be discussed between us which should have been discussed a long time ago.'

'You know our family,' Brij Mohan told his brother-in-law. 'It is not the kind of family' – and now he sat up very straight on the settee with his cheeks puffed out and his eyes rolling impressively – 'with which one can deal in any way one pleases.'

Gulzari Lal irritably clicked his tongue.

'A woman from a family like ours,' said Brij Mohan, 'cannot be so easily divorced.' And having got it out, he sat there, all stern dignity.

'Now you are old-fashioned!' cried Kusum.

50

Gulzari Lal said, with all his authority: 'Perhaps this is not the time to discuss the matter.'

'Oh, I am disappointed in you,' said Kusum, making her eyes flash prettily at Brij Mohan. 'How can you talk like that – a man like you, with education and from such a family? People like you should be leaders of society: you should always hold only the most modern ideas. How can our poor India ever become advanced like western countries if you don't lead the way for others?'

Brij Mohan could not help being flattered – not only by what she was saying but the way she was saying it, all those feminine charms concentrated on him. He found himself anxious to maintain her good opinion. 'You speak of modern ideas,' he said. 'I am also very interested in modern ideas. I have travelled abroad a lot and I have learnt quite a few things.'

'I could tell at once,' Kusum said, 'that you are a man who has seen much of the world.'

'I have been to London and to Paris and Rotterdam and many other places, and I talked to people there – for instance, once I was in a railway carriage, I was going from London to Oxford, and there was only one other person with me in the compartment, he was a clergyman of the Church of England. We had a very interesting discussion, about psychology – '

Kusum clapped her hands to call the bearer and when he came, she made him fill up Brij Mohan's glass. And all the time she leant forward and listened to him with an attentive face.

'We exchanged many ideas and when we parted at Oxford, he shook hands with me and said how much he had enjoyed our talk.'

Gulzari Lal got up and walked around with his hands behind his back, tall in his tall room with the tall furniture.

'So you see I have had opportunity to learn about modern ideas and also I have been very interested in the subject.'

Kusum nodded. 'It is our duty nowadays to keep up with all these things.'

'But it is different,' cried Brij Mohan suddenly, 'when it is a matter of family feelings!'

Kusum had a little shock, which however she quickly overcame. Gulzari Lal stood still in his tracks and wheeled round to stare at Brij Mohan.

'I sit here,' cried Brij Mohan, 'and talk of modern ideas, but what have all these to do with a brother's feelings?'

'I will explain,' Kusum said.

'You will explain to me that divorce is modern, and I agree with you – yes yes, I know it is very good to have divorce, and abolition of dowry and remarriage of widows – these are all excellent things and we are proud to have them. But my own sister!' he suddenly roared and stood up, glass in hand.

Gulzari Lal faced him sternly: 'I told you this is not the time to discuss the matter.'

'I am not discussing! I am telling you my feelings as a brother!'

'I think perhaps if you would like to go home now, I will come myself to visit you some other day.'

'I see. You are telling me to leave your house. Now it has come to this.'

'The time is not convenient,' Gulzari Lal said.

'You are right to tell me to leave your house. Why have I come here? Who am I to defend my family's honour? I am nothing, I have nothing – how dare I come and stand before a man like you and ask for my sister's rights?'

'But this is exactly what he is giving her!' Kusum cried. 'Her rights to divorce – and what greater rights can there be for a woman today?'

'I will tell my chauffeur to drive you home,' Gulzari Lal said.

'In the old days it was different. Then I could have come in my own car with my own chauffeur. I could have driven up to your house and come in and spoken with you and you would have listened to me.'

'But we *are* listening!' cried Kusum. 'We are very interested in everything you are saying!'

'Please be quiet,' Gulzari Lal told her in a low voice.

'When my compensation comes, I shall be a different man. Then people will treat me again with the respect which is due to me and I shall be a worthy brother for my sister.' He passed the silk sleeve of his suit across his eyes.

'Why should I keep quiet?' Kusum said.

'Sh,' said Gulzari Lal.

She stamped her foot: 'I have every right to speak! Please sit,' she told Brij Mohan, 'there is no need for you to upset yourself.' She pressed his arm and was very sweet with him so that he sat down and gave another wipe at his eyes. Then she called the bearer again and pointed at the empty glass; but before he could fill it, Gulzari Lal took the bottle and told him: 'Go and have the car taken out.'

Kusum compressed her lips and folded her arms: 'Very well, I shall also go home.'

'Just wait,' said Gulzari Lal in a low imploring voice.

She turned away from him. She sat down next to Brij Mohan and patted his sleeve in a soothing manner. And he really was soothed – it was good to have someone caring for him and understanding his difficulties, the way she obviously did.

The chauffeur stood in the french windows. Kusum gave Brij Mohan his solar topi and watched to see him put it on properly, and then she stuck his stick under his arm for him.

'If you wish to go home,' Gulzari Lal told her, 'I will take you myself in the other car.'

'Excuse me,' said Kusum. 'I don't wish to give any trouble.'

He watched them being driven away, side by side in the back of his car.

It said *Joginder Nath & Brothers Furnishing House* over the doorway of the open-fronted shop. Joginder Nath himself was sitting in one of his own chairs outside the shop, fanning himself with a bamboo fan to give some relief from heat and flies. The flies were attracted by all the food in the bazaar. Next to Joginder Nath's shop was a sweetmeat-seller and opposite a meat-shop with big chunks of raw meat hung from iron hooks. There were little barrows lined up all along the street, selling fruits that were bursting and oozing in the heat. Many people and a few cows thronged the bazaar, they pushed against each other and trod discarded mango-peels into the dust.

Joginder did not seem particularly pleased to see his visitors. He kept on waving his fan with a weary and bored expression.

'We are starting a school,' Gautam said. 'I have told you about my school and how we need land for it.'

Joginder spat red betel-juice out of his mouth and watched it land, with some satisfaction, on the spot he had evidently had in mind.

'About that land of yours at Chandnipat,' Gautam said briskly.

Joginder jerked his head towards Vishnu. 'Who is he?'

'He is my partner,' Gautam said. 'You may speak quite freely before him.'

Joginder studied Vishnu. One leg drawn up on his chair and his arm dangling lazily across it, he looked up at Vishnu with half-closed eyes. 'What does he do?'

'He is in his father's business.'

Joginder kept on looking at Vishnu. He himself had an unprepossessing appearance, with a stubbled black chin and his shirt open almost to his navel, exposing a great deal of sweaty, hairy chest. 'Who is his father?'

'What does it matter who his father is,' Gautam said. 'I told you he is my partner and we have come to talk with you about that land of yours.'

'What sort of business does his father do?' said Joginder. He put out his strong and not too clean hand and felt the material of Vishnu's bush-shirt.

Vishnu took an indignant step backwards.

'Just see,' said Joginder, 'now he is angry.' Then he laughed and got up and slapped Vishnu on the back. 'Come inside,' he said.

Inside there was furniture – chairs, wardrobes, beds – very dull upright furniture, all made of the same medium-class wood and to the same stiff pattern. Each of the chairs had a design stamped on its seat – a large lotus with vague leaves around it – and the tops of the wardrobes and the tops of the bedsteads were decorated with a head-piece that curved at the sides and met in another, higher curve at the centre.

A boy was going round, flicking at the furniture with a piece of cloth. He stared at the visitors and wiped the cloth thoughtfully under his nose. A man slept curled up on the floor. Joginder nudged him and he sat up and rubbed his eyes and his hair. 'He is my younger brother Som Nath,' Joginder said.

The boy was made to bring out chairs for everyone. One side of the shop was open to the street, but it was blocked by furniture and only a narrow passage left for the entrance. Through this entrance they could see the hot white sunlight and people passing. All the noise of the bazaar came as loud as if they were in the midst of it, and yet there was a sense of seclusion as they sat there on their chairs in the dark little shop.

Gautam said: 'My school is going to be quite different from all other schools.'

Neither of the two brothers seemed to be interested in the school. Joginder's attention was mostly on Vishnu; he said: 'Where do you live?'

'We are interested in your land,' Gautam said. 'If you can just let us have one or two thousand square yards with a few trees, these are all our requirements.'

Joginder turned to Vishnu: 'Why are you joining with him?'

Vishnu said: 'It is a good scheme.' He did not think so at all, nor really had he much intention of joining; but he was on the defensive with Joginder and wished to show himself firm of purpose.

'We shall run our school on completely new principles of education,' Gautam said. 'The children will be quite free: free to enjoy the air, free to enjoy the song of the birds, free to swim like fish in the river – '

'The river is a long way away from Chandnipat,' Som Nath said.

54

'All these are revolutionary new principles, but they are based on ideas which may be read about in our ancient writings.'

'And will it be good business?' Joginder asked, with a wink at his brother.

'You know very well that I am not concerned with whether a thing is good business or bad business. I am concerned only with ideals.'

'You also believe in ideals?' Joginder asked Vishnu. And he looked at him with a little half-mocking smile, so that again Vishnu was on the defensive and ready to say what he did not mean.

Gautam said: 'He and I are quite in agreement.'

'But why don't you let him speak?' Joginder said, and Som Nath laughed. He was younger than his brother but taller with broad shoulders and a round, cheerful face. Together the two brothers gave an impression of great energy and confidence.

'What use is your land to you?' Gautam said. 'It is only lying there, you told me yourself. You should never let land lie idle when there is some useful purpose that it could serve. It is like a man's brain: you must use every part of your brain and concentrate your energies.'

'What are you thinking of offering me for my land?' Joginder asked, good-humouredly, like one playing games with a child.

'Don't worry,' Gautam said, 'you will get a good price from me.' Vishnu looked at him in surprise, so he said: 'I am thinking of applying for a Government grant. Education is very important, it is the duty of Government to subsidize those of us interested to further the advance of education.'

Two customers looked in at the doorway and Joginder got up to deal with them. They were two sturdy peasants who stood scratching their heads suspiciously while they looked at chairs. They nudged each other and, after a time, one of them took courage and sat down on a chair, stiff and upright and as if afraid that something would happen to him from this unfamiliar piece of furniture. 'Sit back,' Joginder encouraged him, 'be comfortable. Nowadays everyone sits on chairs.'

'We are not selling the land,' Som Nath said.

'But it is lying there doing nothing! You are businessmen – you need capital, not land.'

'We want to build a factory there.'

Vishnu asked: 'You and your brother are partners?'

'We are together,' Som Nath said, and it sounded so staunch and strong that Vishnu felt quite envious.

Joginder was arguing about his price while the two peasants looked at him shrewdly and clutched the money tied into their dhotis. The transaction took some time, but at last two chairs were trussed up and carried away. Gautam watched with disgust and, when the customers had left, he said: 'Why do you encourage people to buy what is useless to them? Chairs – as if ever in their life they have sat on chairs.' He kicked his foot angrily against a piece of furniture. 'And all these monsters which no one needs! This is the trouble with our people – they hear of such things and the moment they feel a little money in their pockets, they must rush out and buy them. And what for? No one knows. Once they were happy enough to sit on the floor and keep their possessions in a good stout trunk. But now: chairs they must have, almiras they must have! It is all such a waste and also slavish imitation of ways foreign to us.'

Joginder shrugged: 'I care only that people ask for these things, so I make them and sell them.' He held a chair and banged it on the floor several times. 'You see? It is good strong stuff, people can sit on it and feel comfortable. You speak of ideals. I know only that I have a family and that we have to live. Is that also an ideal? I don't know. I sell to people what they want to buy, that's all.'

'Then you can sell me your land,' Gautam said, 'because that is what I want to buy from you.'

Joginder put out his hand and pushed away the face of a bullock which had, in passing, looked in at the entrance and stood thoughtfully moving its loose pink jaws. 'Perhaps I have some other use for my land,' he said.

'We want to make fountain-pens,' Som Nath said.

Gautam looked cynical: 'And what do you know of making fountain-pens?'

'Nothing,' Joginder said. 'But what did I know of making furniture when I started this business? You learn if you have to. Only start something, that is important, just make a start.' He looked at Vishnu.

'Why fountain-pens?' Vishnu asked.

'Why not fountain-pens? It is something that people need – just think of the hundreds and thousands of people who need fountain-pens.'

Vishnu leant forward and said: 'How will you start?'

'We are wasting our time here,' Gautam said. 'It is no use talking with these two. For them it is only money and how to make more of it.'

But Joginder was looking at Vishnu and Vishnu at Joginder, and Som Nath watched them both.

'How will we start? We have our land in Chandnipat. Put up a shed, get the machinery and start work. It is simple.'

'And capital?' Vishnu asked.

'We have some, we may get a grant from Government, and also,' he said and he yawned a bit and put his hand inside his open shirt to scratch his chest, 'we may take another partner.'

Gautam felt it was high time the subject was changed. He had, after all, come to talk about his school.

Vishnu could not stop thinking about this encounter, and it disturbed him. He did not care for such disturbance and told himself that he had nothing to do with people like Joginder and Som Nath, nor with factories, nor fountain-pens; and to keep his mind off them. he looked round for some more suitable and familiar distraction.

That evening he found Sumi at home, and he at once suggested that they take her to the club. Mala dressed her up in one of her saris – a sky-blue one which Sumi chose herself – and when she was ready, Vishnu looked at her with raised eyebrows and a little smile; which made her defiantly spin round in this splendid sari, her hands on her hips: 'Perhaps I look very funny?'

'Oh no no no!' cried Vishnu, flinging up his hands in protest, but spoiling it by laughing.

Sumi pretended to be cross with him till they got to the club, but then she got too excited to pretend any longer. They sat at one of the little tables on the lawn and drank lime-juice. The air was still heavy and hot from the day's sun, but the grass had been well-watered all day and there were fans between the tables giving out cool little breezes. Somewhere behind some bower a band played western dance-tunes with an Indian lilt to them, and Sumi's eyes were large and round and her mouth a little open, showing a pink tip of tongue.

But Mala yawned, and when she looked round at the other tables, she did so with a bored and slightly hostile look. Sometimes people came over to their table and Vishnu got up to talk to them; there was a lot of laughter and banter and Sumi in her sky-blue sari leant forward eagerly, while Mala drank her lime-juice and put her hand up languidly to her hair. Afterwards Sumi always asked 'Who was that?' and Mala would study her nails and say: 'They are my husband's friends.'

And then a girl came bearing down on them, a bold pretty girl with short hair, and she cried 'Vishnu! Darling!' flinging both her arms on to his shoulders and looking fondly into his face.

'This is Gogo,' Vishnu told Sumi. Gogo turned to Mala and said, 'Hallo, Mala', quite easy and careless and as if she hadn't just called her husband darling.

Mala's face was severe, she returned the greeting with joined hands and eyes sullenly downcast. But Gogo was not in the least put out, she concentrated only on Vishnu. 'Haven't seen you in a million years,' she said, and she put her hand into his shirt-pocket and pulled out his cigarette case and helped herself. He lit it for her, and she bent her head down to the flame, and then she looked up and their eyes met meaningfully, and it was, thought Sumi all a-flutter, just like the cinema, so exciting and romantic.

Gogo flung back her head and blew cigarette smoke debonairly into the air. 'And why do I have to come to this stuffy old club before I can see you? Why don't you come to any of our parties any more?'

'I am respectable now,' Vishnu said. He smiled at Sumi who could not keep her eyes off Gogo. 'Just see,' he said, 'you are shocking my little friend Sumi.'

Gogo was delighted, she flicked cigarette ash in a sophisticated manner and said in a drawling voice: 'Don't be shocked by me, darling. I am all bark, no bite.' Sumi did not smile at all, only went on staring in wonder. 'You must have been telling her stories about me,' Gogo said, shaking her finger at Vishnu.

'No, she is too young for such stories.'

'Oh, you *are* a bad boy!' She turned her lively head right and left and peered into the distance. 'I promised to meet – oh cripes, there they all are, waiting for me, how they must be cursing. His there!' she cried in an uninhibited voice, standing on tiptoe and lifting a well-shaped arm to wave across the tables. 'Bunny! Iqqi! Here I am!' She took Vishnu's wrist and began pulling him away with her. 'Come and mingle with the crowd. You are not going to get away from us so quickly now I've caught you. Jrst for a minute,' she added politely to Mala, who gave no sign.

'Who is she?' Sumi asked eagerly, as soon as they had gone. 'Isn't she pretty? And how she talks! She is very modern I think, Mala?' She craned her neck and saw Vishnu being slapped on the back by young men smoking pipes and one girl ruffled his hair and Gogo leant on his shoulder; she could make out Gogo's voice above everyone else's, and even through the music which the band was playing with discreet gaiety. 'I have never met anyone so modern, Mala. You see, in Mathura it is not like in Delhi and my family are quite strict – '

'It is better for you not to meet such people,' Mala grimly said.

'Why, Mala? She is so much fun, I would like to be friends with her.'

'What is he doing?'

'Who? Oh, you mean Vishnu?' She craned her neck again and rose half-way from her chair. 'He is having a very good time, everyone is laughing a lot – why can't we also go, Mala?'

'Please sit down,' Mala said quite kind and patient. 'It is not his fault,' she said. She twisted her hands, her full shapely fingers, on the table. 'It is these girls . . . In Bombay we also had such society girls but I,' she said proudly, 'never moved in these circles, my family would never have allowed me. What is he doing now?'

'He is still having a very good time. He is lighting another cigarette for Gogo. How she smokes, Mala! Have you ever smoked a cigarette? I would love to try.'

Mala kept on twisting her fingers on the table. 'She says to him Come, and he goes. And his wife is left sitting here – oh!' she cried, as if in pain.

When he got back to their table, Vishnu was in a hurry to take them home. Their drive was rather silent. Vishnu tried to appear easy and careless behind the wheel, but it was difficult with Sumi beside him, disappointed at being hustled away so quickly, and Mala sitting heavily in the back, right in the middle of the seat, taking up most of it with her broad hips and maintaining a brooding, sullen silence which spread unease throughout the car.

They dropped Sumi first, and when they came home, Vishnu did not drive into the garage but stopped outside the front porch with his hands on the wheel and the engine still running. Mala did not move, so he said over his shoulder: 'Go in.'

'Where are you going?' she asked in a smouldering voice. For answer he reached his arm over to the back door and opened it for her.

He drove straight off to the party to which Gogo and her friends had invited him. It was held at Toto Saxena's house, in one of the new colonies of smart pink and blue houses which were let out at high rents to embassy officials and junior executives. Toto lived in a first-floor apartment, and already on the stairs Vishnu could hear the sounds of the party and the gramophone playing.

And there they all were – Toto Saxena and his wife Ushi, Iqqi Singh and Premola, Pitu and Shila, Chuchu Bhatt and Kimi, Bablu and Bibi – all the up and coming young men and their modern wives. It was a fashionable party, so men and women sat not apart as at Gulzari Lal's party but intermingled, some of them in casual attitudes on the floor, and there was drinking and smoking and even some harmless, sexless flirtation. Gogo was dancing with Chuchu Bhatt, she leant back in his arms, one hand holding a cigarette, the other laid on the back of his smartly brilliantined head; she hummed lazy and lascivious to the music.

Toto's apartment was furnished like all the apartments of their set – very chic with little black chairs and folk-art cushions, cacti in hand-painted wooden pots, rush-mats on the wall, tubular lampshades and big, carved, brightly-painted dolls from Puri. Toto in a hand-loom bush-shirt (the party was strictly informal) was mixing drinks at the cocktail cabinet, while his wife Ushi passed round with plates of tiny kebabs which she had stuck on toothpicks. Ushi and Toto were a charming young couple; very sociable, very up-to-date, leaders of the young married set. Toto was employed in an English petroleum company, where he was a junior executive and regarded as one of their most promising young men. And Ushi was the perfect wife for a man with a career to make. In spite of two children, she had kept her figure and she managed to look fashionable on a modest budget (Toto's prospects were excellent, but his salary was not yet spectacular). She was an excellent hostess and took a lot of trouble over her parties, always serving something original like chicken with mushroom and banana, or trifle à la mode, which she made with her own hands in the kitchen while the cook looked on and learnt. She also had a lot of conversation, for she kept up on things: she read a lot – the *Illustrated Weekly* and *Femina* and *Time* magazine (which kept her up on international affairs) – and she went to the local art exhibitions, and she and Toto always bought tickets for the productions of the UK High Commission or the Army Headquarters Dramatic Groups.

Everyone knew Vishnu, for he had once been a popular member of their set. After his marriage he had tended to drop out, and it was tacitly understood that this was on account of his wife, who was unfashionable and could not very well be brought into their circle. But they were pleased to see him again and he was pleased to be there. It was a long time since he had attended any of their parties, and now he felt excited. His eyes shone, his nostrils were slightly dilated: he had the poised expectancy of a hunter. The women were young and pretty and all of them emancipated, drinks were served in cocktail glasses, the gramophone played *Going Crazy in this Moonlight*.

He sat on a low divan with Shila, a dazzling beauty in a black transparent sari and a diamond necklace. 'We haven't met for a long time,' he said; and 'Yes,' she said, smoothing her sari over her lap, 'it has been a long time.' Her voice was deep and thrilling and invested all she said with a special meaning.

'How are we to absorb all those tons of steel?' her husband Pitu, a gross and ugly young man, was saying. Some other guests standing round him nodded and looked thoughtful. Pitu was the most influential member of their set (his father, once a wealthy barrister, was now the Governor of a State) and this entitled him to a great number of opinions.

'Our whole economy is based on waste,' he snorted. 'So much for our wonderful government.'

'Very hot again this evening,' said Vishnu to Shila.

'In summer the temperature always goes up very high,' she said, looking at him with her veiled, dark pools of eyes. He could smell her scent and it made him dizzy with pleasure. But Pitu stuck his head between them and shouted: 'It isn't as if we can compete in a world market!'

'But surely, Pitu,' said Toto, 'the basis of industrial expansion is our steel output.'

'Poppycock,' said Pitu. Toto, holding a drink in either hand for his guests, smiled to show he wasn't offended; unnecessarily so, for Pitu turned his back on him anyway and suddenly dug Vishnu in the shoulder. 'Are you aware how many steel plants they've been putting up?'

Gogo stopped dancing with Chuchu and flung herself with exaggerated fatigue on the floor near Vishnu's divan. 'For Pete's sake, give me a drink someone, quick!' She smiled at Vishnu as she reached up to accept another drink from Toto.

'Are you getting off with Vishnu now?' said Toto, for Gogo – unmarried and bohemian – was the target of all their romantic jokes. 'After all the vows you've made to me.'

'Toto darling, if you give me any more of those wickedly potent martinis of yours, I shall be making vows to all of you.'

'One steel plant, all right, two – well, maybe: but four! Four steel plants!' Pitu held up four indignant, incredulous fingers. Vishnu nodded and tried to look interested. But he was thinking not of Pitu but of Joginder, not of steel plants but of fountain-pens.

'Please, Pitu,' Gogo pleaded, 'don't let's get intellectual.' But the others had all put on serious faces and were ready for a discussion. Toto and Ushi were pleased: they liked to get such discussions going – it showed that they were not just flighty young socialites but, on the contrary, deeply concerned with questions of national importance.

'Our whole economy is based on a false premise!' Pitu shouted. He was pacing up and down and had got very excited.

Toto, however, kept a cool head. He turned his glass in his hand and gazed down into it with the critical alertness he brought to board meetings: 'Of course, it all depends in which direction we are deciding to expand.'

'I think we ought to concentrate more on our cottage industries,' said Premola Singh, a very intelligent and well-educated girl (she had a higher degree in Home Science). 'I was reading such an interesting article the other day on village handicrafts.'

'Village fiddlesticks,' said Pitu. 'That's all sentimental rubbish.' He made a sound of disgust, waved his hand in the air and stumbled over a hand-loomed rug. 'Careful!' everyone cried, and at once several hands were held out to steady him. 'It's time we got rid of all that village hocuspocus,' he snorted.

'Don't forget, Pitu,' said Premola Singh, 'that ninety per cent of our population are still living in villages. Village uplift is a very urgent programme.'

'You are a bunch of spoil-sports,' pouted Gogo. 'Who comes to a party to talk about village uplift?' She turned her back on everyone and knelt on the floor to select another gramophone record.

Chuchu Bhatt, who was rather witty, said: 'Gogo feels she is being neglected.' He helped her put a new record on the record-player and as he did so, he said. 'Never mind, Gogo, I still love you.'

'Anyone with any economic sense in his head can see at once that we won't get anywhere except by industrialization,' Pitu declared. He lit a large cigar and puffed it with authority.

'It would be the greatest pity,' Premola Singh argued, 'to let our old traditional crafts die out.'

'All our lovely pottery and hand-embroidery,' said Ushi.

Pitu sneered: 'We're going to get very far in the arms race with hand-embroidery.'

'I bought a beautiful embroidered shawl the day before yesterday,' Shila confided to Vishnu. 'It was costly, but it will look so nice on all my winter saris.' She looked down into her lap and smiled secretly to herself.

Gogo danced on her own in the middle of the room, her hands on her hips, her head flung back; she sang as she danced – *Can't Seem to Find My Way, Honey Hold My Hand* – attempting the same throbbing cabaret voice as the one on the gramophone record.

'Of course, I have packed all my winter saris away,' Shila breathed. 'As soon as March comes, I wear only my thin, thin summer ones.'

'Honey Hold My Hand,' sang Gogo and she stood in front of Vishnu, swaying her hips and tapping her feet, till he got up to dance with her. She danced in a dreamy, passionate way, with her eyes half-shut; but her body hardly touched his.

'Surely, Pitu,' said Premola Singh, 'you are not suggesting we give up all our own traditions.'

'A nation on the starvation line such as we are,' said Pitu without taking the cigar out of his mouth, 'has no right to any traditions.'

'Pitu,' said Gogo as she dreamily danced, 'will you stop your bloody argument.'

There was a gasp from all the other girls: 'Gogo, please – *language!*' but Gogo tossed back her short hair defiantly: 'I am only quoting Bernard Shaw.'

'Darling Gogo, we didn't know you were an intellectual,' said Chuchu Bhatt. Everyone began to laugh but Pitu shouted. 'How much longer are we going to stay a backward nation!' so they all looked serious again.

Afterwards Vishnu took Gogo home in his car. Chuchu Bhatt humorously called after them: 'I'll give you a ring in the morning, Vishnu, to see if you got home all right!' Gogo talked about the party and all the people who had been there. She talked fast and sat quite a long way away from him. Vishnu did not listen to her much; nor was he thinking about the party. Instead he was wondering about fountain-pens and how exactly they were made.

'Oh gosh,' said Gogo, 'it's so late – Mummy will be *wild.*'

And then Vishnu thought of Mala and the scene she would undoubtedly make him when he got home. She would shout and he would shout back, and they would both be fierce and angry. He stepped on the accelerator, thinking of her waiting there for him, and went too fast, so that Gogo cried: 'Oh, Vishnu, hold it, I'm too young to die!'

Sarla Devi wandered into the house, rather vaguely, and was stopped by a servant who did not know her. She had shuffled off her sandals before entering and was dressed in a plain cheap cotton sari; she did not look the sort of person who usually visited the house. It was indeed some years since she had entered it.

She asked for Vishnu, Mala, Pritti, and the servant stared at her suspiciously. Mala emerged from one of the inner rooms and was as startled as the servant. But, recollecting herself, she led her mother-in-law into the drawing-room where Sarla Devi, ignoring the furniture, sat down cross-legged on the floor. Mala could only follow suit, though she saw how ridiculous it was, the two of them sitting there in the best room in the house as if on the floor of a mud-hut.

'Please call the child,' Sarla Devi said. Pritti was fetched and stood with her finger in her mouth, refusing to come nearer. She knew her grandmother – Vishnu sometimes took her on visits – but did not care for her. Sarla Devi, though fond of children in theory, did not have any soft and petting ways with them.

'Come and kiss your Dadi,' Mala said. But she was not really trying and Pritti knew it and stood where she was. Only the ayah got excited; she whispered urgently, 'It is your Dadi,' and stared with intense interest at Sarla Devi, whom she had not seen before.

'The child is feeling shy,' Sarla Devi said, without rancour. She had lost interest by this time, so Mala told the ayah to take Pritti away. But the ayah, wishing to prolong her sight of Sarla Devi and perhaps take part in some interesting scene, urged Pritti: 'Look, your Dadi.'

'Go now, go!' cried Mala.

When they were alone again, Sarla Devi said: 'Please forgive me for coming today.'

Mala halted any aberration from the conventional, and an apology from a mother-in-law to her son's wife for coming to visit her was certainly unconventional. She did not know how to deal with it, and was consequently irritated.

'I was near,' Sarla Devi said, 'and I thought why not? I would like to see them.'

'I am happy you have come,' Mala said coldly. Sarla Devi felt the chill, but did her best not to mind it. She felt guilty for not being more attached to Mala and Pritti, and had come in a mood to make amends.

'It is wrong of me,' she said, 'not to come more often.'

Mala turned her face away. She had no use for such frankness and was indeed deeply suspicious of it.

'You are my Vishnu's wife, I ought to – ' Suddenly she switched to: 'I want to speak with you about Vishnu, I am unhappy about him.'

Mala stiffened even more, but waited in silence.

'He is not leading the right kind of life for him.' Servants, alerted by the ayah as to who had come, appeared at the door and stood and looked.

'You are his wife, you will understand what I mean.'

'No, I don't understand,' Mala said sullenly. 'Why do you speak of him like that?'

Sarla Devi was patient. 'You see, Vishnu is not like his father. He is my son also.'

'No, he is not like you!' Mala childishly shouted. 'He is like his father!'

'How can you say so?' Sarla Devi appealed with a sad face.

'Because it is the truth.' She got up and turned round and saw the servants looking in. 'What do you want?' she cried and stamped her foot. 'Why are you here?' and she was the more vehement because it was what she wanted to say not only to the servants but also to Sarla Devi.

'Don't,' Sarla Devi said and she seemed pained. 'You must not shout at poor people. You must always respect their feelings.'

Mala thrust open the french window leading to the veranda and went out, hot as it was. Respect was due to a mother-in-law so she did not want to speak any more. But her face was flushed and her ripe bosom went up and down.

Sarla Devi followed her. She breathed the air with pleasure. 'It is better out here. I don't like to sit in such rooms. Where is my son?'

'In the office.'

'Of course . . . But it is good he is not here. You and I are free to talk.'

It was intensely hot on the veranda; heat seeped from the stone floor and the tall pillars. And the garden, all that beautiful green, lay dead in the white sun.

'It is not right for him to live here; and not right for him to work in his father's business.' Sarla Devi began to talk with passion. But Mala was too excited, too angry, too hot to listen. She understood only the general drift of what her mother-in-law was saying, and she interpreted it as meaning that Vishnu was to leave everything – the office, the house, his child, his wife. Perspiration ran down her face, her eyes were pierced by the glare from the garden, head and heart thumped; and still Sarla Devi talked.

Mala, unable to bear more, ran back into the room and sank down on to a small fat stool covered in gold brocade. She wiped her wet face with the end of her sari; she shut her eyes and her breathing came as if she had been running for a long time. Sarla Devi, following her, said: 'But it is much nicer outside.'

Mala cried in a low voice: 'Why don't you leave us alone?'

Sarla Devi saw with surprise that Mala was upset. 'What is the matter?' she asked with genuine concern.

Mala hid her face behind her sari and gave a sob. Kusum would at this point have known exactly what to do: she would have rushed up to Mala, smothered her in kisses, overwhelmed her with comfort and love. But Sarla Devi only stood and twisted the end of her sari between her thin fingers.

Mala lifted her face and looked at her mother-in-law: 'It is you who have made him the way he is. It is all your fault.'

'But no, no! It is all his father's influence – this is what I have been saying.'

'Who has taught him not to care for his home? He roams about God knows where and gives not a thought to his duties. It is you who have taught him like that!'

'It is necessary for him to roam about. I told you, he is not like his father – he is *my* son,' and she clutched the cloth about her chest proudly. 'He will never let himself be tied down by ordinary worldly things but he will soar above them. That is his nature. Only now you are trying to hinder him, his father and you – yes, you also, I must speak out – '

'I am not listening to you!' Mala cried and put her hands over her ears. 'And I will tell my husband not to listen to you either, I will tell him never to go and see you again!'

'You fool!' cried Sarla Devi, and she forced Mala's hands down from her ears and held her arms tightly. 'Why do you shut yourself away from the truth? You sit here among all this furniture, you load yourself down with clothes and jewels, you feed yourself on rich foods – you have padded yourself with all the comforts of life, and now it is only comfort for you and no more life.'

Mala wriggled her arms to try and free herself, but Sarla Devi's grip was remarkably fierce. Mala cried 'Let me go!' and tears of fury welled from her eyes.

'But I will never allow you to make my son like that!' and in her agitation Sarla Devi shook Mala's arms up and down and Mala twisted here and there shouting: 'Don't touch me!' The servants came running, they stood round and implored 'Bibiji!' and Pritti cried 'Don't touch my Mama!' and tugged at Sarla Devi's sari.

It was at this point that Vishnu came home. He had left the office early and had come home for a bath, prior to going out to see Gautam. He was glad to be free from the office, he hummed a gay tune and swung his car-key.

He was soon in the midst of it. The servants crowded round him and Pritti beat her fists against his thighs, crying: 'Make her go away, she is hurting my Mama!'

Sarla Devi released her hold. She suddenly looked crestfallen and guilty. She remembered with what good intentions she had come.

Vishnu chased Pritti and all the servants away. 'Why are you here?' he said to his mother, when they had all gone.

'Yes, ask her!' cried Mala. She had got up from the stool on which she had been sitting and stood there, strong again and full of indignation.

'Why do you come if only to quarrel?' Vishnu said to his mother. She hung her head and twisted her sari between her fingers. 'It was for your sake,' she said in a low voice.

'She told me you must leave me and Pritti and your father and the office!' cried Mala. 'That is what she came for!'

'Be quiet,' Vishnu told her.

'Let her speak,' Sarla Devi said. 'It is all my fault. Please don't be angry with her.'

'My husband can be angry with me if he wants! I don't need you to defend me!'

Vishnu turned away in despair.

'Let me go home,' Sarla Devi pleaded. 'I was wrong to come. You see, I had wanted to explain to her – ' And then she was angry again: 'Why is she like that? What sort of a wife have they married you to?'

'And you stand there and permit her to say such things!' cried Mala, rounding fiercely on Vishnu.

He laughed. Both of them were so angry now, there was nothing else to do.

His mother walked abruptly out of the room. He called after her and followed her out on to the front veranda and watched her walking away. 'Do you want me to take you home?' She never even looked back.

He returned into the house and tried to get unobserved into his bedroom. But Mala was on the watch for him and followed him as quickly as her ponderous body would allow.

'Look at my arm!' she cried. 'See the mark where she hurt me!'

Just as she reached the bedroom, he slipped deftly into the bathroom and turned on the shower.

'She is a madwoman! Are you listening to me?' She banged on the door. Vishnu had taken off all his clothes and was blissfully turning himself to and fro under the spray of cold shower. 'It is dangerous to let such a woman into the house! Listen to me!' Now she was drumming both fists on the door and kicking it with her feet, but Vishnu went on enjoying his bath.

There was a meeting in Gulzari Lal's office. Gulzari Lal himself sat behind his desk, and grouped round the other side of the desk were his engineer, his accountant, a land broker and Vishnu. They were discussing the advisability of acquiring a certain piece of land for development. A site-plan lay unrolled on the desk and everyone except Vishnu looked very intent and, in making a point, tapped the plan.

The broker, a heavy Sikh called Rattan Singh, who had worked his way up from small beginnings, was very keen for Gulzari Lal to buy the land. Not unnaturally, for there was a good commission in it for him. He said: 'A first-class offer and at such a price – if you buy now, by next week I promise you I can get you a profit on it of two lakhs.'

The engineer was more cautious. He twisted his head this way and that, wishing to see the plan from all angles. He did not commit himself to any outspoken opinion but tapped a pencil against his teeth in a thoughtful manner.

The accountant was as volubly against the scheme as Rattan Singh was for it. He was an excitable young South Indian Brahmin, who took himself and his job very seriously. 'At this stage we cannot afford an expenditure of this magnitude,' he said in his rolling South Indian accent which made all the syllables run into each other and, by its near incomprehensibility, gave his utterance an oracular air.

'It is a first-class investment,' Rattan Singh told Gulzari Lal. His broad hairy fingers went along the outline of the plan. 'All the surrounding area is due for development so the price of the land will rise very high in a short time.' He struck a fist on his burly knee: 'Now is the time to buy!'

The accountant looked prim: 'We are not in a position to make such a large-scale investment at the present time.'

Gulzari Lal listened to both of them with an air of impartiality. The engineer was still not committing himself to anything, though he looked more and more thoughtful. Only Vishnu was not in it. He crossed his legs one way and then he crossed them the other way. He stared out of the window, across at the open ground facing the office. This was a public rallying place, which was used for political meetings and mass celebrations. Now it was deserted, vast and empty with a dusty flag flapping from a flimsy rostrum which had been built to simulate a Moghul throne, with a dome-like canopy and scrolls of gold paint which had already faded and peeled.

'I can find ten customers – what am I saying? – one hundred customers for this land this very day!' cried Rattan Singh. 'But I tell everyone, first I must see Gulzari Lal, Sahib: he is the man to whom this, the biggest bargain of my business career, must first be offered.' He had a loud, raucous voice with a broad Punjabi accent. Vishnu, who sat next to him, could smell his breath laden with drink and spicy food.

Gulzari Lal turned to his accountant: 'Perhaps if we pull out from somewhere . . .' He made it as a mild suggestion, but the accountant flushed furiously: 'It is not,' he said, and his hands were trembling, 'sound economy.'

'I see,' said Rattan Singh, tipping his chair back and with his thumbs in his armpits. 'To make a profit of three lakhs within a week, that is not sound economy. I see,' and he swayed his head with a kind of threatening knowingness.

'This is talk only!' cried the accountant. 'We have no interest in talk but in facts and figures. Facts and figures!' he cried and tapped a ledger on his thin knee with a thin forefinger.

Rattan Singh swung his chair back again and sat bolt upright: 'I will give you facts and figures!' he roared.

Vishnu's gaze left the empty parade ground and lingered lazily over the few booths that skirted it: a municipal milk-booth built of aluminium sheets, a cold-drink and betel-leaf seller with a thatched roof, a tea-stall under a tree built on upturned kerosene tins. He was about to yawn when he caught his father's eye and checked himself and leant forward with his elbows on his knees, pretending to be intent on the discussion.

'The municipality have taken over the adjoining colony of Bundi Busti,' Rattan Singh was saying, 'and once they have demolished that whole slum, you have no idea how much the price of our land will rise. Fantastic! Colossal!'

Vishnu wished to show himself an active participant in the discussion, so he said: 'I have heard that the people of Bundi Busti are going to take out an injunction against the municipality.'

'Where have you heard?' Gulzari Lal took him up rather too quickly.

Vishnu said: 'I have forgotten.' After which both of them wished to say no more.

'Very fine,' sneered Rattan Singh. 'You have heard. I would like to ask – what chance have those people to bring an injunction against anyone?'

'They have a case,' Vishnu said, with not much enthusiasm.

'What case? One of these five-rupee lawyers must have got hold of them and filled their heads with rubbish. Case! You won't worry about Bundi Busti. I myself' – and he thrust his chest out and beat his fist against it producing a loud sound – 'will bring you guarantee that there will be no trouble that side.'

The engineer cleared his throat: 'The engineer's problem in this case must also be considered.'

Gulzari Lal beamed on him: 'Yes please, by all means, let us hear what our engineer has to say.'

The telephone on the desk buzzed. Gulzari Lal lifted the receiver and his telephone operator said: 'There is a call for you, sir.'

A moment later Kusum's voice came out loud and fluent over the wire. Gulzari Lal looked at his son and gave an apologetic smile which Vishnu pretended not to see.

'I am in conference,' Gulzari Lal said with weak pompousness. But the voice only became louder and more fluent.

'After all, he is your brother-in-law, some consideration must be shown to him,' Kusum was saying into Gulzari Lal's ear.

He fidgeted and drummed his fingers on his desk. The accountant had opened his ledger and was shaking his head over the rows of figures. The engineer studied the plan. Rattan Singh was murmuring to himself indignantly Outside the parade ground, beyond the steel-framed office window, a group of workmen stopped by the tea-stall and fumbled for coins under their sweat-stained shirts.

Gulzari Lal said, 'I will ring you later,' and replaced the receiver rather hastily.

As soon as he had done so, the accountant raised a finger and, fidgeting excitedly on the edge of his chair, cried: 'Sir, there is one other point, sir!'

But obviously, though Rattan Singh and the accountant were still in fighting mood, Gulzari Lal was now in a hurry to finish the meeting. He let them carry on for some time, then said: 'I think we ought to give our engineer some further time for thought.' The engineer tapped his pencil against his teeth and looked thoughtful. 'We will meet again in a few days,' Gulzari Lal told Rattan Singh, who cried: 'With such a bargain there is no time to lose!'

Only Vishnu stayed behind in his father's office. He stood by the window and watched the cycles and bullock-carts go by.

'What do you think?' Gulzari Lal asked him. Vishnu turned round and looked puzzled. 'About the land,' Gulzari Lal said.

'Ah yes, the land,' said Vishnu with feigned eagerness. He bent over the map which still lay spread on the desk and pretended to study it closely.

'It is a good proposition,' Gulzari Lal said. He traced his forefinger along the plan. 'You see, it is very favourably situated – open on this side, and on that side a good commercial area. It is only here – ' And he stopped short over Bundi Busti and drew up his finger as if the place were hot.

'Rattan Singh seemed to be quite sure that things would be settled there?'

'Yes,' Gulzari Lal said, and nothing further, and then he rolled up the plan and turned to something else: 'The Bombay question is still open, son.'

Vishnu took up a pencil and played with it and smiled a little sadly.

'You are really needed there,' said Gulzari Lal, sounding hollow.

'Forgive me,' Vishnu said. At this point he would have liked to talk to his father about Joginder and his factory, but he did not know how to broach the subject. Besides, there was really nothing as yet to broach.

Vishnu, Gautam and Sumi sat on a shaky little wooden bench outside a sweetmeat-seller's and drank buttermilk out of tall brass tumblers. It was evening and the bazaar crowded, with everyone come out to enjoy the cool air. The shops were all lit up with electric bulbs and the barrows with flares of naphtha light, and there was music blaring out of various radios, sweet-sad music played at top volume, and horse-drawn carriages came trotting through with a merry jingle of bells from the harness of underfed but bravely plumed horses.

Gautam said: 'Of course it is the duty of Government to help those of us who wish to undertake some important work for community welfare.'

Vishnu watched Sumi. He felt very fond of her. He had never had a sister and – as a child and even as a young student – nad envied those who had. He smiled a bit, looking at Sumi's bony little wrists and the way she swung her feet from crossed ankles; most of her face was hidden by her tumbler of buttermilk. If he had had a sister, probably he would have felt about her the way he did about Sumi.

'I think perhaps I shall be able to get a grant of land from the Ministry,' Gautam said. 'I have already filled in a form.' He gave a scornful laugh: 'A form!'

'You have a white moustache,' Vishnu told Sumi, and indeed she had, a line of buttermilk along her upper lip. She flicked out her tongue and tried to lap it up, and Vishnu took out his handkerchief and carefully wiped it away.

'I told them: what are your forms to me? Shall I build my school on a piece of paper?'

On the opposite side of the road there was a small patch of empty ground where a cloth-merchant's stall had recently been gutted by fire. Here a hawker of medicines had taken up his stand and was extolling the virtues of his product. He had an assistant who squatted on the ground, beating a little barrel-shaped drum and singing a song composed in honour of the medicine:

71

'Is your wife happy in the nights?
Or are there big fights?
Make your wife like a dove
With your strong manly love!
Take Maha Purush Elixir
That surely will fix her!

'This is no empty boast!' cried the hawker. 'Out of this little bottle'
– and he held it up, a very ordinary little bottle with what looked like
very ordinary water inside it – 'has flowed the happiness of thousands
of wives!' Quite a crowd had already gathered round him. Children
wriggled their way to the front and listened round-eyed and en-
tranced.

'Forms are only a habit of mind,' Gautam said. 'When I don't want
to do something, then I tell myself yes, I will make a note of it, I will
do it tomorrow. Forms are the social expression of this kind of personal procrastination.'

'Pro-what?' said Vishnu, with a smile at Sumi who was craning her
neck to see the hawker. 'What is he selling?' she asked.

Vishnu instantly diverted her attention: one did not talk about such
matters with one's sister. 'You are not listening to Gautam,' he re-
proved her, 'and he is using such fine long words. How will you ever
become clever and educated if you don't even listen when people talk
clever things with you?'

'What to listen,' said Sumi. 'All day I hear him.'

The hawker's assistant, drumming his drum from both ends, lustily
sang with head thrown back and mouth wide open:

'Has God blessed you with sons?
Given you boys strong as guns?
Maha Purush is fine as tissue
And guaranteed for male issue!'

'There was a very respectable gentleman from Bharatpur,' said the
hawker. 'A Government officer in a high post, fine salary, nice house,
everything first class. But he was not happy. Why not? Please listen
carefully, it is an interesting story. He had been married for seventeen
years, God had given him eight daughters but no son. Then he came
to me.'

Gautam said: 'A man should not be allowed to stand in the bazaar
and fool poor ignorant people with such lies.'

'But perhaps it is not lies,' Sumi said in a challenging way and
looked at Vishnu for support.

'What is the matter with her?' Gautam said irritably. 'Everything I say she must say the opposite. She is becoming like a married woman already.'

'You always say that women must have their own opinions,' said Sumi, lifting her chin defiantly and swinging her legs, and aware of Vishnu's amused approval.

'By opinions I mean real thoughts, not shallow chit-chat – quack quack like a duck.'

'When I say yes to you it is opinions, when I say no it is quack quack.'

'She is not wrong,' said Vishnu with a laugh.

'It is you who encourage her in this new foolery of hers,' Gautam accused him.

'Fertility sterility,' cried the hawker. 'This medicine will settle all your problems!' More and more people, strolling through the bazaar and ready for a little diversion, stopped to listen. A man with an earthenware pot came and squatted on the edge of this crowd and sold brownish and almost cool water, served in one of two glasses which he washed alternately in a bucket.

'I shall pay another visit to the Ministry shortly,' Gautam said, 'and I think you had better come with me.'

Vishnu yawned: 'Once you start with Ministries – '

'We must leave no stone unturned. Our scheme must be pursued with energy and purpose.'

Reminded perhaps by these last words, Vishnu said: 'Why don't you ask Joginder to join you?'

'Joginder is a businessman. First of all, he would have no interest in an idealistic scheme like ours, and even if he had, he would soon turn the whole thing into a money-making concern.'

'Would that be bad?'

'Also,' cried the hawker, 'this medicine is guaranteed to dissolve the stones in your kidneys and bring relief from piles!' His assistant was now drumming his drum with the frenzy of the artist, swaying to and fro and his hair falling into his eyes. 'Even cases that have been given up by doctors in big hospitals have been known to be cured by Maha Purush Elixir!' The audience listened respectfully, and there was some earnest whispering here and there and groping for money.

'I am willing to admit,' Gautam said, 'that our society needs people like Joginder. To some extent I even have admiration for him, for he started with nothing and makes his own way. But it so happens that my aims are different from his.'

73

'How was it he started with nothing?' asked Vishnu, more interested in Joginder than in Gautam's aims.

'His family came as refugees from the Punjab – they had lost everything and lived for several years in a niche in the old wall at Kashmere Gate. Like animals in a cave!' he cried indignantly.

'Mana Purush also has very thorough cleansing action and will cure all disorders of the bowel system!'

'How different his life has been from yours,' Gautam said. 'You have always been soft in the lap of luxury provided by your father and have been content to roll in it, like an unborn child in its mother's womb, without even wishing to be born into the real world.'

'I think you are only jealous of Vishnu,' Sumi said. But Vishnu was thinking it was true, he was very different from Joginder, and rather wished it were not so.

'Only twelve annas!' cried the hawker. 'All these benefits for annas twelve only!' The crowd began to disperse, and a toyman with toys stuck on the end of a long pole wound his way through, blowing on a reed-whistle and drawing the children after him.

A group of young men, who had hovered on the edge of the crowd and had listened, half bored, leaning on one another's shoulders, now came strolling over to the sweetmeat-seller's. They tossed money on to the tin slab which served as a counter and demanded buttermilk.

'For ten annas you are buying health and happiness!' cried the hawker. Only a few people remained, looking irresolute and fingering their money tied in bits of cloth.

'Ten annas will give food for a family for one whole day,' Gautam said, 'and this quack is stealing it out of their mouths.' He looked angry enough to walk over and make a scene. Vishnu said 'Shall we go?' relieving Sumi of her empty tumbler.

The young men leant against the wall of the shop and looked about them for amusement. They were sturdy youths with heavily oiled hair and flowered bush-shirts hanging loose over their trousers.

Gautam got up and said in a loud voice. 'People should be enlightened as to the real nature of such men.' He turned half round, addressing everyone within earshot – the youths leaning against the wall and the sweetmeat-seller who continued heedlessly to pick dead flies out of his vat of cream. 'It is bad to rob the poor, but worse to rob them with lies and false hopes.' He stood there, thin, intense, indignant, with his long hair and his wilting homespun clothes. The youths looked at him, half grinning, winking at one another and hoping that something interesting would develop.

'Come on, Gautam, we are going,' Sumi said, and now the youths looked at her. Their interest quickened: Sumi was not a pretty girl but she was a girl and close at hand.

'When there is some work of importance to be done, then you run away,' Gautam said to Vishnu.

Sumi was aware of the youths staring at her. Their eyes were hot, and moist lips were parted over their teeth. She straightened her net scarf and turned her head away with instinctive coyness. 'O sweet words, O beware of sweet words,' sang radios into the bazaar.

Gautam turned to the shopkeeper: 'You as proprietor of this shop must make some protest. If a thief robs a poor man in front of your shop, do you sit only and pick flies off your cream?'

The youths swayed their heads to the music, their eyes on Sumi. Her head still averted, she put one hand up to the back of her hair and stroked it.

'Come on now,' Vishnu said to Gautam, impatient and angry.

'It is hard enough to make a living,' said the shopkeeper, 'I cannot also look out of my shop and see how the rest of the world is getting on.'

'Hallo sweetheart,' one of the youths said in Sumi's direction and another pursed his lips and emitted a sweet, wet, lingering kiss-sound.

Vishnu stood in front of them: 'Did you speak to my sister?'

'Your sister?' one youth said innocently. Vishnu struck him across the face. Sumi gave a loud feminine shriek.

'All your problems solved for eight annas only!' cried the hawker and his assistant gave a final flourish on his drum.

One youth stood holding his cheek. The other two edged in on him and glared at Vishnu, who glared back at them.

The shopkeeper had stood up behind his vat of cream. He clutched his slipping dhoti with one hand and with the other waved the wooden stick with which he had been stirring his cream. 'Get away from my shop! I don't want any trouble!' Passers-by quickly gathered.

'Are you mad?' Gautam said, attempting to hold Vishnu's arm.

Vishnu shook him off and called to the youths: 'Have you anything more to say?'

The youths muttered: 'Beating up people . . . he is a hooligan.'

People began to ask one another what had happened. Vishnu was pointed out as a hooligan.

'It is nothing to do with me!' cried the shopkeeper. 'I sit here, minding my business, I didn't ask them to come to my shop!'

'What did we do?' the youths asked him. 'We have paid our money, we were drinking our buttermilk and not disturbing anyone. It is he –'
They pointed at Vishnu. Everyone pointed at Vishnu and said: 'See

how he is dressed, just like a Sahib.' It was murmured that he was a
dacoit from the mountains of Madhya Pradesh. A respectful ring
formed round him.

'What sort of people are you,' cried the hawker, seeing the last of
his crowd melt away in favour of the spectacle opposite, 'that you
grudge spending even six annas for the sake of life-long health and
happiness?'

The youths smoothed their hair, dusted off their shirts as if something had been thrown at them and assumed martyred airs. 'It is a fine
thing when one can't even come out into the bazaar and buy a glass of
buttermilk without being molested.'

'You behaved very badly,' Gautam told Vishnu.

'If you have something more to say to my sister, then say it now!'
Vishnu called to them in a proud voice.

'He also speaks like a Sahib,' the onlookers commented with admiration.

The youths put back their half-drunk glasses on the tin-counter and
prepared to go, truculent with innocence.

'Why are you all standing here?' the shopkeeper called to the
crowd. 'There is nothing going on here! If you want to buy, then
come in, if not, then don't wear out the ground in front of my shop.'

'Look at his watch,' people said to one another. 'Gold – it is worth a
fortune. He is one of the big ones.'

Vishnu was disappointed. He was all ready for a fight, surging with
strength and courage.

The crowd parted respectfully as he left the shop. He was even
followed for some distance and people pointed out interesting
features about him to one another. He walked along, frowning and
with his face bent to the road.

Gautam was angry and scolded him all the way, but Sumi slipped
her hand into Vishnu's and she tickled his palm with a moist loving
little finger.

'Mala, he was so wonderful: like a king.'

If she expected Mala to be pleased and proud, she was disappointed. 'In the bazaar you said?' Mala asked incredulously.

'In the city, near the old gate, what is it called, Mori Gate.'

'But what were you doing there?'

'We were drinking buttermilk. There is a shop there very famous
for buttermilk. But I didn't think it was so very good, I have drunk
just as good or even better in Mathura. Oh, but Mala – you should
have seen him!'

'Only you and he?'

'And Gautam. You see, these people were rude to me – you know how people are rude sometimes to girls – ' She looked down and arranged the scarf over her inadequate little breasts in a knowing way. 'And Vishnu was angry, and he rose like a tiger. To protect me.'

'Oh!' cried Mala.

'And they were so frightened of him, they dared not look at me any more.'

Mala clasped her hands and said: 'Oh God.'

'They went away with eyes lowered like punished schoolboys. And all the people said how brave Vishnu was. As a matter of fact' – she began to giggle, putting her scarf to her mouth – 'yes, you know, as a matter of fact they thought he was a dacoit. How funny, Mala.'

Pritti came skipping in; she danced up and down in front of Sumi and challenged: 'You can't catch me!' Mala said: 'Go and play outside.' Then she shouted at the ayah: 'Why do you let her come here!' Pritti began to cry, the ayah to protest. But Mala outshouted them both and firmly shut the door behind them.

'What is the matter?' Sumi said. 'I like to play with little Pritti.'

Mala sat down and tried to sound calm 'Sumi, do you think it is right for a young unmarried girl to go into the bazaar and sit in a shop with two men?'

Sumi was astonished. 'What two men? They were Vishnu and Gautam.'

'Are you married to Gautam?' Sumi stared at her. 'Well are you?' cried Mala, forgetting to be calm.

'What is the matter with you, Mala? Why do you ask such silly questions?'

'Yes or no!'

'No, of course not – but why do you – '

'No.' Mala breathed heavily, getting herself together for the next question: 'Are you married to my husband?'

'I think you are mad today, Mala!'

'Yes, I am mad. It is I who am mad. It is I who let myself be taken into the bazaar by another woman's husband.' She wrung her hands: 'And shamelessly she comes and tells me!'

Sumi began to pout. She decided that Mala had no right to talk to her in this way and that it was time to stand on one's dignity. 'I am not a child,' she said. 'What is wrong? We are not in purdah, we are free like western women. I can go where I like with my friends.'

'You call my husband your friend!' cried Mala in a terrible voice.

Sumi gave her head a grown-up toss of coquetry. 'Can I help it if he is fond of me?' But then she found Mala standing over her and she quickly covered her head with her arms and cried: 'Don't hit me!'

Mala contemptuously drew away. She said: 'You had better go home to your sister.'

Sumi was sobbing, her face in her hands. She did not move, but dared say nothing further.

'And if I were your sister, I would not allow you to run here and there wherever you please and with whomever you please, oh no. How do you ever expect to be married if you behave like this? What family will take you?' She looked down on Sumi's bowed head. 'It is no use crying now,' she said harshly. 'If you had behaved properly, there would have been no need of crying.'

'Mala, it is not my fault. Gautam is always saying how women must be free and go everywhere, and they made me come with them, Gautam and Vishnu – '

'Don't talk of my husband, don't dare say his name!'

Sumi sobbed some more.

'And if I hear that you have been with him again – ' Her hands clenched and her face took on a very threatening expression: of which Kusum, entering at this moment, got the full impact. She said, 'Mala, child,' nervously, then glanced down and saw sobbing Sumi.

'Go home now!' Mala commanded Sumi.

'What is the matter? What has she done?' said Kusum, grimly ready to take part in the proceedings against Sumi.

Sumi looked up and cried bitterly: 'Yes, what have I done? I thought we were friends – '

'Don't talk like that,' Kusum severely admonished her. 'How dare you come to this house and talk in such a way?'

Sumi looked pleadingly towards Mala, who however turned her back and looked out of the window, where she saw Pritti playing in the garden and sharply called to the ayah to take her out of the sun.

Kusum realized that she was allowed to take charge of the situation and did so immediately and with relish. 'You heard this lady say that she does not wish you to stay any longer,' she told Sumi.

'I am her friend,' Sumi said.

'What talk can there be of friendship between a girl like yourself and the daughter-in-law of such a house as this?' She took Sumi's arm and led her to the door. Sumi turned round and cried to Mala: 'I will tell Vishnu of the way you have treated me!' and then she fled, holding her net scarf to her weeping eyes.

'Wait till I – ' Mala made to go after her, but Kusum held her back in an affectionate embrace. 'Such a girl is not worth your anger,' she said. 'I told you long ago not to let her into your house. I could see straightaway what type of girl she –'

'It is not only her fault! He is even more to blame!'

'Who, child? Who is he?'

Mala sat down again, and now it was her turn to cry.

'Tell me,' said Kusum, warm and motherly, her arm round Mala's big shoulders. When she had heard everything, she was as indignant as Mala could wish for; so that at once Mala was prompted to bring out something else: 'His mother was here.'

'Here?' cried Kusum in excitement.

'And for the last time!' cried Mala, equally excited. 'How badly she behaved – oh, I can't tell you!'

Nevertheless she did so, and at length; and even when she had finished, she looked as if she would have liked to start all over again. So Kusum gave her hand a little squeeze and said: 'I know it was a great upset for you. She must be a very difficult woman.'

'She is a madwoman.'

'Oh no no,' said Kusum in gentle reproof, 'it is sinful to speak such things.'

'It is not sinful, it is the truth.'

'It is true that she is different from other people, this I have heard from many sides. But we must be patient with her, child. Just think how patient God is with us! And in every human being we must see God and worship Him.' She looked tolerant and good.

'Please ask Papaji not to allow her to come into the house again,' Mala said unmoved.

'No sweetheart,' Kusum said, 'please don't talk in this way. On the contrary, there is something quite different we must ask your Papaji.' She settled herself nearer still to Mala and put a loving arm round her waist. 'I think her brother is in great difficulties.' Mala looked hostile, but Kusum pretended not to notice this and carried on: 'It is hard for a man from such good family, who has always had money and nice clothes and also travelled a good deal in England and such places – yes, it is hard for him now to have nothing. Just think, one day you have so much and then the next day comes Partition and your family properties are all in Pakistan and you are here in India and you have lost everything. Yes child, it is hard.'

'But he is not the only one. It is the same in all our families. Papaji has lost all his family properties too –'

'But he is such a clever man, so good in business and, of course, he has been in Delhi such a long time. That is why it is his duty to help his brother-in-law,' she said, loud and clear.

Mala was amazed. 'How do you mean, help him?'

Kusum sighed and made wistful eyes. 'It is always our duty to help others.' She sighed a bit more and slowly stroked the sari over her thighs. 'Where I see suffering and hardship, there I feel pity; this is the way God has made me.'

'What suffering and hardship?' Mala said scornfully. 'Whatever money he has had, he has drunk away and also' – she lowered her voice – 'he goes to bad women – '

'Who are we to judge the faults of others?' said meek Kusum.

'One should not encourage people in their immoral ways.'

'Ah child,' said Kusum, 'you are too young to understand how it is in the world. When we are older, we understand and we pity and forgive.'

Mala remained silent, sitting there on her large haunches and staring in front of her with stubborn eyes.

'Sweetheart,' said Kusum, taking Mala's hand again, fondling it and stroking it and holding it against her own warm, powdered cheek, 'you have such a sweet, loving nature, such a soft heart.' Mala let her hand lie inert and heavy in Kusum's and continued to look in front of her. 'Now you see, your father-in-law also has a good heart, where there is help to be given he will give. But he has so many things on his mind, there is his office and many business worries, so that he doesn't have time always to think and find out where a helping hand is necessary. You are his only daughter, and it is for you to point this out to him.'

'I only want to point out to him that my husband's mother must not come to the house again.'

Kusum dropped Mala's hand and even gave it a little push. 'I don't know what is the matter with you today.' She was used to finding Mala malleable and it made her cross to have to work harder with her than she had expected.

Pritti came in with a drawing she had made – a house, a tree and a swing – which she showed to Kusum with silent pride. 'How nice,' said Kusum, just glancing at it and sounding a perfunctory kiss in Pritti's direction. 'Please remember also,' she tartly told Mala, 'that it is your duty to love and obey your husband's family.'

'Here is a house with a window,' said Pritti, pointing it out with a colour-smeared finger.

Mala, sitting straight and stiff and with eyes downcast, said: 'Has his father ever complained of me?'

'And this is my swing,' said Pritti.

'There is not only a father.'

Mala turned her face away and shut her lips tight.

'I have drawn a bird in the tree – can you see it? There it is, pink.'

'Sometimes one must hide what one feels in one's heart and show a smiling face even to those one cannot love. You must learn all this, child, if you are to be happy in life.'

'You are not looking!' cried Pritti angrily.

'Come darling, show Mama,' Mala said.

'But of course I am looking – such a beautiful drawing!' Kusum cried effusively. But too late, for Mala had already taken it and Pritti was pointing out its charms to her.

Kusum watched them and felt – for the first time with Mala – rather worsted.

Sarla Devi cleaned her room herself every day. She swept it with a big bundle of twigs tied together and then she got down on her hands and knees and scoured it with a wet floor-cloth.

Brij Mohan, standing in the doorway, said: 'Fine work for you.'

She took no notice. As a matter of fact, she rather enjoyed such work and did it very thoroughly.

'If you wish me to talk with you, then leave that and stand up,' Brij Mohan said. 'I am not very much used to holding conversation with sweepers.'

'No, I don't wish you to talk with me.'

'This is because you are no longer in the habit of talking with civilized people. When I think of it, what you were, what we all were – ' He beat his fist against his brow. 'Get up,' he cried, 'what pleasure do you take in stabbing my heart!'

She wrung her floor-cloth out calmly in a bucket. 'If you are coming in, then take off your shoes.'

'Like peasants,' he grumbled, but took them off.

The tiny room was very clean now, with the stone floor glistening moistly and a fresh smell of water. Sarla Devi lit a stick of incense on the little table in the corner where she performed her prayer rituals.

'It would be a fine thing,' Brij Mohan grumbled, sitting on her bench and fondling a large naked foot, 'if she came here and found you doing sweeper's work.'

'Who came here?'

He groaned. 'For days I have been telling you that she wants to meet you – what is her name – your husband's – '

Sarla Devi put up her forearm to brush away the hair which had fallen into her face with her exertions. 'Why should we meet? There is no cause.'

'No cause,' said Brij Mohan, casting exasperated eyes to the ceiling. 'Here I have taken the trouble to get in touch with this woman on whom the honour of our whole family is now depending – '

Sarla Devi went out through the door and into the little hut which served her as a bathroom. It had one tap and a bucket of water. She unwrapped her sari and threw the water over her wizened body. When she came out, in a fresh sari and with her hair wet, Brij Mohan had gone to sleep. He lay sideways on the divan with his feet sticking out on to the floor. His mouth was open and chins and neck hung down in folds.

She shut the door quietly so as not to wake him and walked down the stone steps. Just as she was leaving the compound, she met Tara, accompanied by the old woman who acted as her chaperone. Sarla Devi stopped and greeted them. 'He is asleep upstairs,' she told them.

The old woman scratched her nose and looked cunning. She always scratched her nose when she met someone from a class not her own: it was both a defensive and an offensive gesture for one never knew, on the one hand, what one had to guard against, nor on the other what unexpected advantage one might not, with tact and cleverness, be able to gain. But Tara only looked sullen and stared straight past Sarla Devi, her jaws working on a betel-leaf.

Sarla Devi would have liked to prolong the conversation, to say something courteous and friendly to show them how intensely she respected them. But she could think of nothing of that nature and so passed on, feeling inadequate. Tara looked after her and spat red betel-juice in an eloquent manner.

Sarla Devi walked for a long time. She pulled her sari up to cover her head, but still the sun beat down on her and the glare of it pierced her eyes. Dust and stones from the unpaved roads got into her sandals, and she had to stop from time to time to take them out, sitting on some low wall by the wayside and holding her shoes in her hand. No one paid any attention to her; she was just one more old woman, in the plain cotton sari worn by the poor, sitting resting herself by the roadside. It was an effort for her to walk on again, but she always made it. She walked on the bank of the river, then under the bridge and along the walls of the Fort. Sometimes she stumbled with tiredness and heat, but she willed herself on. Her very exhaustion was a triumph for her: it brought her closer, she felt, to all the poor with whom she so much longed to identify herself.

It took her an hour and a half to get to Bundi Busti. The colony was just off a busy main thoroughfare and she climbed down a bank by a railway bridge, into a kind of trough. Here there was a sea of huts, side by side, row upon row, tiny squat huts crowded one against the other. The colony was built out of the salvage that came floating down from a more prosperous world – rags and old bicycle tyres, battered tins and broken bricks. Walls were made of dried mud or of tattered matting, roofs were a patchwork of old tiles, rags and rusty sheets of tin held down at the corners by stones. Sarla Devi walked through the narrow lanes between the rows of huts. The earth was streaked with runnels of dirty water, vegetable waste and peels were trodden into the mud and scratched up again by mangy dogs and pigs and a few sick chickens. And the lanes were all crowded with people carrying on their domestic lives in public – eating, cooking, washing clothes, carrying water – and hordes of underfed children playing games with gusto.

Sarla Devi made her way deep into the colony. She had come to see Ramchander, who was one of the self-appointed leaders of the colony. His qualifications for leadership were that he worked less and consequently had time to talk more than the others. He had even developed some oratorical skill, for he spent a lot of time talking about the grievances of the poor and how they must stand up and fight for their rights. People liked listening to him, for he always spoke with passion and used some fine long words; they would stand round him and nod in agreement, and this gave him confidence so that he became louder and more impassioned, waving his arms in the air and letting his hair fall over his face.

But now he was asleep inside his hut. His wife sat outside, sorting a few old rags which she kept turning over and over, considering their possibilities. 'Sleeping,' she told Sarla Devi contemptuously, 'lying there like a stone,' and she stroked one of her rags and held it up against the light. Ramchander's mother – tiny, frail as a dry twig and bent almost double – squatted on a broken string-cot with a child in front of her. She was squashing lice in the child's head with her fingernail; she seemed to enjoy this work, cackling, 'There you devil, get to hell', every time she caught one.

Yes, grumbled Ramchander's wife, that was the sort of husband she had: when other people's men went to work and did their best to fill their children's stomachs, he laid himself down and went to sleep. But in the nights now, oh then it was different; then no sleeping, then plenty of roaming about and talking and drinking of spirits ... She seemed ready to continue for some time but was interrupted by her neighbour who inquired, indicating Sarla Devi, 'Who is she?'

Ramchander's wife shrugged: 'She is one of the social workers'; and the way she said it suggested that she saw plenty of those and that for all the good they did her, they could stay where they came from.

'What about the other tap we have been promised?' the neighbour challenged Sarla Devi.

Outside an opposite hut squatted two women who were turning a pile of old examination papers into little dolls holding tiny parasols that twirled on a stick. When they heard talk of taps, they shouted: 'Have they come again with their big promises?'

'Two taps for the whole colony, that is what we have to put up with,' Ramchander's wife said, and now all the women were looking indignantly at Sarla Devi.

'Every time one of you comes we hear fine things,' said the women making paper dolls. 'This you will get, that you will get, everything will be done for you.'

The neighbour laughed hollowly: 'And what is done? Not this much – ' and she spat, sideways and with great vigour, hitting a pale little pig running across the lane.

Sarla Devi glanced into the hut. It was very low and dark but she could make out a figure huddled on the floor. 'Perhaps you would call him?' she timidly suggested. 'There is some important business – '

'For God knows how many years now you people have been coming and telling us certainly, you will get more taps, as many taps as you need. Go and wake your father!' she shouted at one of the children who were playing at fishing in a puddle.

'That is all we ever hear,' cried the women making paper dolls, 'promises – yes, on promises our bellies have grown good and fat.'

Sarla Devi would have liked to disclaim any connection with social workers who made promises for taps; but she felt too personally guilty to be able to disclaim anything. So she only looked down at the ground and suffered; and the women began to regard her suspiciously for she was not like the other social workers they knew, who were brisk and self-confident and told them in loud voices about hygiene and family planning.

Ramchander came crawling out of the hut, yawning and rubbing his hair. 'This is the time he gets up from sleeping,' said his wife. The neighbour and the women making dolls shook their heads and clicked their tongues at him.

'I have been working till very late in the night,' he quickly told Sarla Devi. 'I have found out some important news.' He invited her to sit on the string-cot with his mother who shouted 'Wait till I catch you!' at a louse.

'I would have something to say to my man if he played such tricks on me,' said the neighbour.

'They are trying to sell the land next to us,' Ramchander told Sarla Devi. 'There is a Sikh – a broker they say he is – who comes here to threaten us. Of course, if they can clear us out, their land will fetch a higher price.'

'Clear us out,' his wife said indignantly. 'I would like to see them try. For fifteen years we have – '

'Keep quiet,' Ramchander told her. 'Look to your own work.'

But the neighbour took her up lustily: 'Perhaps we are not human beings? Perhaps we have no right to live that they should come to us and say clear out?'

'Where are we to go?' shouted the women making paper dolls. 'They come and tell us get out, and then are we to wander in the streets with our children on our backs?'

Sarla Devi averted her eyes and again felt full of shame.

'This Sikh comes every day,' Ramchander told her. 'He says if we don't go quietly the police will come and beat us all up and take us into jail.' He scowled and clenched his fist. 'Go quietly! We also have our rights, we are not dogs. Let them send their police. They will see.'

'There is no need for you to put yourself forward and get into trouble with the police,' said his wife.

'He is right,' said the neighbour. 'We must show them.'

'Don't let any police come near!' cried Ramchander's mother in a knowing, warning voice.

'Who is he to show them?' said his wife. 'Let him go to his work properly first, and see to his family instead of talking talking all day long.'

'What work is there for me in this season,' said Ramchander. 'She knows it and still she eats my life up.' He was a cotton-beater who in winter went from house to house and fluffed out the cotton in people's quilts.

'For those that seek there is work,' said his wife. 'There is always coolie work – look at Shanti's man, all the summer he carries loads from a workshop and brings home two rupees every day. Even though he has a lump as big as a cabbage in his stomach and they say he hasn't got much longer to go.'

'Lump or no lump a man must work,' the neighbour observed.

'No working, no eating!' cried the women making paper dolls, their fingers nimbly folding and twisting.

Ramchander was sitting on the ground, leaning against the mud-wall of his hut. He was dressed in a torn sweat-stained vest and a loin-cloth. 'The poor don't matter,' he said. 'We can be cleared away like rubbish so someone else can make money. Who cares for us?'

'I care for you,' said Sarla Devi, with a sudden flash of eyes and a rear of the head.

'If tomorrow a rich man should come to me and say strip off your skin to make me a new pair of shoes, who am I to say him no?'

The old woman gave Sarla Devi a nudge. 'The poor need food in their bellies. Eat eat,' she said, poking a forefinger into her toothless mouth stretched open like a bird's.

Ramchander pointed at a pariah dog snuffling along the ground: 'If you are poor, this is how you are – like this dog, to be kicked by anyone who passes. For fifteen years we have stayed here, doing no one harm and only trying to stay alive and put a little food in our stomachs. And now they come and kick us like dogs – get out, they say, get out, dogs, there is no place for you here.'

Sarla Devi cried 'No one will kick you!' in anguish and guilt; but Ramchander's wife turned over her bundle of rags quite placidly and said: 'How he talks.'

'Just wait, my beauty!' cried the old woman to a louse she was about to squash with her murderous finger-nail.

'Instead of sitting talking so much, he should go out and work for his wife and children. There would be some sense. Words we can't eat.'

The neighbour laughed: 'Some for talking, some for working.'

'That is how God has made us and put us into the world,' said the women making dolls, and they too laughed and gave a merry spin to a newly finished paper parasol.

3

Rattan Singh sat in Vishnu's office. Vishnu's office was smaller than his father's but equally comfortable, with an air-conditioner and a pile carpet. Unfortunately it did not have a very interesting view, for it faced on to the back of the building and looked down into a small deep well and into the windows of the offices opposite. Young clerks sometimes appeared at these windows, leaning out for a smoke, and down in the narrow courtyard the sweepers of the building stacked their brooms and quarrelled with the porter. So there was not much incentive for Vishnu to look out of the window; and he spent a lot of time just staring at the wall of his office which was decorated with a trade-calendar featuring a lush and jewelled film star.

Rattan Singh filled the armchair facing Vishnu's desk. He had disposed himself at ease, his mighty hairy arms with the steel bracelet hanging over the sides of the chair and one large leg bulging in white trousers laid flat over the other. He wore a pink turban and his beard stretching across his broad face was curled and oiled.

'You are a young man,' he told Vishnu. 'You must be full of plans and drive. Yes, drive,' he said. 'It is very important. Without drive you can't make a success in business.'

Vishnu agreed with him, though he felt hot and sleepy and singularly lacking in both plans and drive.

'A young man like you will go like a tiger after every good scheme you hear of. That is why I am talking with you.' He stretched his mouth right back with his finger and picked a big lump out of his teeth. 'You will understand that an offer like I have brought must be snatched up at once with both the hands.'

Vishnu glanced up at the film star smiling sensuously out of the calendar; but she interested him no more than Rattan Singh did.

'What could be better?' said Rattan Singh. 'A fine piece of land in a fine situation, a bargain price. What is there to think about? Believe me,' he said, putting a sincere hand on his heart, 'no one has as great a respect for your father as I have. What a man! Such a head for business, such a fine personality, a king of a man. Only, you see, he is not so young any more.'

Vishnu said: 'You mean he doesn't care to take risks.'

'Risks? What question is there of risks? It is a straight-forward bargain and nothing else. No, what I mean is he has not got that fire of youth that makes a man leap on a bargain when it is offered to him. That is why I am here talking with you.'

Vishnu laughed. He knew how absurd it was that anyone should think him or even pretend to think him keener to drive home a business proposition than his father. He got up and said: 'I will try and set my father on fire, if that is what you want.' He hoped that the interview was concluded. Rattan Singh had an overpowering effect on the room, exuding a hot smell of perspiration, scented oil and spicy food.

Rattan Singh also got up. His chest was heaving with laughter and he put a huge hand on Vishnu's shoulder. 'Now you are making fun. Believe me, when you think about this offer I have brought you will see it is not a matter for fun.' He turned round and saw the picture of the film star which made him smack his mouth and sway his head. 'Hai hai,' he said humorously, 'let me also come in.'

Just then Sumi entered. She looked very small and miserable and held a handkerchief balled in her hand.

'What is it?' Vishnu asked with concern. He turned to Rattan Singh: 'I will talk things over with my father.'

Rattan Singh looked over Sumi. He was evidently not impressed by what he saw, but all the same assumed an expression of tact and discretion. He hit Vishnu on the back and said in a hoarse whisper, 'We will talk later', and then he almost tiptoed to the door. Sumi sat on the edge of the sofa, pressing her handkerchief to her eyes.

Vishnu sat down next to her and put his arm round her shoulder. This made her cry more. He felt her thin shoulders shaking; how frail she was, how childlike, how much she needed his protection. He held her and passed his hand upwards over her arm, her cheek, her hair, pressing her nearer against him.

'I thought we were all friends,' sobbed Sumi. It took some time before he pieced the whole story together, how Mala and Kusum had turned her out of the house.

'Never mind,' he said, 'you and I are friends.' But he could not blame Mala: on the contrary, it was Sumi he blamed for being so indiscreet as to tell her about that incident in the bazaar.

'But she won't let me be friends with you either,' Sumi wailed. 'She said so. Oh, and I have been so happy with you all. I have liked coming to your house and that time you took me to the club – ' She had another cry. 'I am only from a very simple family and in Mathura it is so dull – ' She was overcome with great feeling for herself. Vishnu began to comfort her again, pressing her head against his shoulder.

At this point Gulzari Lal came in, looking businesslike with his spectacles on and some papers in his hand. When he saw them sitting there like that on the sofa, he took off his spectacles and swung them in the air.

Vishnu unwound his arm from round Sumi and stood up. He said: 'Rattan Singh was here just now to talk about that land.'

Gulzari Lal put on his spectacles and took them off again. He cleared his throat. Finally he said: 'He has been to see me also.'

Sumi sat there and snivelled into her handkerchief.

'If the slum in the adjacent area can be cleared,' Gulzari Lal said, 'it is a sound deal.'

'It sounds like a very sound deal,' Vishnu said eagerly.

Sumi gave another loud sob. Vishnu shifted uneasily, looked at her and then at his father who pretended great interest in the papers in his hand. 'She is not feeling well,' Vishnu said.

'Ah,' said Gulzari Lal. He looked down at Sumi with an expression of concern. 'Perhaps an aspirin?'

'She felt faint in the street so she came up here and I made her sit on the sofa to rest herself.'

'Ah,' said Gulzari Lal again, and he and Vishnu avoided one another's eyes.

Afterwards Vishnu took Sumi home. He felt slightly annoyed with her: she had made his position unpleasant both with his wife and his father, and though he cared less about Mala, he disliked appearing in an unfavourable light before Gulzari Lal. Sumi talked of the dreariness of her life, how hard she had to work at her sister's and how her parents could not find a husband for her because of the smallness of the dowry they offered; and how she longed for excitement, for beautiful things, for interesting people. She had stopped crying and sat close to Vishnu while he drove; and listening to her, he began to feel sorry for her again and that same urge to comfort her the way he imagined he would have comforted a little sister, if he had had one.

But when they got to Shankar's house, there was Mrs Shankar in a very angry mood. 'Where does she go?' she cried. 'What does she do? And I sitting here with all the work!'

Sumi pushed out her lower lip and looked sulky. Vishnu tried to make himself agreeable. 'I brought her home in my car. She was not feeling well and it is so hot.'

Mrs Shankar suddenly swung out at Sumi and thumped her hard with her fist. 'Now get into the kitchen and do some work!' Sumi cried out loud and clutching her shoulder, where the blow had fallen, rushed into the house.

Vishnu felt angry and humiliated. But he could say nothing, for Mrs Shankar was Sumi's elder sister and it was her right to do what she liked with her.

'She is a girl from respectable family,' she told Vishnu in a furious voice. 'A girl like that can't sit in a young man's car and be taken where he pleases.' Then she shouted: 'Please remember her marriage is still to be made! What decent family will take her if she is seen sitting in cars with young men like you!'

He drove away and, after some time, his anger gave way to melancholy. His feelings for Sumi were so pure, yet everyone – his wife, his father, her sister – suspected them. Such, he reflected, is the society we live in; and it seemed to him sad and deplorable that he could not feel brotherly affection for a girl without interference from relatives.

Kusum looked severely round Brij Mohan's room. She said nothing but the expression on her face and the way she fastidiously chose to sit only on the very edge of the chair made her opinion sufficiently clear. Brij Mohan felt uncomfortable: never had he been so acutely aware of the shortcomings of his household. He began at once to justify himself.

'It is difficult for a man to live when everything has been taken from him.'

But Kusum continued to look severe.

Brij Mohan sighed. 'Often I think, what has become of me? What has become of my life? And then it seems to me that it is time for the end.' He sighed again and rather longed for the bottle which stood under his bed: but he was afraid it might make an unfavourable impression on Kusum. 'What else is left for me? For both of us, for me and my sister – '

'I have come to see your sister.'

'Yes, she is upstairs. We are an unhappy pair. Here we sit in this house which is falling in ruins over our heads, like our lives, just like our lives – '

'It is a good house,' said Kusum. 'Only it needs a little care and cleaning. Perhaps you will take me to your sister?'

'I will send for her.' He called for his servant who after a time appeared, rubbing his eyes from sleep, and was dispatched upstairs.

Kusum looked round the room, which was high and of good proportions. 'You can make it so nice here, just with a little trouble. And then what a fine impression your home will create on people who come to visit you.'

'Who comes to visit me?' Brij Mohan asked tragically. 'I am a forgotten man. How different it was once! You should have seen me in the old days at Lahore, the friends I had then – every day parties and outings, when we went on picnics we took oven-baked chickens and bottles of beer with us and a whole party of servants carrying our silver cutlery and special English picnic sets made of bakelite.'

'It is little use to dwell on things of the past. I would be in a poor way if I looked back only on the past, on that time when my dear husband, Major Mehra, was still with us. You don't know what it was like to be an army officer's wife in those days, what privileges we had, what position, what respect. Well it is finished, it is all gone, and however much I cry for it, it won't come back. So I look only to the present and the future. That is why I am here today,' she added with a determination which chilled Brij Mohan.

The servant returned to say that Sarla Devi was out.

'Where out?' Kusum tackled him.

'There is a lock on her door, but I called through the door, even though I saw the lock, I called Bibiji, are you there? They are asking for you downstairs, a fine lady has come. But she did not answer. Who knows where she has gone? She runs here, she runs there, nobody knows.'

'Go go,' said Brij Mohan, 'we have heard enough.' He felt guilty. It seemed to him that he had promised Kusum that, any time she came, Sarla Devi would be there and ready to talk to her.

'She must have gone out,' he said.

'So it seems.'

'She does a great deal of good work. She goes out to see poor people, she helps them. She has a lot of feeling for the poor.'

'It is our duty to help the poor, God expects it from us.'

'She is a saint!' Brij Mohan cried. 'For herself she wants nothing, only for others, always for others. If someone comes to her and says give me your jewels, give me your clothes, your food, the house you live in, she would give without one thought, she would strip herself of all.'

Kusum nodded. 'There are such natures.'

'They go too far. And in such cases it is the duty of those close to them,' he said and, narrowing his eyes, looked shrewd, 'to guard their interests and see to it that people don't come and take from them what is theirs by right.' After which he had enough moral courage to put his hand under the bed on which he was sitting and bring out his bottle, with a glass conveniently poised on it.

Kusum smoothed her sari over her lap. Her face assumed a soft, thoughtful expression. 'Certainly,' she said, and her voice too was soft and thoughtful, 'it is necessary to look after those near and dear to us.'

'Our duty,' he said and took a drink which refreshed him considerably. He sat up straighter, there on the bed with his knees in crumpled trousers set apart and his fists, one of which held an empty glass, planted sturdily on them. 'I am still a proud man, a very proud man, Mrs Mehra, and the honour of my family is dearer to me than my life.'

Kusum smiled, a very charming feminine smile. 'It is a great thing to esteem the honour of one's family. It shows breeding and courage – oh such people one must honour and admire!' She looked at him and her eyes were shining. She was wearing a pale muslin sari that billowed about her with a design of hand-embroidered roses. And she smelt all fresh and cared-for with powder and eau-de-Cologne, and her cheeks, though not young, were soft and rosy.

'And how true it is,' she said. 'How true that we must look after the interests of those near and dear to us, and guard them and be fierce and watchful for them – yes yes, you are right and noble to say it!'

Brij Mohan cleared his throat, shifted his thighs a bit and lowered his eyes modestly: 'A brother must look after his sister, that is what he is there for, it is his duty.'

'But how many brothers are there who follow this duty? So many cases you hear and read of, where a brother is quite heedless of his sister, and even worse, where he is bad to her and takes her money from her and is worse than a stranger. Only the other day I heard of one lady, who has been left a widow with quite a lot of property: in such cases one often hears that the husband's family persecutes the widow – well that is bad, but it is not quite unnatural, but in this case, just think, it was the lady's own brother, her own mother's son, who set lawyers on her and took her to court and altogether made her life so unhappy, on account of her property, that she didn't know which way to turn or look for help.'

Brij Mohan shook his head and made righteously disapproving noises.

'Yes,' cried Kusum, 'a noble heart like yours feels for such a woman, even though she is a stranger to you! And how much more will you feel then – oh I know it! – for your own sister, what will you not do to save her from suffering?'

Brij Mohan rose to the occasion: his hand on his heart, he declared: 'A sister's happiness should be dearer to a brother than his own.'

'How beautifully you say it. A sister's happiness – ;' and she said it again, with even more feeling: 'A sister's happiness,' and smiled and shook her head in silent appreciation. But a moment later she grew thoughtful, laying her head to one side and folding her hands in her lap: 'Only there is one thing,' she said in a slow, hesitant voice.

Brij Mohan listened.

'We must know what we are doing for someone is really for their happiness. Just think for one moment: do we always know what will make another person happy and what not? My dear father, God rest him, had at one time the habit of smoking a hookah. One day I thought I will make him happy and give him a new hookah. It was a very costly piece – beautiful work from Lucknow, all silver with flowers and little birds on it in red and green. But it so happened that just at this time he had been forbidden by the doctor to smoke at all,

92

so my present instead of making him happy made him more unhappy. This is only one small example.'

Brij Mohan scratched the stubble on his chin with his finger-nail and was on his guard.

'Happiness, what is happiness? It is in a person's heart, and who can read another's heart? That gift is God's only. It is a little stuffy here, perhaps we can open a window?' Before he could move, she had got up and moved swiftly over to the window; it stuck rather and a lot of dust flew, and afterwards she daintily wiped her hands on her handkerchief. 'And a person like your sister – no, let me speak, my heart is so full – I have heard how independent she is, what a fine free spirit! I admire her so much and often I think of her and love her already like my own sister. Her happiness is my happiness – but then also I think to myself: what is happiness? A person like she is wants to be free, this I know, she has no use for the ties by which other women, ordinary women, are bound.'

Brij Mohan opened his mouth to speak, but changed his mind about what he was going to say; and before he could rearrange his thoughts she had come and laid a hand on his arm.

'Who would wish to bind such a woman?' she said, sincere and urgent. 'Who would wish to bind the wings of the bird that wants to fly and soar away high into the sky and there nestle in the heart of God?' and she showed with her hand the upward flight of the bird and Brij Mohan's eyes involuntarily followed.

'It is wrong,' Kusum said. 'We must think of her – that must be our most important thought: what is best for her. And is it not best for her to give her what her nature needs, that is, freedom not only from the usual family ties but also from all legal ties? Of course,' she said hastily, checking anything that he looked as if he wanted to say, 'at the same time we must see to it that all her material needs are also satisfied and that she and those near to her can live in comfortable circumstances such as they are used to and their family honour demands. That will certainly be seen to. Perhaps we can open some door also to give us a little fresh air.' She opened the door nearest to her and discovered a bare little connecting room without any windows and nothing in it except some empty bottles in a corner and Tara sitting cross-legged on the floor, crackling her toe-joints.

'Now who is this?' Kusum said, though it was rather obvious who and what Tara was, as she sat there in a lilac-spangled transparent sari, filling that little room lavishly with the smell of her sweet scent.

Brij Mohan had jumped up. He ran to the door and attempted to close it. 'It is my niece who has come to visit.'

Kusum made no pretence of believing him. She looked severely at Tara, at the same time preventing Brij Mohan from shutting the door till she had looked her fill. Tara remained apathetic, ready to stay as she was till she was told to get up.

At last Kusum turned away. She made straight to the door that led out of the house; she had the air of one carrying off an affront with dignity.

Brij Mohan hastened after her. 'My niece,' he urged; and after a while, 'She understood nothing of what we said'; and then again: 'What am I to do? I am a lonely man.'

Kusum marched on, stately, high-bosomed, indignant. She took no notice of Brij Mohan pressing on her heels and made no reply to his protestations. But as a matter of fact, in spite of her stern mien, she was not ill-pleased with the way her visit had gone.

Mala paced up and down the drawing-room, wringing her hands and haranguing Vishnu. He had come here away from her, hoping that she would not follow him; she usually confined their scenes to their bedroom. But now she was desperate and did not care who heard her.

'And with a girl like that,' she said. 'An uneducated girl from poor family whom I had allowed into the house out of pity and who pretended to be my friend.'

Vishnu was sitting on one armchair with his feet up on another, reading the newspaper. He pretended to be engrossed in it, making a lot of show of running his eyes up and down columns and turning pages with a great rustle.

'Kusum auntie warned me against her. She said don't let this girl into your home, she is a bad girl. If only I had listened to her!'

'One should always listen to one's elders,' Vishnu said from behind his paper.

'Oh what am I to do!' cried Mala, striking her fist against her forehead.

Gulzari Lal came in, holding Pritti by the hand. Usually his entrance would have been enough to make Mala curtail her scene, but today she wanted help from every quarter.

'What quiet moment can I have when I know he is running here and there with such a creature?'

Gulzari Lal looked embarrassed. He bent down and kissed Pritti on the head. 'Go little darling, go and play with the new dolly I have brought for you.'

'I want to listen to Mama and Papa quarrelling.'

Gulzari Lal looked more embarrassed than ever. Vishnu began and stifled a laugh behind his paper. 'What is there to laugh!' Mala pounced on him. 'It is a matter for shame that your own little child should know what goes on between her parents.'

'I know why they are quarrelling,' Pritti announced, rather pleased with the effect she had made. 'It is about Sumi, auntie. Ayah told me.'

'At once that woman shall leave the house!' Mala cried.

Gulzari Lal told Pritti, 'Your ayah was only making a joke with you'; but when he saw the sceptical expression on her face, challenging him to substantiate his lie, he felt ashamed and looked the other way.

'Now it has come to this limit,' Mala said, 'that the servants are whispering about us, and even the child knows – '

'If you didn't shout so loud,' Vishnu said, 'who would know anything?'

'And if you were a different type of person, what would there be to know?' she came back at him, uncommonly quick.

'Children,' implored Gulzari Lal.

Vishnu tossed aside the newspaper and got up. 'I wonder you don't feel ashamed to make such scenes before my father.' He looked so angry that Pritti took her grandfather's hand and clung to it.

'*I* should feel ashamed?' cried Mala indignantly, pointing her finger at herself.

'The child,' warned Gulzari Lal without much hope.

'Let her know what sort of a mother she has,' Vishnu said.

Mala put her hands over Pritti's ears. 'What words are these for a child to hear from her own father? In my home, my father would rather have torn out his tongue from his mouth than let his children hear such words.'

'Then why don't you go to him? Why don't you go home? We hear so much about how you are going to Bombay, but till now I have seen very little of your going!'

'Not like that, son,' said Gulzari Lal.

'I shall be gone soon enough, then you will know!'

'Good,' said Vishnu, leaving the room, 'I hope this time it is a definite promise.'

Mala sat down heavily on a sofa. Pritti said, 'Are we going to Bombay, Mama?' pleased and excited.

'No no,' said Gulzari Lal, 'you must stay here with your Papa and your Dada, what would they do without you and Mama?'

'But Papa says he wants us to go!'

'He was only saying in joke.' Gulzari Lal looked down on the top of

Mala's sad head. He wished to pat it and say comforting words. He felt guilty, before her and before her father, that she was not happy in his house.

Kusum, appealed to, promised to try and take Mala out of herself. It was not an easy task. Kusum took her on shopping tours, car drives and to cinema matinée shows; but Mala remained sullen and unhappy. The only time she showed any animation was when the talk turned – as she so often made it turn – to Vishnu. Then her eyes flashed and she had plenty to say. Kusum did not encourage her on that topic; and sometimes she tried to explain to her that it might be better not to think so much about Vishnu: 'Show him that you lead your own life and don't care what he does, then you will see, he will soon come running to you. You must broaden your horizons, child.'

And with a view to broadening Mala's horizons, Kusum took her to tea with Mrs Bhatnagar. Mrs Bhatnagar was the widow of a rich industrialist (Bhatnagar Silks) and she was much respected for the wide variety of social work in which she was engaged. She was President of the All-India Society for Bringing Hygiene to the Depressed Classes, Vice-President of the All-India Care for Widows Association, Secretary of the All-India Rehabilitation Centre for Immoral Women and Treasurer of the All-India Home-Crafts for Industrial Workers Society. She would, Kusum was sure, be a wonderful example for Mala.

And there was also her daughter Ushi Saxena, wife of Toto Saxena of Burma Shell. Ushi, with her many interests and her advanced views, was calculated to be another wonderful example: but unfortunately Mala had already met her and had not liked her sufficiently to be pleased to meet her again. When she was first married, Vishnu had taken her to some of the parties of the Saxena set and Mala had not enjoyed them. She suspected and disapproved of the easy talk, the dancing to the gramophone, the educated girls with their educated views. It had been altogether too modern for her liking.

But she was somewhat reassured by Mrs Bhatnagar's drawing-room, which was not in the least modern. There were Burma teak sofa-sets and armchairs with carved legs, a big clock with Roman numerals and a glass-fronted cabinet which had angels carved on it and inside which could be seen the fine German china and cut-glass dishes which Mrs Bhatnagar had brought back with her from her trips abroad. On the walls were two dark oil-paintings, one of a lady in a crinoline holding a fan, with a foot-stool and a lap-dog, and the other of gondolas in Venice; these too had been brought back from abroad and were said to be very authentic.

Although Mrs Bhatnagar was devoted to good works and the uplift of the poor, she liked everything about her to be elegant and in good taste. Grey-haired and stately, she wore expensive sombre-coloured silks and big rings on her fingers. Her servants were dressed in turbans and with red cummerbunds round their uniforms. The tea and cream and sugar came in a heavily ornate silver set and there were dainty refreshments on leaf-shaped china dishes with a design of rosebuds.

But Ushi, smart and young in turquoise, teased her mother about the elaborate arrangements of her tea-table. 'People don't have these things any more, Mummy,' she said. 'Everything is much more casual today.' And she smiled as she thought of her own gay parties, the buffet-suppers and the long-playing records.

'We are the older generation,' said Kusum. 'We can't try and keep up with you young things.' And she comprised Ushi and Mala in one glance: but Mala sat there stiffly with her teacup and made no attempt to look like a young thing.

'But everything here is so beautiful,' said Mrs Dass who was the only other guest present. She was the wife of a small-time dentist and lived in rather cramped circumstances in an overcrowded suburb. Her devotion to various of Mrs Bhatnagar's committees, as well as to Mrs Bhatnagar herself had allowed her the privilege of much coming and going in Mrs Bhatnagar's household and even to be invited to an occasional tea-party like this one. She looked round her with genuine appreciation: 'Who would wish to change anything?'

'Oh, we must always be ready for change,' said Kusum. 'If we don't change, these young people will call us' – she clapped her hands and gave a delighted laugh – 'old fogeys! Yes yes, that is what you will call us. And you are right. Even if we are not so young any more, we must always be modern in spirit.' She turned to Mala: 'This is the trend for us women today.'

Mrs Bhatnagar nodded gravely. 'Many wonderful opportunities are open to us today.' She spoke slowly and with weight, tapping a teaspoon to emphasize her point. Kusum nudged Mala to pay attention.

'We need workers,' said Mrs Bhatnagar, 'sincere and willing workers to help us in our task of uplift and rehabilitation.'

'Mummy,' said Ushi, with a wink at stolid Mala, 'you are giving us a presidential address.'

'Just listen to her!' cried Kusum. 'These naughty girls are always making fun of us. They think only their husbands and babies and parties are of any importance,' and then she cried: 'God bless them!'

'Oh please,' said Ushi, 'that's not fair. Just because we don't sit on all your committees and keep up with all your good works – '

'It is difficult to keep up with a person like your mother,' Mrs Dass said. 'Sometimes I think to myself: how is it possible for one lady to undertake so much work.'

'When there is work to be done, we have to do it, shoulder to the wheel,' said Mrs Bhatnagar.

Ushi said: 'Mala, you haven't been to any of our parties for such a long time.' She took a bite from a cheese pakora. 'Vishnu was at our house the other day. We had such a good time. Mummy, I wish my cook could learn from yours how to make cheese pakoras like these, they are absolutely yum-yum.'

Mala was suddenly alert. She said: 'When was he at your house?'

'They are so light,' Ushi said. 'When ours makes them they come out like lead.'

'I will send him to teach your cook,' Mrs Bhatnagar said.

'When was he at your house?'

'I have forgotten – some time ago. How nice it was to see him again. We all asked him – Vishnu, why don't you come more often and bring Mala with you?'

'Who else was there?' Mala asked, with an intenseness which was, under the circumstances, almost rude. Kusum quickly turned to Mrs Bhatnagar: 'I hear you are doing some wonderful new work for the slum colonies.'

'Always busy,' said Mrs Dass. 'She will not give herself a moment's rest.'

'Who else was there with you when he came to your house?' Mala said doggedly.

'Let me think: Pitu and Shila and Gogo – the whole crowd. It was fun.'

'What did you do?'

'I hear you are resettling a whole colony,' Kusum said. 'Such wonderful work.'

'There is this slum colony Bundi Busti that is to be resettled,' Mrs Bhatnagar said. 'Our aim is to build it up into a model colony. Once they are established in proper housing, it will be our task to educate them to a hygienic and useful life.'

'She has drawn up such a fine report,' said Mrs Dass. 'I think Government ought to print and distribute it everywhere, it will be a great step forward in our national life.'

Kusum swayed her head in admiration and Mala said: 'Was there dancing?'

'I have raised several points in my report,' Mrs Bhatnagar said. 'For instance, I have stressed that mothers must be taught to keep their homes, however humble, scrupulously clean. Also all fruits and vegetables must be washed in potassium manganate to prevent outbreak of cholera.'

'Once disease is checked,' said Mrs Dass, 'the mortality rate will be much lower.'

'Then there is family planning. Our choice lies between oral pills and rubber sponges. There is also the bead system.'

'Did he dance with Gogo?'

Kusum firmly grasped Mala's arm and squeezed it a bit harder than affection warranted. 'Come child, I think we must be going – these are all very busy people.' She laughed, got up, smoothed her sari over her prettily rounded hips. 'How I would love to read your report some time,' she told Mrs Bhatnagar as she kissed her good-bye. 'It is a very interesting subject for me.'

Gulzari Lal had made up his mind to buy that land. It was an excellent scheme, marred only by the proximity of Bundi Busti. But he had in the last few weeks shown favour to several sanitary inspectors and municipal clerks, all of whom had assured him that Bundi Busti was no problem.

And there was Rattan Singh who said: 'Leave it to me, I will settle them. It will only need a little – ' He rubbed thumb and forefinger together and looked shrewd.

'Yes yes,' said Gulzari Lal. What he was thinking of was the scheme itself, which excited him. It was a beautiful piece of land, and a lot could be done with it.

'There are a few ring-leaders, that is all we have to worry about. Once we have fixed them, the others will go quietly.' He sat on a chair, big and confident, with his legs astride. 'It won't come very costly. A hundred rupees is a lot of money to people like that.' He slapped the inside of his thigh and laughed with pity and scorn.

'When can you get me the title-deeds?'

'What is there to wait for?' said Rattan Singh. 'At once, this minute – '

Gulzari Lal picked up his telephone to fix a time with his solicitor. When they had done so, the solicitor said. 'About that other matter.' By the change of tone Gulzari Lal realized that the solicitor wished to talk about his divorce proceedings. He said, 'Some other time,' and hung up. But his mood was spoilt.

He tried not to, but he could not help remembering Sarla Devi's self-assumed protection of Bundi Busti. Though he persuaded himself that this was of no importance, that it was nothing but a temporary hysterical fixation, yet he was uncomfortable. Especially when he talked to Vishnu: for he remembered that Vishnu was aware of his mother's interest and wondered uneasily whether he would mention it.

'I have looked at the scheme from every angle, and the more I look the better I see it is.' Then he said: 'What do you think?'

Vishnu knew that this question was only a matter of form, and that what he thought would make no difference to his father's decision. But he said dutifully: 'It seems like a very good scheme.' He too was thinking of his mother and Bundi Busti; though of course – as Gulzari Lal might have known – he had no intention of discussing it with his father.

'A first-rate colony,' Gulzari Lal said, 'with three different types of houses, Class A, B and C.' He became enthusiastic and took up a piece of paper and drew on it with a pencil. 'And here perhaps we can have an ornamental lake.' Vishnu bent over him and also tried to seem enthusiastic. 'And this would be a good spot for an open playground,' said Gulzari Lal, 'and here the bazaar area would come.' He swept his pencil about with relish and he was smiling.

But when he looked up and saw the vacant expression on Vishnu's face, his own pleasure went and he laid down his pencil. 'Yes,' he ended in a flat voice, 'we must look into it.' He pushed aside his piece of paper and after a while he said: 'Son, the Bombay question is still open.'

Vishnu said: 'I wouldn't do any good there.'

'You would be quite on your own, and all decisions would come only from you.' Vishnu was silent. 'And there is your wife also – ' But he remembered having said that before.

Vishnu got back to his own office as soon as it was politely possible. He was sorry he could not do what his father asked, but he was also irritated that he should keep asking. He felt as if everybody was asking something from him: and he longed only to be free and on his own. There were a few uninteresting files lying on his desk, which he opened between finger and thumb. Then he sighed and got up and looked at the picture of the film star on his calendar and out of the window down into the deep grey well where the sweepers' brooms lay piled up.

Soon he was sitting in his car and driving, without any great sense of purpose, towards Joginder's furniture store. He parked his car near a taxi-stand and walked through the bazaar. When he got to the shop, Joginder was not there, only his brother Som Nath who was standing by patiently while an Anglo-Indian couple were trying to make up their minds whether to buy a rather ugly table or not.

'Where is your brother?' Vishnu asked.

'You give us for twenty-two rupees and we'll take,' said the woman.

'Fixed price,' said Som Nath.

Vishnu sat down on a bed at the rear of the small, crammed shop. The couple looked as if they were going to be a long time making up their minds. The woman suddenly darted her finger at another table and demanded 'How much?'

'When will he be back?' Vishnu asked.

Som Nath hit his fist on the top of the other table: 'This one is also of very good quality.' To Vishnu he said: 'Why don't you come and see him at our house?' and he told him the address.

The woman opened the big worn handbag that dangled from her arm and peered inside it, perhaps to make sure her money had not been swindled away from her. 'Your prices are too high,' she said. Her husband nodded in gloomy agreement.

Som Nath protested, he pointed out the high quality of his goods and how nowhere else, anywhere in the city, would they be able to get such good pieces at such a good price. Vishnu looked up and saw himself reflected in the mirror of a wardrobe. Behind him were some chairs trussed together. He looked very much out of place and wondered why he had come. He got up and walked out of the shop.

On his return he found Gautam sitting in his office. He looked as if he had been there for a long time, but also as if he were prepared to wait for a long time more. He had made himself comfortable in an armchair, having taken his shoes off and drawn his feet up.

Vishnu did not feel like having any conversation at all. His eyes were heavy, a great unspent yawn held his jaws like a paralysis.

'How would it be if we went to the south?' Gautam said. 'We could start our school there.'

'Leave me alone.'

'I have never been to the south, and I think it is time I went. We are too parochial. The whole country is free and open to us, from the Himalayas down to Cape Comorin, and here we sit in one place and twist our hands and say we are bored.'

'When did I say I was bored?'

'No, you didn't say, you are too fast asleep even to realize it.'

Vishnu's head ached, his eyes watered with weariness. 'Please stop trying to make a better man of me. Please give me up as a hopeless case.'

'Don't make jokes at your own expense. For a man in your state it is very bad policy.' He was squatting in his armchair on his heels, with his hands swinging loose over his knees; he looked shabby and poor but entirely comfortable.

Vishnu shut his eyes and pretended no one was there.

'Once you start making jokes of yourself, you will start making apologies for yourself, and then you forgive yourself everything.'

Vishnu kept his eyes shut and his head buried in his hands; but his irritation was mounting.

'And in your life there is everything to forgive. At least let me have one of your cigarettes.' Vishnu threw the pack with such force that, in his effort to catch it, Gautam toppled over backwards in his chair. He lay there and looked surprised: 'That was not a nice way of offering me a cigarette.'

'I didn't offer, you asked. Also I have work to do, so perhaps you will go now.'

'Slowly, slowly. I have come to discuss one or two things with you. Perhaps you have forgotten about the school, but please remember I don't give up so easily.'

'But I do,' Vishnu said. 'I give up very easily and I have given up your school.'

Suddenly Gautam said: 'And Sumi?'

'What about Sumi?'

'I don't know what about Sumi. It is you who should know. Every day she wants me to go to you – tell him this, tell him that, why doesn't he come to visit our house.'

Vishnu yawned: 'She is such a child.'

'Perhaps she is a child but this doesn't prevent her from having some very grown-up feelings.'

Now Vishnu felt he had every excuse to be as angry as he pleased. He picked up a box of matches from the desk and flung them against the wall (there was a marble paperweight which would have been even more effective: but his mind worked sufficiently coolly to calculate that the noise this would create might disturb his father): 'Have I ever promised anything to her that you should hold her up to me like a murder I have committed?'

Gautam looked at him for a moment and then he looked away again. And the way he looked away, it was not in disgust, not in counter-anger, but only as if he were ashamed.

'I don't even want to hear her name any more!' Vishnu then cried, beside himself.

'All right,' Gautam said. He knelt down and picked the matches from the floor and put them back into the box. Then he pocketed the box and made for the door.

Vishnu let him go, and for quite a time afterwards assured himself how right he had been to be angry.

Brij Mohan sat on a chair outside his house. His chair was placed on what should have been the lawn but was now only bits of stubbly grass with big brown patches. A cow which had wandered in from the road was munching at the foliage growing rough and thick along the sides. Brij Mohan felt lonely and neglected. The old woman in charge of Tara had quarrelled with him about money and in revenge had not brought Tara for several days. And his servant had fever and lay shivering on the rear veranda. Sarla Devi had come down and given him medicine, but after that she had gone straight up again without talking to Brij Mohan at all. When he had followed her, she had locked the door.

He bent down and picked up a stone to throw at the cow. He missed and she continued to eat at her leisure. He wished his sister were not so different from other people. It was all very well boasting to Kusum about how altruistic and noble she was; but he did not really feel very boastful about Sarla Devi. He burped, an empty, painful burp: since his servant was sick, he had eaten nothing. Why would she not talk to him? Always with her wild schemes and her wild thoughts and wild prayers – there was more virtue, he thought with a deep sense of being done wrong by, in looking after a brother and living with him in peaceful companionship. He gave a scathing look up to her room on the roof. She had someone up there with her again, he knew; he had seen him walk up, one of her wretched poor about whom she showed so much concern. His stomach rumbled; he felt sick, sour, sad.

But then he saw Vishnu coming in at the fallen gate. The sight of Vishnu always did him good. 'Oh-ho,' he called, 'the Don Juan of Delhi!' Vishnu had parked his car round the corner so that his uncle would not hear him drive up; but now that he was caught, he put a good face on it.

'How are all the milkmaids?' Brij Mohan asked humorously but eagerly, and he patted his nephew as he always did, squeezed his arms, looked with love and nostalgia into that young, smooth, handsome face. Embarrassed with these attentions, Vishnu stamped his feet and clapped his hands at the cow, which made off with a clumsy clatter of hoofs and a piece of foliage still drooping from his mouth.

'What are you doing?' Brij Mohan said 'If your mother saw you, she would give you a lecture about how this cow must be encouraged to eat its fill from your garden.'

'She is there?' Vishnu asked, looking up to the roof.

'Don't disturb her, she is giving succour to the poor up there. Come in, we will have a drink.' He wished desperately to entertain his nephew. If only Tara had been there, she would have sung for them and they could have had an agreeable evening. But the house was empty and dull; there wasn't even anyone to send out for soda and cigarettes. Again his stomach rumbled and turned, and the sour taste came into his mouth. 'Leave her to her good deeds. We two will enjoy ourselves – we are both people who know how to enjoy ourselves.' He hit Vishnu's chest and winked and laughed and coughed loosely.

Sarla Devi's visitor was coming down the stone stairs at the side of the house. Sarla Devi leant over the parapet to call something after him and saw Vishnu. She was delighted: 'You have just come at the right time . . . Wait, Ramchander!' she called to the man and then she came down the stairs herself, all light and skipping in her enthusiasm. Brij Mohan gave an exaggerated groan: 'Now we shall all be pressed into social service.'

'Ramchander, my son will be able to help us.' Ramchander kept his eyes fixed on Vishnu's shoes, which were handmade of the finest kid leather. 'At least he will be able to find out for us who is buying that land next to Bundi Busti. From there we can see.'

'Leave the boy alone,' Brij Mohan said. 'He has come to see me, not you. We are having a good time together.'

'Once we have found out who they are, we can organize some kind of counter-offensive against these money-lenders.'

Ramchander kept his eyes fixed stubbornly on Vishnu's shoes. He stood in an attitude of aggressive lowliness – his eyes downcast, his hands meekly folded, a poor man, a hungry man, a man who had nothing and was nothing – so that Vishnu felt all too conscious of his own good clothes and healthy well-fed appearance.

'For you it is easy,' Sarla Devi said, 'you can find out all we want to know, since your father is' – here she hesitated a little, trying and not succeeding in keeping the note of contempt out of her voice – 'in the same line of business.'

But Vishnu was guilty and tongue-tied. He thought of Gulzari Lal Properties and wished he were not of it.

'Why do you trouble the boy?' said Brij Mohan. 'These things are all very well for old women like you whose life is finished, but this boy has something better to occupy his time.'

Sarla Devi looked from Vishnu to Ramchander and back again. It was as if she expected something momentous to happen from the meeting.

Afterwards Vishnu followed her upstairs. Brij Mohan shouted 'Come back, son! She will make you as mad as she is herself!'

'Somebody is buying the adjoining land and that is why they want Bundi Busti cleared,' Sarla Devi said. 'Already one of their men is going round threatening them. Some broker, they say.' She looked very small against the sky and the tops of trees massed round the roof. And how thin she was, how lined, how ageing.

He leant with both hands on the parapet. In the garden where he had once seen pretty girls shelling peas there was now only an old man smoking a hookah.

'Send him down here to me!' cried Brij Mohan from below.

Sarla Devi put her hands over her ears. 'If only he would leave me alone! How he talks and talks – his latest is that now I must meet what is her name – your father's – '

'Mrs Mehra? Kusum?'

'It seems that if she and I meet all the problems in the world will be settled.'

'Come down, son!' cried Brij Mohan. Sarla Devi took Vishnu inside and shut and locked the door.

'I have nothing against her, God knows,' she said.

Vishnu stuck a joss-stick into a brass-holder and lit it. Soon a warm, decaying, sweetish smell floated into the room.

'I wish her everything that is good. But why should I meet her?'

Vishnu fiddled with the things on her little prayer-table. There was a tiny plaster of paris Siva she had once bought at a fair and which was already considerably chipped, a copy of the *Gita*, a garland of marigold and a few sweetmeats she had offered in the morning. 'You are having divorce?' he asked. He ate one of the sweetmeats.

'If your father wants it, why not? What is there? My brother talks so much nonsense.'

Vishnu turned the pages of the *Gita*. He did not want to pass any comment; he was vaguely unhappy, though in principle he had nothing against divorce. *Treating alike pleasure and pain*, he read, *gain and loss, victory and defeat, then get ready for battle.* And they had of course been living apart for such a long time, it would make no difference whatsoever.

'But why are we talking about this?' she cried. 'There is something much more important.'

'Bundi Busti,' said Vishnu, still bent over the *Gita*.

'Something must be done. It is so shameful, so degrading, that hundreds of families must be turned out of their homes because there is some speculator who wants to double his profits.'

He was listening to her, but his eyes on the *Gita*, he read the same words over and over again: *then get ready for battle.*

'And what homes,' she said bitterly. 'There is the double disgrace that people should have to fight for their homes and then that they should have to call such places home. If you saw them, if you saw the conditions there – '

He was still looking at the book, reading *then get ready for battle*, but suddenly she snatched it from him: 'Is it all nothing to you – that people are poor and helpless!' He looked at her in surprise. She was so angry.

'Oh, Vishnu, Vishnu, why are you like that? You are my son, you are beautiful as Krishna and strong as Arjun. But your conduct is that of a little merchant's son.'

He turned away from her, but she came after him and held on to his arm; he noticed that she was not as weak as she looked.

'You must stand up, son, and fight, you must fling yourself into the world!'

'Fling yourself where, how?' Vishnu said, wrenching himself free from her. *Then get ready for battle* – but there was no battle he could take a part in, aching with unspent strength though he was. 'That's all I ever hear, great long words which sound so beautiful but when you want something more, there is nothing, nothing.' He walked up and down in that tiny room, cramped and impatient. 'Now if I wanted to start something really – nothing big, oh no, not like your words, only something small and ordinary – for instance, like making fountain-pens. If I were to come and say this is what I want to do, how you would shout, all of you, how angry you would be with me!' He passed his hand through his black hair, shut the *Gita* with a snap as he passed it, blew out the joss-stick. 'Oh no no, you would say, this is not worthy of you, now you are behaving like a little merchant's son!'

She remained quiet. There was such a silence in the room that Vishnu's angry voice still seemed to echo. Then she said, in a humble voice: 'Do anything you like, son. Only do it.'

Brij Mohan was drumming both fists against the door: 'Why do you lock this boy away from me? Let him come down and have a good time!'

Sumi rang Vishnu in the office. She said in a breathless little voice: 'Sister has gone for a wedding.'

'Gone for a wedding?'

106

'She has gone away for two days,' Sumi explained in agitation. She was telephoning from a neighbour's house. The neighbours were all listening with interest.

'Please come to my tea-party this afternoon,' she said.

'I don't know if I – '

'Please come,' she said desperately. The neighbours smiled and nodded to encourage her.

Vishnu hesitated for a moment, but sensing the agony at the other end of the line, quickly said, 'All right', and put down the receiver. But he was not pleased. He felt uncomfortable about Sumi and would have preferred not to see her.

She received him with a very serious face and lowered eyes. There was almost a hush of reverence about her, as if this was a very solemn occasion on which she had expended a lot of thought and feeling. He was more uncomfortable than ever.

Gautam and her brother-in-law Shankar were in the tiny sitting-room. They too had an air of constraint about them, as if something was happening which they should not allow. Sumi had bought some sweetmeats from the bazaar and had arranged them on thick little plates. She had also bought some fresh marigold garlands and draped them round the pictures on the wall – a coloured picture of Siva and Parvati on a cloudy mountain-top and an enlarged photograph, faded and white, of an old man in a turban and a big moustache. The little room was whitewashed, with large patches of damp and one small curtainless window protected with iron bars. Sumi had arranged three wooden chairs along the wall and there was a small table on which the sweetmeats stood. Otherwise the room was quite bare, but the sweetmeats and the garlands gave it a pathetically festive air.

'Here is our guest of honour,' said Gautam, when Vishnu came in. But Sumi had imposed too solemn an atmosphere for any humorous comments to go down well. They sat on the hard chairs ranged along the wall, reduced to silence, and submitted to the programme she had evidently thought out carefully before. The children, bribed with sweetmeats and sherbet, had been banished outside. They played around Vishnu's car, sounding the horn and drumming on the bonnet, and sometimes they came peering through the iron bars of the sitting-room window to watch the tea-party going on inside.

Sumi handed round sweetmeats. She stood offering before Vishnu, in a deferential attitude, as if they were strangers. And yet, far from feeling a stranger, he felt more than a friend, and it was so embarrassing for him that he dared not lift his eyes. There was not a smile anywhere. Gautam was bent over his plate, eating as many sweetmeats as he could, as fast as he could. Shankar cleared his throat several times, as if about to speak, but then only rubbed the back of his hand against his nose in a nervous manner. Sumi made the tea party go inexorably on, till everything was eaten and everything drunk.

At last Gautam said: 'It is a nice party, Sumi, but it is not very cheerful.'

'Ah,' said Shankar, 'the most important ingredient of any party is good cheer.' He looked round, smiling, pleased to have said something and perhaps broken a spell.

But Sumi remained solemn. She sat with her hands modestly folded in her lap and said: 'If you like, I will sing for you.' She had evidently had this part of the programme ready too. She discovered her small portable harmonium behind the door and sat down with it in the middle of the floor. One hand went over the keys, the other opened and shut the lid to blow the bellows. She sang a devotional song which was very moving and she sang it in a moved voice. 'Beloved,' she sang, 'you are sweetness, you are peace – take me to you in my night, ravish my soul away.' She had a weak little voice, but it throbbed with feeling. The harmonium throbbed too, lumbering gravely after her.

As always when he heard such music, Vishnu was sad and stirred. He thought of everything that was and everything that could be; life was at the same time unsatisfactory and full of possibilities. He looked at Sumi on the floor, singing, with her eyes large and longing; but he yearned for other, unknown things.

She finished, her hands dropped from the harmonium into her lap and sat with modestly lowered head.

There was a short silence, in which they all recovered from their strong feelings. Then Shankar cried 'Wah!' in applause and was seen to wipe a tear from his eye. 'When I hear such singing, my heart rises up, I feel strong and noble, and yet also very humble – ' He wiped again at his eyes, though there were no more tears left.

But Gautam shook his head. 'It is beautiful,' he said, 'but it is wrong.'

'Wrong?' cried Shankar. 'What can be sweeter than a pure young girl singing like that with love to her God?' Sumi kept on humbly sitting on the floor by the harmonium.

'In our country,' said Gautam, 'religion and the senses are mixed very closely. No, I am not saying that is wrong – on the contrary, what could be more right, how should we drink in our religion but through our senses?'

'Yes,' said Shankar, 'when I hear beautiful music I hear God speaking to me, and He is also in the smell of flowers and in everything that is delightful in this world.'

'But there is always a danger,' said Gautam. 'Especially for our women.' And he looked not at Sumi but at Vishnu, who got up and studied the photograph of the old man on the wall.

'Often they mistake what is lower in themselves for a high manifestation. How many of our women do we see hanging around healthy young swamis, they swoon with love and speak words of ecstasy – to whom? To God? Or to the swami?'

'Your father?' Vishnu asked Shankar, turning from his study of the photograph.

'May he be in peace and happiness,' Shankar acknowledged.

'And even when there is no swami . . . All these expressions of love and longing – come to me, I await you, ravish me – who knows whether they are meant to fly up straight to God or whether perhaps they are not meant for someone nearer to earth?'

'There is some resemblance,' Vishnu said, looking at the photograph and at Shankar and back again.

Sumi, though she usually had plenty to say, stayed quite still by the harmonium.

'What does it matter,' Shankar turned on Gautam. 'Love is some thing holy, whether it is for God or for man.' And Sumi looked up, with big eyes shining. Her brother-in-law tried to check himself for a moment, but then was carried away by his own feelings: 'Those who are young don't know it yet, how quickly love is stamped out by the cares that fall on us! In youth we are full of beautiful feelings and our hearts are soft and good. Is it wrong to be like that? Wrong to love and feel delight? Believe me, life loses its savour soon enough – there is no need to suck it out of young souls before it is time.' He had got very excited, but feeling Sumi's radiant, grateful look on him and Gautam's frown, he made a violent effort and broke off, waving his hand in deprecation. 'Perhaps I am talking nonsense, don't listen – ' He took out his handkerchief and wiped his face. 'Sometimes I get such stupid thoughts.'

Vishnu passed from the study of Shankar's father to that of Siva and Parvati on their mountain-top.

'No, you are not stupid!' cried Sumi.

'Oh, you are still here with us?' said Gautam.

'What you say is true – love makes us good – '

'Please take us for a drive in your car!' the children pleaded through the iron bars.

'Yes!' cried Vishnu, startlingly willing.

Sumi jumped up at once. 'Wait, I will also come.'

The children, pushing and jostling each other, piled into the car. Sumi climbed in after them, into the front seat where two children were already wedged beside Vishnu.

Gautam put his head through the window: 'Come out,' he told Sumi, 'let the children have their drive.'

Vishnu waited for her to go, but when she showed no intention of doing so, he started. The children gave yells of delight and bobbed up and down in their seats. 'Now I am going into second gear,' Vishnu explained to them.

'Did you like the song I sang?' Sumi asked.

'And this is third gear.'

'It is true that God is in the person one loves.'

The children in the front seat began to twiddle with the knobs and suddenly the windscreen wipers started up. 'Aie!' they cried, first in shock and then in joy. The children in the back seat tumbled over backwards with laughter.

They were speeding through the Government colony, past rows of yellow peeling little blocks of houses. There were no trees, only dust, and cows sitting in the unpaved roads. 'Our swing!' cried the children as they passed a barren little playground at the corner.

'He is God for us,' said Sumi, 'so that we want to worship and give ourselves to him.'

Vishnu, making for the house again, turned the block by a vast cinema-hoarding which showed a swooning actress in transparent silk against a background of swords and villains and buildings burning in bright orange flames.

'I feel so strange,' said Sumi, a hand on her chest. 'All day I think and at night also I lie awake and think. You don't know how I have waited and waited.'

Vishnu drew up outside the house where Gautam stood waiting, but the children wailed in protest: 'Just once again! Only once!'

Sumi also said: 'Only once.' Vishnu resignedly started up again and the children hung out of the windows and waved to Gautam.

'I don't want anything, only friendship,' Sumi said. 'She is coming back the day after tomorrow. You will come tomorrow?'

'There is Pattu's house! If only he could see us now!'

'Tomorrow unfortunately I am busy.'

'Then should I come to your house? Would Mala be angry with me?' Vishnu turned firmly once more by the cinema hoarding. 'She was such a good friend to me.'

'Just see, children,' explained Vishnu, 'now I wish to stop, so I take

110

my right foot off the accelerator and put it on the brake. Like this.'
Gautam opened the door for Sumi and the children to get out.

Gulzari Lal's favourite dream was of himself as a successful family
man. He was the provider, the mainstay, the prop behind his son, his
daughter-in-law and his little grandchild; and all that they had to do
was to be happy and comfortable in the luxurious setting which he
had devised for them. But although all the conditions for the
fulfilment of his ideal were there, nothing ever squared up to it.
Vishnu was out most of the time and Mala alone and discontented;
and Pritti trailed dully around with her ayah. Gulzari Lal would come
home from the office, all ready to play his part, and sit in the drawing-
room for tea which Mala poured for him out of a large silver pot. He
brought presents for Pritti and tried to make conversation with Mala
as they sat together in the drawing-room in what should have been a
happy family group.

But Mala's face was stern and Pritti was bored which made her
shout too loud and do forbidden things; so that Mala got angry with
her and told the ayah to take her away. And then Pritti could be heard
crying in another room and Mala looked severe and unhappy and
Gulzari Lal was pained.

Yet he could not really wish Mala different. She was as the woman
of a house should be: tall, stately, slow, broad-hipped; she was neat
and did exquisite needlework, she hardly ever left the house and had
no interests outside it. All these qualities ideally fitted her to be the
mother of children and the centre of a happy household. He had
recognized them the very first time he had gone to see her in her
father's house; and that was why he had chosen her. She was everything that his own wife had not been. But, all the same, things had not
turned out as he had anticipated them.

By late evening he was usually tired of his unsuccessful role of
family man and longed to go out. Sometimes he would offer to take
Mala with him – to a cinema, if she wanted, or just for a drive; but
she always refused, pleading that she had some sewing work to do or a
letter to write to her family in Bombay. So he would go out by
himself, for a drink in the club and a chat with business associates; or
– though not before a little struggle with himself – to Kusum.

He tried to prove to himself that he could do without Kusum, but
never succeeded. Even though nowadays his visits to her held little
pleasure, for she had two main topics of conversation with him and
hardly ever let up on either of them: the divorce, and how something
must be done for Brij Mohan. Both were unpleasant to Gulzari Lal,

111

and he often ended the evening by losing his temper and walking out on her. But she knew he would come back, if not the next evening then the one after that, and he did; and then she started all over again.

She never let him guess it, but Kusum was not happy herself. She missed her daily visit to his house and the sense of dignity and possession she had derived from it. She also missed their jolly loving times together, though it was she herself who was preventing them. She knew it was in a good cause, and that she was only giving up present happiness in order to lay up a future one on a more secure basis; but it was often hard. She would sit at home, despondently in an armchair, without even having her bath and in an old sari, sighing to herself; and her servant hovered around, making some feeble dusting gestures at the furniture and waiting for her to unburden herself. This she always did quite soon; she had no secrets from her servant, though he had only been with her a year or two.

'Life is hard when a woman is alone,' she sighed at him; and he sighed with her and beat his duster hard against the sideboard.

She would discuss the whole situation with him. It was like communing with herself, only she did not like communing with herself alone. And he always made the right comment at the right place (he was only a young man but very understanding – she had often found that domestic servants were more understanding than other people, they seemed to have a thorough grasp of life's complex problems). She often spoke to him of Gulzari Lal, sometimes with love and sometimes with anger, as she happened to be feeling at the moment. She sat with her legs drawn up on the armchair and her sari pulled half-way over her shins and she pressed and massaged her own feet as she talked. She felt comfortable like that, and even allowed herself to pass a little wind at times; it was nice to be at home and homely and sit there without having to think of one's society manners. She told him about Sarla Devi too, and about Brij Mohan. She had quite a lot to say about Brij Mohan: still a gentleman, from very fine family, educated and travelled in the west – but he had neglected himself, that was his trouble, and also he *drank*, she whispered; and the servant said ai-ai, what could he not tell of the evil that drink had brought into the lives of people.

So much had the servant heard about Brij Mohan that he had no difficulty in recognizing him when he came to call. Kusum was having a cup of tea in her sitting-room; she sat happily in a crumpled cotton sari with her hair unkempt and her shoes off. The servant whispered should he say she was out or would she go and get ready? She flew into her bedroom and shut the door behind her, but opened it again at once to whisper loudly: 'Show him in here and see he is comfortable.'

Brij Mohan, who had been left standing outside the front door, was ushered in. He swept his solar topi off his head and gave it and his cane in a fine absent gesture to the servant, who took them with aplomb as if every day gentlemen gave him hats and sticks to put away. Brij Mohan, in his faded silk suit, tapped his breast pockets with both hands and looked around the little sitting-room. The servant swiftly whipped away Kusum's half-drunk cup of tea, straightened a cushion here and there, picked a thread from the carpet. Brij Mohan lowered himself into a ruffled, flowered, little armchair. Through the wall – it was a tiny flat – he could hear bath-water filling into a bucket and a little later he heard someone moving about deftly in the next room. Everything was so domestic and comfortable; a little warm nest, he thought, and sighed with pleasure.

Then the adjoining door was flung open and Kusum appeared radiantly on the threshold. She gave a start when she saw Brij Mohan, then clapped her hands and uttered a little cry of delight and surprise. Brij Mohan got up, flushed and smiling. He bowed, but the single button doing up his silk jacket was tight, so he undid it and bowed again.

Kusum clapped her hands over his in a warm sisterly gesture: 'How proud and happy I am that you have come.' Soon she had him sitting with her on her sofa, while the servant made tea and fritters in the kitchen.

Brij Mohan felt happy if a bit bewildered. He had not expected such a warm reception. Kusum talked and talked; she brought down all the framed photographs and showed them to him: 'This is my daughter Nilima; this is Munni on her wedding day; and this is our own little darling, our little Kaka – yes I am a grandmother, don't pretend to be so surprised!' And Brij Mohan admired, nodded, studied, so that soon she had all her cupboards open and was bringing out envelopes stuffed with more photographs which she poured into his lap. 'Here we are on a houseboat in Kashmir, the whole family – this was in the year, let me think now, Nilima must have been fourteen – '

Brij Mohan had come in an apologetic and defensive mood. He had wanted to explain about Tara and had expected to have some difficulty doing so. But it appeared she had if not forgotten then at least forgiven; so he was content to let it rest for the moment and admire her family.

'Here we are in Mussourie – every year Major Mehra sent me with the children to the hills, from May to July, all through the hot season.'

Brij Mohan looked tenderly at the photographs. He murmured: 'Family happiness is a wonderful thing.'

'It is the greatest blessing granted to us,' Kusum said. 'Such warmth, such love as there is in a happy family group – it is God Himself laughing in our hearts!'

'My life has always been a solitary one,' Brij Mohan said in a hoarse and tragic voice. 'A life of loneliness.' There was a silence pregnant with sympathy and understanding. Then he said: 'That is why I have sometimes had to take for company people not quite of my social class.'

Kusum got up. She went over to her sideboard and took out a bottle of whisky which Gulzari Lal kept there for his occasional evening drinks. She poured generously and Brij Mohan took it with a look of such gratitude that she was instantly convinced she had done right. It was true, one should not encourage the terrible vice of drinking, but there were moments when a man's weakness must be condoned.

'She is a good girl,' said Brij Mohan. 'If circumstances had been different for her, she would have led a good life.'

Kusum picked her photographs from out of his lap and began to pack them back into their envelopes.

'I am like an elder brother to her. A girl like that, Mrs Mehra, needs someone to take an interest in her and raise her up to a higher level. Just think what her life has been, how she has been brought up and educated only to serve the weakness in men.' Impassioned, he drained his drink and moved nearer to Kusum on the sofa. 'It is to save her from such fate that I have her brought sometimes to my house where I can look after and care for her as for my own sister.'

Kusum got up to put away her photographs. He followed her, talking with conviction, hopefully holding his empty glass: 'In the eyes of the world I may perhaps be blamed for bringing such a girl as Tara to my house. But do I care for the world? It is only the opinion of those I esteem which is of any value to me.'

'Did you tell your sister that I came to see her?'

'Did I – ?'

Kusum sat down in one of her flowered armchairs, primly on its edge, with her hands in her lap.

'I told her,' Brij Mohan said, putting down his empty glass. She at once called to the servant to take it away.

After a while he felt compelled to say: 'She was very sorry she missed you.'

'She said so?'

He cleared his throat, swayed his leg, looked longingly at his solar topi and cane which the servant had laid on the window-sill. 'Perhaps I should be going.'

'What sort of friendship is this you are offering me? When the talk turns to matters that are close to my heart, then you say you should be going.'

'Please understand my position also,' he murmured, ashamed.

'Understand your position! I! When day and night I think of you and feel for you and turn over and over in my mind what I can do to help you. How often I have talked about you with him – '

'With Gulzari? You have talked about me?'

'Again and again! We are both very concerned. Of course he will do anything he can for you – ' How she wished at this point that she had something concrete and definite to offer him! For a moment she hated Gulzari Lal who – though she had begged and pleaded and stormed with him – still had not committed himself to do something for Brij Mohan. And because she could not tell him anything definite, she instead redoubled her warmth to Brij Mohan, she sat next to him again on the sofa, looked at him with tender feeling eyes and talked of friendship. And he, though there was some doubt somewhere in his mind, some feeling that he should not perhaps give himself over too completely, was yet so overwhelmed by the regard and affection she seemed to be bestowing on him that he allowed himself to rejoice in her friendship.

The servant stood in the doorway and watched them, glad that the visit was going so well. He enjoyed having visitors and hoped that Brij Mohan would come again.

Mrs Bhatnagar, with Mrs Dass and a young male secretary behind her, hesitated for a moment outside Sarla Devi's door. She had known Sarla Devi in the old days, when she was still living with Gulzari Lal, and did not relish meeting her again. But that was on a personal level: and where her work was concerned, Mrs Bhatnagar had no regard for the personal. She entered boldly.

Sarla Devi did not extend a cordial welcome. She had been sitting in her room in a sombre mood; Ramchander had found out and told her who had bought the land. She did nothing to disguise the displeasure Mrs Bhatnagar's unexpected visit gave her.

But Mrs Bhatnagar could take a cool reception in her stride. She sat down, uninvited but with some firmness; whereupon Mrs Dass followed suit, while the young man stood modestly outside the door, holding some files.

Mrs Bhatnagar looked round: 'A charming room.'

'So simple,' said Mrs Dass.

'Simplicity must be our aim in our daily living,' said Mrs Bhatnagar. 'In our country there is no place for pomp and show.'

Sarla Devi thought about Vishnu and how he was on his father's side after all. He could have told me, she thought; what harm would it have done if he had told me, instead of saying nothing. She felt bitter and betrayed.

'Our aim in life,' said Mrs Bhatnagar, 'must be not to create luxury for ourselves but to help our more unfortunate countrymen.'

'In this endeavour,' agreed Mrs Dass, 'we are all united like sisters.'

Sarla Devi was not listening to what they were saying, but their presence irritated her. They were the sort of people she had thought she would not have to meet any more. And her heart was heavy for Vishnu.

'That is why we are here today,' Mrs Bhatnagar said. 'I have come to know that you too are taking an interest in the people of Bundi Busti.'

At this name, Sarla Devi began to take notice, and at once looked suspicious.

'We have been working on a survey of the colony for some time,' Mrs Bhatnagar said. Without turning round, she snapped her fingers towards the young clerk standing in the doorway who at once began to fumble hastily in his files; but not hastily enough either for Mrs Bhatnagar, who expressed impatience by continuing to snap her fingers soundlessly in the air, or for Mrs Dass, who stood over him and said: 'Why are you keeping our President waiting, is this the way you do the duties you are paid for?' When the relevant papers were found, Mrs Dass passed them to Mrs Bhatnagar and the young man mopped his face with relief.

'Yes,' said Mrs Bhatnagar, looking with satisfaction at the papers lying in her lap, 'we have put in a lot of field work here and made a thorough study. We are now in an excellent position to assess the future needs of this colony. Some preliminary recommendations have already been made, which we propose to put into execution as soon as the new site has been occupied. Preliminary recommendations!' she called and held out her hand, and another sheaf of cyclostyled papers was quickly passed to her from the young man via Mrs Dass.

'Why don't you come in and sit?' Sarla Devi unexpectedly asked the young man, who became flustered.

'There is no need to bother,' said Mrs Dass, looking at him furiously as though it was he who had suggested a seat for himself.

'These recommendations will be further worked upon. We intend to have a very careful scheme prepared by the time the colony is moved.'

'Moved?' said Sarla Devi. She was interested now and forgot the young man, whose right to sit down she would otherwise have stoutly insisted upon.

'A very fine plot has been earmarked for them beyond Shahdara,' Mrs Bhatnagar said.

A beautiful airy place,' Mrs Dass corroborated.

'But they don't want to go,' Sarla Devi said in a tone which, if Mrs Bhatnagar had known her better, would have put her on her guard.

But Mrs Bhatnagar only smiled in a tolerant manner. 'It often happens that children don't know when something is done for their good. We must regard them like children.'

'Like children they must be guided by their elders and betters,' Mrs Dass said, smiling likewise.

But Sarla Devi did not smile at all. 'Elders and betters?' she inquired like thunder.

'We have already explained to them,' Mrs Bhatnagar said, 'that however far away they are moved, our workers will still come to them. As a matter of fact,' she said with an air of quiet efficiency, 'I have begun to make arrangements for jeeps to transport our social workers to the new site. The U.S. Ambassador's wife has kindly taken an interest in our work and is arranging for the jeeps to be delivered to us as a gift from the American people to the people of India. Only the other day we had morning coffee together to discuss the project.'

'And are you also providing jeeps to take the inhabitants of Bundi Busti to their work in the city?' Sarla Devi said, ominously calm.

Mrs Bhatnagar and Mrs Dass looked at each other. They realized they had someone very unpractical to deal with.

'Of course, this will not be possible,' Mrs Bhatnagar said with praiseworthy patience.

'Then also it will not be possible for them to move!' Sarla Devi shouted angrily. Mrs Dass and the young man were shocked: no one ever spoke in such a disrespectful tone to Mrs Bhatnagar.

Sarla Devi had a lot more to say and, in saying it, would have got even more disrespectful. But just then Tara and her chaperon appeared. The old woman peered into the room, bending round the young man who stood in the doorway and who, on seeing her, moved hastily aside.

'One word,' said the old woman to Sarla Devi. 'Only one,' and she held up a modest little finger.

'Come in,' said Sarla Devi.

The old woman's toothless betel-stained mouth was stretched wide in an ingratiating smile. 'We are not disturbing?' Tara stood behind her, looking sullen and reeking of scent.

'He is not there,' the old woman whispered into Sarla Devi's ear. 'I have brought my girl and he is not there to receive her.' So that the other ladies would not think badly of her for holding this private converse, she smiled at them again and joined her hands to them in greeting. 'He is not angry?' she breathed into Sarla Devi's ear, coming very close.

'Why should he be angry?'

'There was some misunderstanding.' She nodded, full of benevolence, at the other ladies, but there was an anxious look in her eyes. 'It has been very hard for my girl. How she has been weeping and weeping – even in her sleep she cries out "Take me to him, I can't live!"'

Tara, for one who had gone through such torments, looked very placid. She was aware of the young man's hungry look on her but she lowered her eyes and sniffed, genteelly holding her finger under her nose as she did so.

'She has a very soft heart,' whispered the old woman.

Sarla Devi said: 'Go down and wait for him. He will be happy that you have come.'

Mrs Bhatnagar tapped the papers in her lap: 'I shall be glad to discuss our recommendations with you. There are one or two points that will be of particular interest to you.'

'It is a very important memorandum,' said Mrs Dass. She looked furiously at the young man whose interest in Tara had not escaped her; but he was too preoccupied to notice.

'He has been asking for us?' the old woman whispered. 'He has been missing her?' She shut one eye shrewdly: perhaps there was more to be gained than she had reckoned on.

Mrs Bhatnagar addressed the old woman: 'We have come here on important business and there is still left much to discuss.'

'We are very busy people,' Mrs Dass added sternly. 'Our President is not a lady to be kept waiting.'

The old woman threw up her hands in horror. 'Aie! To have kept these fine ladies waiting, foolish old woman that I am, sinner, dirt!' She struck her forehead with her fist; there was a mischievous glint in her eyes.

'There is nothing to discuss,' Sarla Devi told Mrs Bhatnagar.

'Tara, beg forgiveness!' commanded the old woman, and she herself made a gesture as if to touch Mrs Bhatnagar's feet in humble submission.

Mrs Bhatnagar drew her feet away. 'You will find that our recommendations are calculated to have a far-reaching beneficial effect. Hygiene,' she said impressively; 'child welfare.'

'Literacy classes,' said Mrs Dass.

'Did he miss her?' the old woman whispered.

'We intended to make the new Bundi Busti a model colony by teaching these people a clean and healthy way of life.'

'He asked for her, he was unhappy?'

'It is difficult to be clean and healthy if you live in a hovel and don't have enough to eat!' Sarla Devi cried.

Mrs Bhatnagar looked serious. 'The answer is moral reform. The evils of drink must be eradicated.'

'And family planning is also very important,' said Mrs Dass.

'We are arranging classes in conjunction with the Prohibition League and the Family Planning Association.'

'Demonstration classes,' said Mrs Dass.

Tara lifted a plump arm and scratched herself under the armpit with a soft, refined motion. The young man's eyes burnt as he looked at the breast swelling tightly in satin under her lifted arm.

'Our expenses are very high,' the old woman whispered. 'And always she needs new saris and blouses – how long it is since he has given her saris.' Her breath was hot on Sarla Devi, laden with the smells of country liquor and of betel in a decaying mouth.

'Now our first task must be to get them moved to the new sites,' Mrs Bhatnagar said.

'Our workers will supervise them while they are putting up their huts and also give them some directions,' said Mrs Dass.

Longing for air and freedom, Sarla Devi cried: 'They are not going to move, they don't want to move!'

Suddenly Tara too cried out: 'What is he looking at? What does he want from me?' She wrapped her sari round her shoulders and glanced indignantly at the young man.

'Now, daughter,' said the old woman, 'don't upset yourself, he is a good young man, he is with these ladies.' To Sarla Devi she whispered: 'You see what a fine girl she is, how careful of her honour.'

The young man's face was swollen with shame. 'I was not looking,' he protested. 'I was only – ' Mrs Dass fixed him with a savage glance.

'Why don't you go away?' cried Sarla Devi. 'Why don't you leave me alone?'

Mrs Bhatnagar gathered the papers in her lap and stood up with dignity. 'We shall come again when these people are not here to take up your time.'

'I was looking there!' the young man cried, desperately pointing at the wall. 'I was looking at a lizard, it was eating a fly!' His eyes were brimming with tears.

'You made a mistake, daughter,' the old woman said. 'He was looking at a lizard which was eating a fly.'

'I am sure we shall be able to combine our efforts,' said Mrs Bhatnagar, passing the papers to Mrs Dass.

Sarla Devi said: 'Please go, go.' She shut her eyes and put her hands over her ears.

It was a quiet time in Bundi Busti. Most of the men had gone to work, and those who did not have any sat around outside their huts or drank tea on credit at the betel-seller's. Nobody was much disposed to listen to Ramchander, though he was in an eloquent mood. He squatted on his haunches under a big banyan tree and told them how they must all stand up and fight for their rights as workers and human beings. But his audience was scanty. There was a sick old man who had dragged his cot under a tree and lay there coughing, and a few children, and one or two men chewing betel in quiet enjoyment. Only Sarla Devi, sitting cross-legged on the ground with her hands folded in her lap, had the patient look of a listener.

But as a matter of fact she too was not paying much attention. She had heard Ramchander often enough before, and thought willing to grant that everything he said was true and more than true, she saw no point in only saying it. What was wanted was action, but here neither Ramchander nor anyone else seemed to show any resolution. It was true, they had presented a petition to the Prime Minister – but that had been more of a gesture than an approach to effective action. A chosen delegation had marched up to the Prime Minister's house and been received by a secretary, who had been polite and had taken their petition. After that there had been nothing else to do, so they had turned homewards; but because it seemed an anti-climax to do nothing but go home, they had visited one of the country liquor shops on the banks of the river and had had a pleasant evening of it.

'Because we are poor, we are not any the less citizens of this state. There are laws and statutes in which it is written that every man, whether he is rich or poor, has his rights. If they come and tell us "be off with you", we have the right to stand up and say "read your laws and statutes, see what is written there about poor people and how they

120

also are entitled to freedom and justice!" ' He had become very excited and beat his fists in the air. The old man on the cot coughed and, as he did so, groaned and clutched his abdomen. 'Are we men, or not? Don't we have wives and children to look after? Isn't it our duty to protect them and fight for our rights?' The children gazed at him with joy and wonder. 'Look,' they told one another, 'spit is coming out of his mouth.'

Sarla Devi had heard many popular orators like Ramchander. They always spoke with great passion and with many noble abstractions. She said: 'Now that you have presented your petition, you must also put your case to the corporation.'

'Nothing will be left undone!' cried Ramchander. 'We will fight like men and die like men!' But she knew it would be as difficult to persuade him as it was to persuade the others that any action of theirs could be effective. They were too used to the role of victim to be convinced that they had any power to act against an aggressor. The forces that decreed they must be moved out of their colony seemed to them as omnipotent and as irresistible as the tides of physical disaster which washed continually over their lives. One did not argue with disease, with famine, with death: one accepted, for one was after all only human and weak.

But she persisted: 'And if you can't get the corporation to revoke the order, then you must go to court and take out an injunction.'

The men sitting around looked at one another and shook their heads: 'It is difficult to get mixed up in these legal matters,' they murmured and spat out the juice from their betel.

And Sarla Devi had silently to admit it: it *was* difficult. If you had nothing and were noboay, corporations and injunctions were not to be dealt with lightly. And while you sat, like this under a tree, others – men like Gulzari Lal – who understood how things were to be accomplished, quietly approached the right persons, set the correct wheels in motion, and their work was done.

'We must claim our rights as citizens!' Ramchander declaimed. He wiped perspiration from his forehead. It was getting very hot under the trees. Flies hovered thickly and there was a smell of sewage mixed with that of cow-dung and food frying in cheap oil. Ramchander's audience slowly drifted away. Soon only the old man remained, and he had gone to sleep with his head drooping over the side of the cot.

'They are all frightened,' Ramchander told Sarla Devi. 'That broker has been here again – Rattan Singh he calls himself – and he has been threatening them with all that will happen if they don't quit.'

Sarla Devi got up to go. Nothing had been achieved. Ramchander said: 'And your son? He is helping us?' She looked down at the ground, at the cracked earth streaked with runnels of soiled water. She knew she should have told him that it was Vishnu's father who was buying the adjoining land; but she felt too ashamed.

Afterwards she went and sat on the banks of the river, all by herself in a little patch of shade thrown by a clump of bushes. There was no one about, only some buffaloes wallowing in the water and in the distance lorries carrying loads of sand. The river was in flood now and the water stretched as far as the horizon where it merged with the sky and lay all still in a shimmer of heat. There were only sun and river and sky, and Sarla Devi felt flooded with peace. The burden that lay on her heart had lifted and all the poverty and misery of the world had melted from her. She felt so pure, so blissful that tears came to her eyes; her body felt light as a straw blown on wind. If only it could be so always, if only she could be thus free for ever: free from her own body and from the sense of that of others. All her life she had wanted to be free and alone, like this, thinking nothing and being nothing, only a disembodied state of acceptance; and all her life she had been tugged back by her compassion into a world where nothing could be accepted and everything had to be fought against. She was not even a good fighter, but still she felt she had to engage, like an enlisted soldier, and could not opt out.

A tiny breeze blew up and shivered over the water and blew grains of sand into her face. Hot, slow flies crawled over her arms. She sat quite still. She thought if this is what it is like to be dead – but it was not like being dead at all, on the contrary, it was most intensely alive. When she was in the midst of people, she felt scattered along them into a thousand pieces; now she was whole. And she felt the urge, as often before, to forget who she was and never go back to the places where she had lived. Just rise now, from this silent spot, and go wandering she did not care where, as long as she could lose herself and be nothing. She longed for forests and mountains, for wilderness. She thought of herself blown by winds and ecstatic with prayers: never to suffer again for others, but free and filled with joy.

A boy with a long staff went shouting along the river's edge at the buffaloes, who came wading out of the water and shook their big black bodies so that water flew off in drops. 'Oy-yoh!' shouted the boy, dancing around the buffaloes and poking his staff into their glistening hides. Patiently they fell into line and, turning their backs on the water in which they had wallowed with such joy, plodded heavy and dutiful up the sandy incline and out on to the road.

And Sarla Devi too got up and went home, as if she too had been goaded and herded by a boy who poked with a stick.

4

Joginder lived in a colony some way out of the city. It was a newly built colony where small self-made businessmen had bought plots and put up houses out of their modest profits. Vishnu left the outskirts of the city behind him and then got on to the Grand Trunk Road, passing fields and wild hedges and many monkeys that went scrambling up trees and leaping across the road. But the city was creeping up: already here and there, among the fields and monkeys, there were little factories – brick-kilns and a paper-mill and a motor workshop; and every now and again a board set up in the wilderness advertising Plots for Sale on this Superior Site.

In Joginder's colony the site had already been cleared, many plots had been sold and a number of houses built. But nothing green – no trees, no grass – had yet begun to grow, many of the plots were still lying vacant and on others work had only just begun. Joginder's house stood all by itself, with raw land beside and around it; it was a small and rather ugly house, but it was finished and stood there proudly, amid the empty plots, the unmade roads, the litter of building materials. Some old women were sitting outside it, but as soon as they saw Vishnu they pulled their saris farther over their heads and hastened inside. Joginder was lying on a string-cot in a small inner courtyard, with his legs cocked up and crossed one over the other. Two young boys sat on the threshold between the courtyard and the inner rooms, ostensibly studying in books, though as soon as Vishnu came they concentrated more on him.

Joginder looked just as much of a brigand as Vishnu had remembered him – with his bad shave, his close-set eyes, his shirt unbuttoned over his great chest – but here he was a brigand at home, at rest, relaxed and expansive, a king. He asked at once 'How do you like my house?' and while Vishnu was still looking right, left, up in careful appreciation, added proudly: 'It cost me Rs 15,000 to build.' Several rooms opened out from the courtyard and they were full of busy noises – the clatter of pots and the sizzle of frying food, the swish of a broom, a W.C. flushing, women shouting instructions. 'It is all paid for and finished now,' said Joginder, 'the wood, the floors, the sanitation, I have paid everybody.' A baby started crying inside and at once there were soothing noises and snatches of lullaby as it was rocked still screaming, to and fro. 'It is all ours, our own house,' said Joginder; and then he added: 'Things were different for us when we first came to Delhi.' He lay back at his ease on his cot, and from that position told Vishnu how it was when they first came to Delhi and had lived in a niche in the old city wall; seven of them and in winter they had put a piece of sacking in front, to keep out the cold. The baby was still crying, so Joginder called out: 'Bring him here, none of you even knows how to keep a child happy!'

Vishnu was aware of girls behind doors, watching him; there was soft whispering and giggling and jingling of bangles; he rather enjoyed it.

An old woman in widow-white brought out a very large baby. 'My youngest,' Joginder said proudly. 'I have five of them, all boys.' He cradled the baby and made soothing noises at it. It had a big head covered with curly black hair plentifully oiled and wore a dress of shiny red satin. Its eyes had been lovingly painted with kohl and round one fat-layered arm it wore a black thread against the evil-eye. Joginder hummed to it and rocked it to and fro in his big arms, and soon the baby really was quiet. The old woman stood by, toothless and grinning and pointing with her finger: 'Look at that – only with the father does he find peace.'

Joginder looked down at his son, whose eyes were slowly closing. 'When I hear a child crying, I don't know how it is with me ... My younger brother was born when we were fleeing from the Punjab and when we got to Delhi there was no money, my mother was hungry herself so what milk could she give him? So always he was hungry, crying crying day and night with hunger.' The baby had gone to sleep now, but when the old woman made a gesture to carry it away, Joginder shook his head and kept it in his lap, rocking his thighs gently up and down. 'You have children?' he asked Vishnu.

'A little girl.'

'Never mind, God will give you sons also.' And, half lying there, across the cot with the fat baby on his thighs, he smiled the complacent smile of a man with five sons.

Vishnu cleared his throat and asked: 'And your business?'

'Thank God, things are going on well.' There was a short pause, neither of them wished to embark too openly on the matter on which Vishnu had come. Joginder yawned, the luxurious off-duty yawn of a hardworking man. 'In the beginning it was difficult, but now we are very well known in the market. I am even thinking of leaving this business entirely in the hands of my brother Som Nath.'

124

'You are retiring?'

Joginder flung back his head and gave a great laugh which made the baby start up in its sleep. 'I am not ready for that yet,' he said, hastily patting the baby on the chest. 'I still have some sisters to be married and two of my brothers are going through College – one of them is studying to be an engineer and the other is taking a course in book-keeping. Those two,' he said, pointing at the boys sitting with their books in the courtyard. When they were pointed out, they both turned pages and wore the engrossed expressions of boys studying hard. 'And my own sons will be growing up now and then they too must have education, and also my sisters' children, so it will be some time yet,' and he laughed again, 'before there can be talk of retiring.'

An old man in an unstarched dhoti drooping about his legs and a wilting turban wound round his head shuffled slowly across the court-yard to enter a door opposite to that from which he had emerged.

Joginder jerked his head in that direction. 'When I get to my father's stage of life, perhaps then I can think of leaving my business.' Vishnu thought of his own father, still very far from leaving his business.

Shrill voices came from the room which the old man had entered. There was an old woman's voice and an old man's. The old woman's had a raucous, earthy kind of strength but the old man's was much weaker, which made it tremble in impotent rage.

'Quarrelling with my mother is the only pleasure left for him,' Joginder said. 'He was the postmaster in our village before Partition and when he came to Delhi he could never get proper work. So,' and he smiled, shrugged and was tolerant, the successful son of his un-successful father, 'he just grew old.'

'You will leave Som Nath in charge of the furniture business?' Vishnu asked, quite casually.

The old people continued shouting. The old man accused the old woman of ruining his life and she accused him of ruining not only hers but that of her children also and her grandchildren. No one took any notice: the clatter of pots in the kitchen went on undisturbed, the girls giggled and jingled their bangles, Joginder rocked his knees under the sleeping baby.

And as casually as Vishnu had asked, Joginder answered: 'I am thinking of setting up a small factory for making fountain-pens.' He called to someone to take the baby away and then, relieved of his burden, stretched himself and gave another mighty yawn. 'I have a piece of land lying at Chandnipat,' he said.

Vishnu made a sound of polite interest, as if this was the first time he had heard of the scheme and was glad, in a disinterested way, to do so.

'You must come and have a look at it with me one day,' Joginder said; and after a while he laughed and slapped Vishnu on the back, for nothing in particular but only as a man will who has taken a liking to another. And Vishnu felt pleased and rather flattered.

Sarla Devi was very displeased with herself. This was not a new sensation for her, for she had always made high demands on herself and had always, in her own estimation, fallen short of them. By way of penance she would then set herself some unpleasant task and the discomforts she thus forced on herself – and often on others – were sops to a conscience which nevertheless hardly ever ceased to trouble her.

In the present instance the penance she imposed on herself was a comparatively light one, and consisted of nothing more astringent than a visit to Mrs Bhatnagar's. However, the prospect of this was to her so disagreeable that it almost compensated for her feeling of guilt; certainly, nothing except her duty to Bundi Busti – which she felt she had not been fulfilling as rigorously as was necessary – would have brought her anywhere near the house.

One of Mrs Bhatnagar's drawing-room teas was in progress and everything was measured and gracious. But Sarla Devi struck a discordant note: her very appearance was wrong, her cheap cotton sari, her untidy hair; and her entrance was rapid and rude, as she glanced impatiently round the room, stared at the elegant tea-tray as if to say, now what is all this, there is no time for this; and she looked as if she wanted to sweep it off the table there and then so that they could get on with whatever business it was she had come for.

However, Mrs Bhatnagar was a practised enough hostess to be able to deal even with so irregular an intruder into her drawing-room. 'Mrs Dass, of course, you have met,' she said firmly, 'and this is Mrs Kusum Mehra.' And then, in accordance with social etiquette, she reversed the procedure and introduced Sarla Devi to Mrs Kusum Mehra, who inclined her head and said she was pleased to meet her.

But Sarla Devi said: 'I have come to speak about Bundi Busti.' She did not even bother to sit down. 'I have already told you that it is not possible for these people to be moved.'

'You are just in time for some tea with us,' Mrs Bhatnagar said, making it sound as if this must please Sarla Devi as much as it did

126

herself. And Mrs Dass, assuming her role of intimate in the house, called to the bearer to bring another cup.

'First of all, the new site is too far away from the city. Then also, what right has anyone to move them? But we have been over that before: now the question is, what is to be done?' Mrs Dass pulled up a chair for her and, looking round at it for a puzzled moment, Sarla Devi sat down with a quick impatient movement. 'Your help is urgently needed. You may have some contacts in the right committees – unfortunately all this, which is a question of humanity, has to be reduced to committees and such nonsense.' Mrs Bhatnagar passed her, via Mrs Dass, a dainty porcelain cup of tea. 'I hope it is enough cream and sugar for you?'

'What? I don't want it, that is not what I have come for – yes, yes, all right, give it,' she said, for a cup of tea was hardly something to be made an issue of; besides, she disliked tea, so swallowing it became a part of her penance.

'Second thoughts are best thoughts,' said Kusum, trying to sound gay though she was rather nervous: for this meeting, which she had so long desired, was too sudden and unexpected.

'What we must do now is to pull some strings from our side and see to it that the eviction order is cancelled.'

'Now what may I pass you?' said Mrs Bhatnagar.

'Perhaps a nice cucumber sandwich?' Mrs Dass suggested.

'You see, these people are helpless. Where are they to turn to, whom to ask for help? That is why we must do everything we can for them.'

'Of course,' said Kusum, 'one must always help those who are helpless.' Sarla Devi turned to her and gave her a look so long and strange that Kusum became quite flustered and felt impelled to go on talking: 'That is a principle in life we must follow very closely, otherwise what is the use of all our health and strength and possessions and all the other good things that God has given to us?'

Sarla Devi's eyes lit up at that and she looked at Kusum as at a friend whom she was the happier to find because she had not expected to do so in that place.

Kusum was delighted with the excellent impression she had created and was determined to keep it up. She turned to Mrs Bhatnagar and exhorted her: 'We must not spare ourselves to do what we can in this case.'

'I think I may say that it is not my habit to spare myself,' said Mrs Bhatnagar with quiet dignity.

'We all know,' cried Mrs Dass, 'how you wear yourself out in the cause of others!'

'The people of Bundi Busti are my duty and responsibility, and I have never yet shirked either my duty or my responsibility.'

'Where these two things are concerned,' Mrs Dass informed the company, 'she is like a rock.'

'But the eviction order has not yet been revoked,' said Sarla Devi. 'And meanwhile a lot of pressure is being put by the people who have bought the adjoining land to have the order enforced.'

'Shame!' cried Kusum.

'If we don't stand by these people, who will? Who will ever care what happens to them?'

'We have studied the problem from every angle,' said Mrs Bhatnagar. 'There are many circumstances to be considered.'

Sarla Devi found herself looking for help at Kusum. And Kusum did not fail her. The fact that she was not quite sure what cause it was she was espousing in no way detracted from her enthusiasm for it. She put down her teacup and sat up in her chair: 'Where the innocent are to be saved from oppression, of course one must not wait, one must act at once!'

'There is no question of oppression,' said Mrs Bhatnagar, with patience.

'Quite on the contrary,' said Mrs Dass. 'By moving to the new site these people will get great benefits.'

'The benefit of walking to their work ten miles and back every day,' Sarla Devi said. 'And all because some speculator wishes to make more money!'

Kusum clicked her tongue in disapproval: 'There is nothing worse than to make your profit out of the sufferings of poor people. When I hear of such behaviour, I ask myself how is it possible for man's heart to be so full of greed that he has no feeling for others?'

Mrs Bhatnagar said: 'It is not for reasons of private speculation that the colony is to be shifted but as part of a larger programme of rehabilitation.'

'Rehabilitation and resettlement of sub-standard housing groups,' said Mrs Dass with an earnest and important face.

But Sarla Devi cried: 'Rehabilitation is only another word for getting them out of the way so that others can make their profits!'

At this Kusum began clicking her tongue again: 'And who are the unscrupulous people who are behaving in this shameful manner?'

Sarla Devi hesitated for a moment, but then she said it out loudly: 'It is Gulzari Lal Properties.'

'Disgraceful,' Kusum said at once and without giving a sign.

'Let me repeat again,' said Mrs Bhatnagar, with her eyes shut as if in pain, 'that whoever is or is not buying the adjoining land has nothing to do with the question in hand. Our argument is based on a misunderstanding.'

Sarla Devi jumped up from her chair: 'But there is no argument! Do you think I have come here to argue with you? I have only come to tell you what must be done and that it must be done very quickly!'

Kusum laid a soothing hand on Sarla Devi's arm.

'Our line of policy on slum rehabilitation,' said Mrs Bhatnagar, 'has already been thoroughly thrashed out in committee.'

'I will send you a copy of the minutes of our meetings on these subjects,' said Mrs Dass.

'And we shall be happy to incorporate you on the relevant committee. We are always glad to welcome sincere and willing workers to help us in our task.'

Sarla Devi turned and with tight lips left the room. The other three looked at one another.

'She is a strange lady,' said Mrs Dass.

'With hot temper no good work can be achieved,' said Mrs Bhatnagar.

Kusum looked at the door through which Sarla Devi had disappeared. Then she too got up. 'Not everyone,' she said with a fervour calculated to make up for her own hasty departure, 'can be as patient and good as our Mrs Bhatnagar.'

She hurried after Sarla Devi and caught up with her in the street. 'Please don't be upset. Everything will be done to help these poor people.'

'Who is there to help?' Sarla Devi said bitterly.

'I am there.' She put her arm round Sarla Devi and caressed her like a very old friend. 'Leave everything to me.'

That evening Gulzari Lal found Kusum as sweet and loving as he could wish for. And it was not until they had had their dinner and Mala had gone to bed, and there were only the two of them walking arm in arm in the garden, romantically by moonlight – it was only then that she said, 'Have you heard about a place called Bundi Busti?' in an innocent inquiring voice.

'It is a slum colony,' he said, calmly enough but on his guard.

'I hear it is to be cleared.'

'Slum clearance,' he said. 'How beautiful is the moon tonight.'

'It is like one of your costly silver dishes.'

'Don't say your. Say our.' He pressed her arm linked lovingly in his. 'What right have I – '

'Chuchu,' he said, tenderly, reproachfully.

She let that drop for the moment, important point though it was. 'You have bought the land next to Bundi Busti?'

'These are all dull office affairs. When I am with you, there is something better to talk of.'

They walked in silence for a while. It was a still hot night, full of moon and jasmine. They should have been very happy, arm in arm like this and alone, the two of them.

But happiness was not what Kusum had come for. 'Your wife,' she said, looking at him sideways and from under lowered lids, 'is very much concerned about Bundi Busti.'

He stopped walking and dropped her arm: 'My wife?'

She smiled, looking down at the ground. 'Oh, we are great friends now.'

He walked slowly back into the drawing-room. He rested himself in an armchair. She followed him and sat demurely on the carpet at his feet.

'How did you meet her?' he asked at length, in a voice full of gloomy resignation.

'Just think, it was quite by chance. Should I get you a drink?' She did so, and then sat back in the same manner as before. 'I felt a very great affection for her at once, as soon as I saw her, even before I heard who she was. This shows that blood is thicker than water, as the English say.' Realizing that, even if true, the statement was not applicable in the present case, she added: 'I am quite sure that in a previous birth we were born as sisters. I was told by a lady once who knows all about what happened in people's past births – she is a very gifted Muslim lady, a great saint to whom even foreigners come for guidance – this lady told me that in a previous birth I had a twin sister who died when we were four years old and ever since my soul has been seeking, seeking her, and one day I would find her. Now I have found her.' She had only just stumbled on this theory, and it moved her.

Gulzari Lal said, 'You are two very different characters'; and indeed, he thought with some relief, they could not have been more so.

'It is a very well-known fact that twin sisters are always very different in character from each other. But there is one thing we have in common and that is the great feeling we have for poor people.' She began tenderly to stroke his calves, prominent in white leggings, with

130

her finger. 'That is why, as soon as I heard about Bundi Busti, I decided that we must take action together.'

Gulzari Lal committed himself to nothing. He sat silent and patient, hoping that the conversation would take an easier turn than it looked like doing at present.

'Of course I know,' she said, running her finger up and down his leg, 'that with you there to help us there will be no difficulty.' And when he still said nothing: 'What can two weak women do alone? Everything is in your hands.'

Gulzari Lal finished his drink. After that he cleared his throat and was bold: 'There are some matters women don't understand.'

'Chuchu! Are you being old-fashioned?' She was mock indignant, prepared to keep everything light and on a humorous note.

'You should never,' Gulzari Lal said, quite firmly and not a bit humorous, 'meddle in business concerns.'

So she stopped stroking his leg and, adaptable as always, quickly changed her tone to his. 'So now trying to do good to people is called meddling,' she said, grimly nodding her head up and down.

'There is no question of doing good or not doing good. It is a business matter.'

'You are only a profiteer!' she cried. He was in no doubt now that she really had met Sarla Devi.

He lit a cigar and walked out with it on to the veranda. The garden, the moonlight, were as before, but he had ceased to find them beautiful. He sighed and, smoking his cigar, felt misunderstood, misjudged.

Left sitting alone by his empty armchair, Kusum began to feel sorry. She admitted to herself that she had been carried away. It was certainly not right to call him a profiteer; a man had, after all, to work and make the most of his business. It cost money, she thought, looking round the drawing-room with some satisfaction, to keep up an establishment like this.

She followed him out on to the veranda and stole her hand into his. 'It is for our sake,' she said softly. She loved the manly smell and look his cigar gave him. 'If you don't do something about Bundi Busti, she will refuse to give you divorce,' she said, very close to him and in a persuasive, urgent whisper.

Gulzari Lal puffed his cheek round his cigar and stared out into the garden through a haze of fragrant smoke.

'She will revenge herself like this on you, and who will be the ones to suffer but you and I?'

'She is not like that,' he said.

'How you talk! Everyone is like that. If she has a weapon against us, she will use it to gain her own ends, that is only natural.'

'It may be natural, but she is not natural.'

'I see. She is a monster. A very fine way to talk about the mother of your son!'

Perhaps she was better than natural. But he did not want to think about that. He himself was no better than natural and he needed a woman who was no better either. 'She doesn't think like other people,' he said.

'You have lived with her for so many years and still you don't know her. And I, after seeing her for only half an hour, can read her mind exactly.'

'It is not *her* mind you are reading, it is your own.' He did not know how to explain to her; except to say she is nobler than you are.

He suddenly threw away his cigar and put his arms round her, quite fierce and protective.

'What waste!' she cried, looking after the cigar now smouldering on the lawn.

'She is very different from us,' he said. 'The things that matter to us in life she doesn't care for at all.' He pressed her against himself. 'It is best for you not to know her.' She had her own opinions about that, but she kept a submissive silence and allowed him to go on holding her in his arms.

A cold reception was what Sumi had expected and had come prepared for. At once she bent down to touch Mala's feet in all humility and said: 'If I have offended you in any way, please forgive me.'

Mala was surprised, but not altogether ill-pleased. She raised Sumi graciously: 'Is this the way to greet a friend?'

At so much kindness Sumi burst into tears. And once she had started, she found it both pleasant and expedient to go on, so that soon Mala was comforting her. Even though there was no exchange of confidences, they had a warm scene together from which, when Sumi finally dried her eyes, they emerged almost as friendly as they had been before.

So it happened that when Vishnu came home he found them both sitting in wicker armchairs on the lawn, enjoying the evening air. From the distance came the sound of home-speeding traffic – motor-cycle rickshaws backfiring and over-crowded buses and rows of cyclists breast to breast – but only as a far-off echo emphasizing the stillness of that well-kept garden; and even the day's heat, which still lay over the city and emanated from the stone of its buildings and its

132

dry, cracked soil, was here reduced only to a fragrance stealing from night-flowers and a vapour hovering over the lawn, which latter had been well watered all day and now was cool and deep and very green.

It seemed to Vishnu that there was a dreadful expectancy in the air. He sat down in the third chair, which had stood ready and waiting, while Sumi looked at him with large sad eyes. He tried to be gay: 'So this is how you spend your time while I am slaving in the office;' but it was received in silence. He stared up into a tree, pretending interest in its foliage.

'It is so nice to see Sumi again after such a long time,' Mala said.

'Yes,' he said, 'very nice.' Sumi continued to look sad. He forced a laugh: 'Only she is so quiet – this is not the Sumi we know at all.'

'What is there always to talk and laugh,' Mala said. 'Of course, she is growing up now.'

'Yes,' Vishnu said. Sumi looked down into her lap.

'And soon her family will find someone for her to marry, and then she will see that there is not much to laugh at in the world.' Mala was wearing a white sari which glimmered in the dusk, and her eyes shone like jewels. Vishnu could smell her scent, which was so familiar to him – that mixture of hair-oil and attar and Mala. She sat there, large and calm, with her bosom draped in white gently moving as she breathed. He wished they were alone. But Sumi was looking at him with demanding eyes, so he jumped up and cried: 'Look, what a beautiful butterfly!' It fluttered in the flowerbed; like a shred of tissue caught in a breeze.

Sumi also got up and stood beside him. She sighed: 'It is so lovely.' Vishnu moved back and stood behind Mala's chair and looked down at the nape of her neck. It was strong and shapely and covered with a fine down of hair which he knew reached down right into her back; he had often followed its path down her spine with his lips and longed to do so now.

'How fine it must feel to be a butterfly and have wings and fly wherever you want,' Sumi said.

'Birds also have wings,' Mala said, 'and can fly.' Vishnu wanted to laugh. He put his hand under her sari and pinched her upper arm, his fingers sinking luxuriously into her soft flesh. She gave a tiny cry but stifled it immediately and sat quite still.

'Only human beings are heavy with sorrow and can't fly from the earth to which they are bound,' said Sumi. Vishnu bent lower over Mala's chair and smelt her warm hair; his fingers were still on her arm, pinching it, while she continued to sit rigid and careful not to give a sign. 'If only we too,' said Sumi, 'could fly away in company with those we love.' Go home, Vishnu silently told her, but it was some time before she did.

Mala served him his food, she stood and watched him eat, and when he had finished she brought water for him to wash. She was calm and silent, and he watched her walking away from him, carrying the finger-bowl in which he had just washed his hands. He looked at her large hips springing out from a small firm waist and her swaying buttocks with the sari clinging to them in silken sculptured folds. He smiled and got up and stretched himself and then he said: 'Today you are behaving like a model Indian wife.'

She turned her face over her shoulder to look back at him. She looked so puzzled that he laughed. 'I think you are trying to make up to me,' he teased her. She continued to look puzzled: she had never responded to any kind of teasing. Then he saw the expression on her face change, she was frowning and he realized that she was remembering something (how well he knew every look of hers, and what it portended! he was always aware of what she was going to say long before she said it).

She said: 'Why did you pinch me today? If she had noticed, how bad it would have – ' He walked up to her and gave in to temptation and began to fondle her luscious buttocks. 'Please,' she begged, 'someone might see us, one of the servants – ' She was still holding the finger-bowl.

For answer he now used both his hands, one remaining where it was, the other exploring her breasts. She did not move but stood there with the finger-bowl. He pressed close against her; they were both breathing hard and short. Then they heard Gulzari Lal's voice outside, calling Vishnu. Mala looked up into his face with panic-stricken eyes, but she could not move away from him. He took the finger-bowl from her and set it on the sideboard. 'Vishnu!' called Gulzari Lal. He held her hand and, one finger on his lips, tiptoed with her hurriedly to their bedroom. 'Vishnu, are you there?' But the door was already locked behind them, and he pushed her on to the bed and fell on top of her, where she lay warm and waiting.

It was a long time before they were spent, and then he lay naked against her naked, his face pressed into her and enjoying her smell. She lay on her back, breathing softly, and he smelt her and tasted her with wet, satisfied lips. He thought of the first year of their marriage and what a wonder and delight she had been to him then; and for the moment she became such a wonder and delight again. And perhaps it was even better now, for she had spread out in the most womanly way possible and her flesh, having lost its girlish firmness, was now soft and yielding and receiving.

He murmured to her, full of bliss: 'Shall we go away?'

'To Bombay,' she murmured back.

'No, not to Bombay.'

'Please,' she begged and drew a loving finger over his naked shoulders.

He shut his eyes and tasted her again with his lips. Wanting only to lie still and drown in her, it was some time before he felt like talking again. 'No, not to Bombay – ' Then he told her, briefly and in short disconnected sentences, with his face still pressed into her, about Joginder and his factory at Chandnipat.

'Chandnipat,' she said.

'It will be very dull and there will be nobody.'

But she was smiling. She thought of the three of them, he and she and Pritti, in a dull place. There would be nowhere for him to go and he would have to be with her and they would lie like this every day and all night.

'And the house we shall live in will be nothing like this. No comforts, nothing.' But she was hardly listening, thinking only of how completely she would possess him there.

'And you will be very lonely.' At which she laughed, but she did not say anything. He passed his hand over her womb and said, almost shyly: 'Perhaps you will have another child,' murmuring into her flesh.

'Perhaps,' she said. And that prospect too held joy even though she had suffered terribly with Pritti, swelling up monstrously so that she could hardly walk, and at the end she had been in labour for three days and nights. 'If you want,' she said and laid her large shapely hand on his as it stroked her womb.

Sarla Devi heard loud voices from downstairs and, peering over the parapet, saw Brij Mohan having a quarrel with Tara and her old woman. He was using some very strong expressions, so that she thought it best to go down and see what she could do to settle the quarrel.

He was sitting on a mat spread on the veranda, eating a meal which his servant had brought for him and cursing the two women between mouthfuls. When he saw Sarla Devi, he waved his free hand in the air and called: 'You go back upstairs, there is no need of your social service here!'

135

'The curses he has given us,' the old woman complained to Sarla Devi. 'And what for? If we have erred and are to blame, we are ready to beg pardon – but what is our fault?' Tara, in yellow georgette, stood chewing a betel-leaf, waiting for matters to take their course.

'Why do you shout at them like that?' Sarla Devi demanded. 'I heard you from upstairs. And the words you used – '

'These ladies have heard plenty of words like those before, don't worry.' He shouted for his servant who came, thin, coughing and tattered, bearing more hot chapattis on a plate.

'He is angry for nothing,' the old woman said. 'This girl has come to him, with such love, and now see how unhappy she is at the treatment he is giving her.' Tara shifted her betel-leaf from one corner of her mouth to the other, sucking its juices with relish.

'You can be at least polite with her,' Sarla Devi remonstrated.

He got so angry that he choked over his food and grew very flushed in the face. 'Careful, Sahibji,' his servant warned him, 'it is dangerous to get warm while eating.'

'With both hands they take my money and then also for that I have to be polite to them! Get out!' he shouted at them. 'Go find someone else and suck the juices out of his body!'

'What do we ever ask for?' wheedled the old woman. 'A little sari here and a little blouse-piece there – we don't ask for costly jewellery, for lakhs of rupees in cash – '

'Everything I have had to give you have taken. There is nothing left now, so you can go.'

The servant, solicitously waving flies off Brij Mohan's food, muttering indignantly: 'Sari and blouse-piece!'

'It is only for love of you that this girl comes here. The offers she has had! A fine girl like that, naturally.' She lifted Tara's plump arm and fingered it appreciatively. 'There is one Chaudhuri from Rohtak who has promised her a house with garden and in the garden there are many peacocks – '

Brij Mohan dabbled his fingers in his water-glass to wash them and flicked off the drops in the old woman's direction: 'Then you had better take her there, for you have nothing more coming here.'

'Sari and blouse-piece!' muttered the servant. 'First it is my turn for new shirt and dhoti, look at what I run around in doing my work,' and he lifted the ends of his truly tattered shirt for all to see.

'Now this one has started!' cried Brij Mohan.

'If he will only be a little kind to her,' the old woman said, 'that is all she wants, a little kindness.' She made kissing sounds at Tara and stroked her cheek pityingly. 'If he likes to give her a little present now and again – of course, we poor people must also live – but what she treasures most from him is love and kindness. I am going now,' she told Sarla Devi, 'and I will leave her here with him.'

'I don't want her,' Brij Mohan cried. 'Take her away!'

'She can stay with me,' Sarla Devi said.

The old woman lost no time in hurrying away. Tara looked sullen and stared straight in front of her, with her jaws working over her betel-leaf.

Brij Mohan continued sitting on his mat. 'If you are so fond of her, then take her with you upstairs.'

'After all this time you can't suddenly say to the girl get out, I am finished with you. She is not an old pair of shoes to be thrown away.'

'Only money money, presents and money, that is all she wants from me.'

'Unfortunately that is the way she has to earn her living.'

Brij Mohan looked gloomy and said: 'It is quite true: love cannot be bought.'

'But what do you want from her? She is ready for all your pleasures. She will sing for you when you want her to, she pours your drinks for you, she serves you, she lies on her back for you – '

'*Chi!*' Brij Mohan rebuked her, ill-pleased to have his sister so well informed.

'What more is there you want?'

'There is more, much more.' And he sighed, thinking of Kusum in her snug little home.

And it was at just that moment that Kusum herself could be seen coming in through the gate, fresh in white voile and under a gay parasol.

Brij Mohan jumped up. He hurried to meet her. 'What an honour, what a pleasure.' He was perspiring with joy and embarrassment. He tried to draw her aside, away from the veranda where Sarla Devi and Tara were. But she made straight for them.

'It is your sister that I have come to – '

'This is my sister.'

Kusum laughed gaily. 'We are old friends.' And she embraced Sarla Devi. Brij Mohan was very much surprised, but while Kusum had her back to him, he took the opportunity to wave Tara away inside. Tara did not see him, she was busy looking at the visitor. But Sarla Devi did. She disengaged herself from Kusum's embrace and took Tara by the hand, drawing her forward into their circle.

Kusum took it very well. She even graciously nodded her head at Tara. Then she smiled, clasped her hands and looked out into the tangled garden and its bits of broken masonry with as much pleasure as if it had been a charmingly laid-out park.

Brij Mohan straightened the collar of his shirt in an attempt to give himself a smarter appearance. He clapped his hands for the servant – 'Bring chairs!' he shouted grandiosely, though he knew there were only two in the house, one of which was broken.

'What need?' Kusum said and settled herself all free and easy on the mat. 'It is good to be sitting here with you.' She patted the place next to her for Sarla Devi to sit down: 'There is so much for us to talk.'

'About Bundi Busti?' Sarla Devi said eagerly.

'That also – '

'Bundi Busti?' said Brij Mohan.

Kusum, calm and smiling, laid her hand on Sarla Devi's: 'Our concern for Bundi Busti is only one of the ties that bind us so closely.' Then she said: 'I am sure we shall learn to understand and love each other.'

'Why not,' Sarla Devi said with absentminded politeness.

'Let me be bold and say I love you already!'

'Ah!' cried Brij Mohan.

Sarla Devi looked at him in amazement, which irritated him. 'Say something,' he told her. 'She has come to you with such heart, such generosity – '

'No!' cried Kusum. 'First I must prove myself worthy of her love!'

'And you sit there like a piece of wood.' And then his eyes fell on Tara, who sat like another piece of wood, her legs drawn up and her back supported against the wall. 'Who asked you to be here and listen to the talk of these ladies? Shameless! Inside at once!' he shouted, shooting out an imperious forefinger.

'She is doing no one harm!' Sarla Devi cried. 'Sit down!' she shouted at Tara who had obediently risen.

Kusum was soothing, gentle: 'Let the girl go. These are family matters we are discussing, there is no need for any outsider.'

'What family matters?'

Brij Mohan gave a shout of impatience. Kusum smoothed her sari in her lap.

Sarla Devi said: 'You have come to talk about Bundi Busti – '

'Bundi Busti!' cried Brij Mohan. 'Your head has become upside down with all these Bundi Bustis of yours, so when people come and talk with you on important business, all you can think of is Bundi Busti, Bundi Busti!' He panted with annoyance and his jowels quivered.

'Not like that,' said Kusum. 'Out of anger no good talk can come.

We are a brother and two sisters, we must be patient and loving with each other.'

'What does she care for brothers and sisters? She cares for nothing except these wretched fellows who come here and join their hands before her and say you are our mother and our father – then oh yes, then she has heart, then she runs here and there for them in the hot sun, then no work is too much.'

'She is so good and noble,' said Kusum, 'we must all take our lesson from her.'

'Don't flatter her! You don't know her, how she is, what a trouble to live with ... Just see, you have come here today in such friendliness, to talk with her about the things between us, and all she does is fill our heads with talk of Bundi Busti – and as if that were not enough, she also drags forward this girl' – he snapped his fingers towards Tara, roaring at her in parenthesis: 'Why are you still here?'

Kusum lowered her eyes and looked down at her hands meekly folded in her lap. 'Perhaps she doesn't even know what I have come to talk with her.'

'For how long I have been telling her that this lady wishes to come and meet you, and now that the meeting is arranged, what does she do? What do you do?' he shouted at Sarla Devi.

'But when did you tell me that she wishes to come and meet me?'

He struck his forehead and cried: 'It is her ambition to make me as mad as she is herself!'

Kusum squeezed Sarla Devi's hand: 'It is quite true – for a long time I have been asking him to arrange a meeting between us two.'

'And every day I have been telling her!' Brij Mohan shouted. 'Ever since there was first talk of this divorce – '

But now the word was out, Kusum tried to cover it up again. 'I had this longing to meet you. I can't tell you how I ached to be with you and talk with you – '

Sarla Devi had understood. She withdrew her hand from under Kusum's caressing one. 'I don't know why you are all so worried about the divorce. It is not important at all.'

'Of course not!' cried Kusum. 'It is a very ordinary matter, why should anyone worry about it? This is exactly my attitude also.' There was a dubious look on Brij Mohan's face, so she carried on quickly, concentrating only on Sarla Devi: 'We are living in modern times, divorce now with us is only something legal, it is nothing more really than signing some kind of agreement, for instance the lease of a house – '

'Yes yes,' said Sarla Devi, not interested at all.

'And in any case,' cried Kusum, her voice rising, 'it is not something that can ever come between two people like us whose hearts are open to each other and for whom there is more in life than only selfish worldly interests.' Her arm round Sarla Devi, she looked at Brij Mohan with what might have been construed as a challenge and which, at any rate, he dared not meet. Instead he turned on Tara, still hovering in the door, to roar at her: 'But how many times must I tell you to take yourself off!'

'Sh,' said Kusum, soothing, tolerant, 'that is not the way to talk with the girl. Even humble people and others not of our class must be treated with respect, otherwise how can we expect to have any respect shown to ourselves. Go, child,' she said, turning graciously to Tara who went at once, with a jingle of jewellery and her hips swaying in yellow georgette.

'One must know how to talk with these kind of people,' Kusum said, 'then also one can get some influence over their character and lead them into a better life.' And she looked at Sarla Devi for approval of these sentiments, and to make sure that they were entirely on the same side. Sarla Devi was really, she thought, a very easy person to get along with; one only had to know how.

Vishnu did not go into details with his father. He only asked him whether he could have some capital to start on a scheme of his own; and Gulzari Lal, embarrassed, a little afraid, but concerned only with doing right by his son and making him happy, committed himself to an uneasy affirmative. Vishnu lingered for a while, wishing he could tell his father more and reassure him. 'It is a small factory,' he said, 'a very sound scheme.' Gulzari Lal nodded; there was a multitude of objections he could have brought up – what did Vishnu know about factories? – but he carefully refrained. He wanted to show himself the most tolerant of fathers. And was this not how he had started off himself? By taking his share of capital from his father and venturing out on his own? But he was not happy, even when he reflected on that precedent. He had worked, he was working, he told himself, only for Vishnu; and everything that Gulzari Lal had built up was there for Vishnu to take and enjoy. He felt some pity for himself when he compared himself to other men – the well-off businessmen who came to his parties and whom he met drinking at the club – men like Tek Chand of Tek Hosieries, R. K. Anand of Raj Motors, P. Nanda of the Britannia Trading Corporation: men who had built up firms and not inconsiderable fortunes like himself and now had the pleasure of seeing their families reaping the fruits. And like the sons of those men,

Vishnu too had everything he could wish for – a beautiful wife and child, a car, a houseful of servants, a bank account of his own, a place in the office. What else was there in a man's life, Gulzari Lal tried to persuade himself, what further need was there of ambition?

His interview with his father filled Vishnu with new energy, and the next day he and Joginder took the first of their trips to Chandnipat. It was a long clear drive out on the Grand Trunk Road and, once they had left the city behind them, Vishnu pressed his foot on the accelerator and they went speeding through the dust-laden landscape, only slowing down, every now and again, for a creaking series of bullock-carts or for camels, their humps loaded with cauliflowers, lifting dainty feet over the stony ground. Joginder sat leaning his elbow on the window, with the wind blowing up his hair; they hardly talked at all – Vishnu smoked cigarettes and Joginder chewed betel, spitting the juice out of the window in silent satisfaction.

The land where Joginder's plot was did not at first sight look very promising. It had been earmarked for industrial expansion but there was as yet not much industry nor much expansion. Washermen had hung up an army of wet clothes and some little girls were playing on a homemade swing fixed in the branches of a margosa tree. Two of them perched squealing on the seat, while two others pushed and a puppy dashed to and fro barking shrilly and attempting to snap at their ankles. But a bit farther up there was already a scattering of small sheds with corrugated-iron roofs and a little factory with a chimney out of which came tufts of black smoke and a smell of burning rubber. Some more building work had started and workmen and their women walked waist-high in the earth, while loads of bricks were tipped and stacked from lorries. Joginder and Vishnu stood at the edge of the land, surveying it like two pioneers with visions of what was to come; while the girls in the tree halted their swing and stared at them and giggled, and the puppy barked at them.

They made their way back into the bazaar, past the very new cinema-house which stood by itself in a waste of empty ground. The bazaar was dense and crowded. A stretch of unpaved, deeply-trodden road wound narrowly between booths that were spilling over with merchandise. Behind the booths could be glimpsed crumbling brick houses with carved pillars and arched doorways and courtyards littered with straw and livestock and discarded boxes and bits of machinery. There were also two little mosques, white and delicate with latticed arches and gilded minarets; but though the booths of the bazaar ran pell-mell up their steps, the mosques themselves were desolate, their forecourts overgrown with grass and haunted by ownerless

141

bullocks and children playing hide-and-seek. But the Hindu and Sikh temples, facing each other at one end of the bazaar, were thick with bells and cymbals and incense and overblown flowers, and pregnant women went in with their babies and offerings, and begging ascetics chanted and beat sticks on tins. Rearing over the bazaar, taller than anything in the town, was a brand-new clock tower of brand-new red brick.

They sat at a cracked wooden table outside an eating-stall called the Palm Hotel and ate food swimming in ghee which ran agreeably down their fingers; their palates burnt with spices and they drank great quantities of sweet brownish water. 'From Delhi?' the proprietor asked them. 'A lot of people,' he said, stirring in his blackened cauldron, 'came down from Delhi these days: there were plans to build factories.' Joginder nodded and picked food out of his back teeth. Vishnu watched a customer in the booth opposite which sold plaster busts of saints and gods and politicians; the customer scratched his head and was unable to decide between a pink-cheeked Gandhiji with little gold spectacles and a pink-cheeked Krishna playing on a flute. The owner of the shop urged the beauty of both of them in turn, while passers-by stopped and gave their opinion.

A textile mill was to be built, said the proprietor of the Palm Hotel, a very big scheme; Joginder gave a grunt of interest; and other schemes also, said the proprietor: a bicycle factory, a tyre manufacturing concern, an ice-plant – all very big schemes and very big people were coming. 'Just see,' exclaimed the owner of the booth opposite, holding up Gandhiji, 'how he is smiling, like a real person!' And the spectators said: 'Exactly like a real person! And how healthy he looks!' Thank God, said the proprietor of the Palm Hotel, business was good with all these people coming (and where else could they eat as well as at the Palm Hotel?) and now more would come and business would be, please God, even better.

It was a small and undistinguished little town, which had been there during the time of the Moghuls and during that of the British. Once it had had a fair proportion of Muslims, but in '47 there had been a massacre and now there were no more Muslims left. There were not many of the original Hindus left either: most of the present inhabitants had come pouring in from other towns and villages where there had been other massacres and their own relatives and neighbours killed by Muslims. But no one seemed to remember about that: they lived here now, and it was as if they had always been here. Now they were to have a textile mill and a bicycle factory; the town would grow and expand and they would all do well. Everything looked hopeful.

And Vishnu too was hopeful. He thought of how he would live here. He would work in the factory all day and only at night he would go to eat and sleep in some rented little brick house. Just a room to sleep in and a courtyard to cook in. At night sometimes he and Joginder would stroll through the bazaar and see what was going on and perhaps eat a meal at the Palm Hotel. When there was a new film showing at the new cinema, they would go and see it, sitting in the best seats at the back and crunching peanuts. It seemed a good life to him, and he could not at this stage think of anything he might miss in it. He remembered briefly how he had promised Mala that he would be taking her and Pritti with him. But that had been just talking: Chandnipat was no place for them. They could stay with his father in Delhi, and he would go to see them several times a month, or whenever he found the time. Though of course – he thought with satisfaction of those powerful days ahead – there would not be much time.

One morning Brij Mohan really threw out Tara and her old woman. He shouted and cursed and when they saw that he was serious and it was finished, they shouted and cursed back. He drove them out of the house, hurling imprecations at them as he stood on the steps of his veranda, while they answered him back from a safe distance out on the road. All the people living in the quarters at the back rushed out to listen and so did the cobbler who sat under a tree across the road, and passers-by stopped, so that there was quite a crowd. Brij Mohan was too angry to care. He kept on shouting at the top of his voice while the old woman took advantage of the audience to appeal to their feelings: 'Such a beautiful girl, and see how he has taken her youth and her innocence!' The spectators, however, refused to commit themselves to either side; they only stood by and appeared vastly entertained. Brij Mohan's servant appeared from behind him; he said, 'Sahibji, why do you excite yourself for such rubbish,' but Brij Mohan, swollen and purple with fury, pushed him aside. 'Get out, you prostitutes!' the servant shouted in a weak voice over Brij Mohan's shoulder, and for answer Tara picked a handful of stones from the road and flung them in the direction of the veranda. Promptly Brij Mohan scooped up stones from his garden and threw them back at her, roaring with each one: 'I'll show you, you — , I'll soon teach you, you — !' At this moment Sarla Devi appeared on the roof, leaning her dishevelled head over the parapet: 'My God,' she cried at Brij Mohan, 'have you gone out of your mind?'

'There is another one!' Tara screeched, pointing up to the roof so that everyone now looked in that direction. 'She is another fine one, that one!' and she shook her fist at Sarla Devi and the old woman too shook her fist.

'Go home,' Sarla Devi exhorted them from above, 'don't listen to him!'

Tara let loose a furious volley of indecencies at her. She used language so pungent, and with such practised fluency, that the spectators shook their heads and laughed, enjoying themselves but a little shamefaced to be hearing such words. Brij Mohan rushed down the path and both fists raised, advanced on the two women; they promptly fled before him, but even in running Tara carried on with her invective while the old woman encouraged her and, though somewhat short-breathed, joined in with some contributions of her own. Brij Mohan pursued them for a little way down the road, then turned and charged at the spectators: 'Is this a public show that you should be standing here with your necks out!'

'Come in,' cried Sarla Devi from above, 'you have done enough!'

The spectators shuffled slowly apart, reluctant to leave in case there was any more to come. Some of them tried to get on the right side of Brij Mohan: 'Very bad women, Sahib,' they said, and the cobbler shouted from across the street: 'We have seen their sort before!'

Brij Mohan walked back into his house and paced up and down his room. His servant stayed with him, making ostentatious tidying actions such as hanging up a shirt on the clothes-hook and straightening shoes under the bed; all the while cursing Tara and the old woman and assuring Brij Mohan what a good brave thing he had done in throwing them out. Brij Mohan hardly noticed he was there. Sarla Devi did not come down which was fortunate, for Brij Mohan was in no mood to listen to her reproaches. 'Siding with prostitutes against her own brother,' he muttered to himself; and it seemed to him so terrible that his own sister should be against him that his thoughts were full of bitterness and soon even tears came into his eyes. And once he felt his tears flowing, the full impact of his tragic situation struck him, so that they flowed faster and he sat down on the bed with his head in his hands. The servant was still talking: 'Sahib,' he said, 'I know my place, I don't speak, I don't hear, but I could tell you some things about those two –' Brij Mohan took a shoe and threw it in the direction of the servant, who picked it up and put it back into its proper place, telling himself as he did so: 'Sahibji is angry, those two jackals have made him angry.'

Brij Mohan, sitting on the bed, poured himself a drink but it failed to cheer him up. He felt a deep need at this stage for some sympathetic heart and he knew only one such; and so it was not long before he was knocking at Kusum's door: She was having her after-noon nap but did not at all mind, she said, being disturbed. She was rosy and dishevelled, and she looked so warm, so plump, so desirable that Brij Mohan could not help imagining to himself the perfect bliss of waking up with her in the same bed. But his respectful demeanour showed nothing of these disrespectful thoughts, and he even delicately averted his eyes while she adjusted her sari and fiddled with her hair.

'It is not that I feel very tired,' Kusum was saying, 'but I think we are all getting a bit old, that is why we need these afternoon naps.' She fixed the last hairpin and gave the lie to her remark with a gay young laugh.

He prepared at once to be gallant and was beginning to tell her how much more attractive she still was than all these young girls; but at young girls he stopped short, and he hung his head, and then he told her in a hoarse, ashamed voice: 'I have sent her away.'

She recoiled from him in horror. 'Sent her away? Your sister?'

'No no – ' He told her about Tara, and she was first relieved, then approving and finally sympathetic. 'You have done right,' she said.

'It is you who have taught me to do right,' he replied. She looked at him with her kindest eyes; she glowed with feminine understanding, so that he was moved to unburden himself:

'My life has not been a happy one. My marriage –' It was years since he had thought of his marriage; and indeed it had been such a short and untried affair that it was hardly worth much thought. But now he was choked with emotion. 'I have had to make do with the company of low women,' he whispered in confession. 'What pleasure could there be for me with such people? It is only since I have enjoyed your friendship,' he said, shifting his chair closer, 'that there has been hope for me again. In what words can I describe the peace and hap-piness that come to me when I sit in this little home of yours?'

Kusum suddenly seized his hand and cried: 'And how much more happiness will there be for you when I am living in a large and beauti-ful home!'

He saw the catch and fell silent.

Now she seized his other hand and held them both: 'Just think, how much more fittingly I will be able to entertain my dear friends when once I am there as wife in my rightful place. How we shall enjoy each other's company in that beautiful drawing-room with so many ser-vants to wait on us and everything the heart can desire.' And carried away by her own vision, she squeezed his unresponsive hands and cried: 'Am I not your own sister, and where can you be happier than in your own sister's home?' At that she felt him weakening, and she redoubled her fervour, crying: 'It will be just like the old days for you again – you will see how nice I will make everything for you!' so that it seemed as if she was prepared to marry Gulzari Lal only for Brij Mohan's sake.

Sumi was very excited. She smiled and her eyes danced; she ran around the house with Pritti and both of them shouted in shrill voices. And afterwards, when Pritti had been taken away by the ayah, Sumi sat with Mala in the little room with the stag's head and the bust of Byron, and she fidgeted, smiled, hummed, admired Mala's sewing and obviously had something on her mind. But Mala, never very sensitive to such outward manifestations, did not ask what it was, so that Sumi had finally to come out with it herself. 'They have found someone,' she said in a low voice, her head bent shyly.

Mala stopped sewing: 'A bridegroom?'

Sumi giggled and buried her face in her hands.

'Oh, Sumi,' said Mala. She was too large and lethargic to show her appreciation in any more energetic way, but she spoke with great warmth.

'They have sent for me,' giggled Sumi from behind her hands.

'Then you are going away?'

'How I shall miss you all.' She managed to look and probably even feel unhappy, but only for a moment.

'We shall miss you also,' said Mala, slow and measured. She reflected for a moment: it was true, she would miss Sumi. Yet she was not as sad as she might have been if she had not had a change of her own to look forward to: and at the thought of that she glowed, and she felt tempted to tell Sumi, about how she and Vishnu were going away together to live in a dull place.

Though she refrained from telling Sumi, she could not resist confiding in Kusum; and Kusum, always ready to enter another's mood, was all enthusiasm. 'We shall be alone,' Mala said, 'only he and I and Pritti;' and Kusum kissed her and said: 'It will be so beautiful for you.' They rejoiced together for a while, till Kusum said in a soft inquiry: 'And your father-in-law?'

Mala had a shock. She had not thought about Gulzari Lal in this context up till now – not so much out of selfishness but because it was difficult for her to take in more than one aspect at a time. Now that another had been brought to her notice, she looked at Kusum in dismay: 'You think he won't like us to go?'

'He will be very lonely without you all,' Kusum gravely suggested.

146

Mala bit her lip and engaged in painful thought; which after a while evidently brought forth some hopeful result, for her face lit up again and she said: 'But you will be there with him.'

Kusum smiled, sadly. 'Ah, child, who am I to take the place of you all?'

'But he is so fond of you, and now that there will be divorce ...' She stopped, not quite sure whether this could be talked about. Kusum gave her no help, only modestly lowered her eyes.

'Oh, auntie,' Mala cried, 'what shall we do if he won't let us go!'

'It is a very difficult situation.'

'But with you here – ' Mala pleaded. Kusum shook her head with a sad, gentle smile to denote her own insufficiency. 'You have so much influence with him – ' Mala knew what she wanted to say but did not know in what tactful words to say it; and this put her into greater distress. She joined her hands in supplication and her beautiful eyes shone with tears: 'If you will only talk with him and tell him – '

And Kusum became all softness. She kissed Mala, she cupped her face in loving hands: 'Sweetheart, what would I not do only for your happiness.' Mala's tears fell gratefully on to her hands. 'Leave him to me, child,' she said with resolution. 'What can be done will be done.' She gave another sigh, emphasizing the difficulty of the task before her; but even as she sighed, there was a pleased little look which she could not quite efface.

There was a restlessness in Bundi Busti. Women were outside their huts, making up careful little bundles, and the children leapt about in a special kind of excitement. The men sat gathered under trees or drank tea on credit outside the banya's shop.

Ramchander was not in his hut, where Sarla Devi went looking for him. 'God knows where he is eating up his time,' said his wife, but with a kind of wifely complacency. She was wearing a new sari of flowered cotton and some coloured bangles which also seemed to be new, for she kept giving them the same critical and pleased attention she gave her sari. Her neighbour was grimly tying bundles with rope and Sarla Devi looked at her and asked: 'Why are you doing this, sister?' But the neighbour tossed her head and turned her back.

'Don't mind her,' Ramchander's wife said sweetly. 'She is a very black-tempered woman.'

The neighbour spun round. She glared at Ramchander's wife and at the new sari and the new bangles; then she spat.

'Should I send for him?' Ramchander's wife asked Sarla Devi, in the same sweet voice as before. She ran her hand up her arm and gave a pleasant glassy clink to her bangles.

The neighbour went back to her tying. She pulled viciously at the rope, muttering: 'We have a fine lot of men.'

'What is it?' Sarla Devi asked.

'To let themselves be kicked out like dogs, after fifteen years – '

'Don't listen to her,' urged Ramchander's wife. 'We are poor people, we must do what others tell us.'

'Your man opened his mouth wide enough before!' shouted the neighbour. 'Now what have they stuffed in it that he has kept so quiet?'

Ramchander's mother, scenting a quarrel, came crawling out of the hut. Some other women also gathered round and stared silently at Ramchander's wife and the new sari and bangles.

Ramchander's wife cried: 'Perhaps he hasn't got a family to think of that he should let himself be locked up in jail and beaten by the police!'

'My son is a good son,' said the old woman. 'He will look after his old mother and see to it that she gets her food.'

'It is not the police who have shut his mouth for him,' said the neighbour.

'And it was with something sweeter than beatings!' one of the other women shouted.

Suddenly they were all shouting. Sarla Devi walked away, but she could still hear their voices for some time. She found Ramchander drinking tea outside the banya's shop. He was not pleased to see her; he put down his metal tumbler and reluctantly joined her.

'So you are going,' she said.

He shrugged and looked surly. 'What else is there for us to do.'

She knew that whatever she might say would sound accusing, so she said nothing. But he began sullenly to defend himself: 'What could I do by myself? No one cared – you saw how they didn't care, you saw it yourself that day I called a meeting under the tree.'

'Yes,' Sarla Devi said, but she did not trust herself to say any more and began to walk away from him. He followed her. 'Perhaps they are right,' he said. 'Who are we to stand up against all those people?' She walked on, avoiding children tumbling in the mud. 'It is a good place they are sending us to,' he said. He kicked at the cracked poor earth and said: 'There is nothing so wonderful about this place that we should fight for it.'

She assured herself, walking swiftly through rows of huts, that she did not blame him at all. How could she blame him? Whatever sum it was they had offered him, it had been a fortune for him; and he was in no position to resist a fortune.

He was still following her, and now his voice had become anxious. 'I am a poor man, I have a wife and children and a very old mother also to support – ' She would have liked to turn and say something to him; only to show that she did not blame him at all and that no one could blame him. But no words like that came to her and all she did was walk faster, as if she wanted to shake him off; so that soon he gave her up and turned back, saying nothing more to her, and she climbed up the incline by the railway bridge and out on to the main road without looking back again at Bundi Busti.

At home she sat still in her neat little room for a long time. She sat on the floor with her legs crossed and her hands laid lightly and palm upwards on her knees. It got dark and she still sat like that. She had forgotten about Bundi Busti, and about everything else. She did not hear Brij Mohan's step outside, nor his voice calling her. He turned on the light and said: 'Now why is this madwoman sitting in the dark?' His voice and the sudden light shocked her, and the return was so violent and unpleasant that she jumped up and the blood rushed into her head and she felt faint with fury.

'Saving on the electricity is her latest contribution to the poor of India,' Brij Mohan grumbled.

She screamed at him 'Why do you come here?' in an unnatural voice.

'I see,' he said, at once on his dignity. 'This is now the reception that is to be extended to a brother.'

She ran trembling hands through her hair in an effort to control, to soothe herself.

'If you don't wish me to intrude on you, certainly I shall be pleased in future to restrict myself to my own quarters.' He considered the effectiveness of turning on his heel and marching off downstairs again. But he had an important announcement to make to her.

Her hands and voice were still trembling, but she said, 'It is all right'; and then half-apologized, 'I was asleep.'

He allowed himself to be mollified and sat down, wondering how to start on his difficult topic.

But she said 'What do you want?' so he had not much more time left to wonder. He was suddenly embarrassed and looked down at the floor and coughed.

She had quite recovered by this time and was sorry. She realized he had something difficult to tell her and wanted to help him.

149

He cleared his throat. 'Perhaps I was wrong,' he said. 'We must move with the times,' he said and coughed, 'with the times.'

'Are you thinking about the divorce?'

He was not at all pleased. Sometimes she was really unnecessarily acute. But that was what he had been thinking of, and now he had to go on from there: 'What is divorce? It is only a legal term and it has nothing to do nowadays with a family's honour and prestige. These are not at all affected by divorce.'

'No.'

'Don't say no like that,' he said, deeply irritated.

'But I was agreeing with you!'

'It is not your place to agree or disagree with me. You are careless in your thinking, to you all things are the same. But I have reached this conclusion after giving the matter deep thought for many days.' He stood and drew himself up to his full dignity. 'I am now willing,' he said, 'to give my consent to your divorce.'

She looked quite grave, so that he was pleased with the impression he had made.

When Vishnu first heard about Sumi, he cared very little. Girls were always being married off, it was only to be expected. But after a while he thought how it had been before, he and Gautam and Sumi, and the times they had had together. Now all that was finished. He began to grow a little sad; and in the evening he drove to Shankar's house. Mrs Shankar came to the door when she heard his car and looked out at him suspiciously, drying her hands on the end of her sari. She stood stolidly in the doorway till he asked for Gautam, and then she moved reluctantly aside. 'Out there,' she said. 'Talking talking, wasting their time. When she is married, she will find out.' She laughed, as if it gave her pleasure to think of Sumi tied down and overworked as she was.

Shankar sat in a broken old basket-chair, Gautam and Sumi on the grass. Vishnu sat down on the grass, his legs drawn up and his arms round them; he chewed a blade of grass. But there was some constraint.

'It is too long,' Shankar told Vishnu, 'since we have seen you with us.' Vishnu agreed, but carried it no farther. Sumi furiously plucked handfuls of grass, while Gautam lay flat on his back and stared up into the sky.

'It happens like that even among the best of friends,' Shankar said. 'They meet every day, and then circumstances come between them and they no longer meet; even though their feelings for each other remain the same. I had a friend once, such a friend, he was in the railways – '

Sumi suddenly said: 'Did Mala tell you?' She looked up and her face was hot and flushed.

'Yes,' said Vishnu; he glanced at her and was full of regrets and would liked to have said a lot more.

'Now her time has come,' said Shankar, smiling but not quite at ease.

'Lamb to the slaughter,' said Gautam up into the sky.

'Listen to him!' cried Sumi.

Shankar clicked his tongue in gentle disapproval. 'Don't talk like that – it is not like that at all.'

'Then how is it?' Gautam said, indignantly sitting up on the grass. 'Is it in your opinion a custom to be commended that a girl should be tied up by her loving family and handed over to the first comer?'

'No no no no,' said Shankar holding up hands of horror, 'why do you frighten her with such talk!'

'Let him talk!' cried Sumi. 'I have heard his nonsense before!'

'And what is worse,' Gautam said, pointing at her, 'she has been so conditioned by her society that she is even happy to be taken to the slaughter. Look at her,' he cried, 'look at her face, how her eyes are shining – look at the happy lamb!' Sumi put her hands before her face so that no one could look; but her thin little shoulders were shaking with laughter.

'How do you know,' Gautam asked her, 'that they haven't taken out some monster for you to marry? Have you ever seen him? What proof have you that he has even all his arms and legs?'

At this suggestion Sumi burst into laughter so loud and clear that it penetrated to Mrs Shankar indoors who at once looked out of the kitchen window and shouted: 'There is the flour to be sifted!'

Shankar was shocked. 'That is no way to talk. Her parents have all concern for her, they chose with love and care.' He stroked Sumi's head and made soothing affectionate noises at her.

Gautam cried: 'Hasn't she a mind and heart of her own to choose with?'

Sumi folded her arms behind and tucked her legs beneath her. 'Who am I?' she cried. Only Vishnu laughed.

'These are our customs,' Shankar said. Gautam gave a sound of disgust and lay down flat on the grass again.

'He is angry,' said Sumi, tickling his cheeks with a blade of grass.

'He is so impatient,' said Shankar. He smiled: 'Everything must be changed – quick, like this, to fit in with his ideas. But that is not the way things are done in the world.' His mood changed suddenly and he sighed and looked sad and resigned. 'People live the best way they can,' he said.

Gautam abruptly sat up again. 'It is people like you who are the ruin of this country! With you it is always: this is the way things are done, who are we to change them?'

Shankar spread helpless hands. 'All my strength is given to keeping myself and my family alive. I have none left over with which to change the world.' He smiled ruefully: 'I am only a poor man.'

'No man is poor,' said Gautam severely. He got up and paced along the grass in some agitation: 'My God, when I think of all our gifts, all our riches – the sky, the sea, the mountains and the sun – everything is there for us to seize and enjoy, and still people sit in their little corners and moan about how they are poor.' He stood by the mulberry-tree and looked up at it hopefully, but of course its season had long passed. 'As for me, wherever I shall be and whatever I shall do, I shall always be a rich man.'

'A millionaire,' said Sumi. Yet he did not sound or look ridiculous, in spite of his shabby clothes and his cracked dirty feet. He stretched himself luxuriously like a real millionaire, and said: 'Tomorrow I am off.'

'He can run here and there and no worries,' Shankar said – not enviously but, on the contrary, pleased that someone should be free to do this.

'He is going to set up his school on the top of the Himalayas,' Sumi said.

'If there is no place else,' Gautam said, 'I will climb up there, why not?'

'I thought you wanted to go south,' Vishnu said.

'I feel like a little mountain air. I am tired of you plodding people down here in the plains. And just wait – once I get up there and collect my children and teach them the right way to live, they will come swooping down on you like a new breed of men, you will see! They will be strong, free people and they will defeat you all, not with arms and swords – no, we don't believe in such weapons – but only with their laughter and their joy in living.'

'Sumi!' cried Mrs Shankar from indoors. 'Am I to sift the flour myself also?'

'One moment,' Vishnu said, 'don't go,' and he held Sumi's wrist, though he had nothing special to tell her.

'And you?' Gautam asked him. 'I hear you are going in with Joginder.' They stood facing each other now, almost like two adversaries.

152

'I suppose you will become a big captain of industry and make even more money than your father.'

'I will try,' Vishnu said.

Shankar swayed his head in admiration: 'That is the spirit I like to see in a young man.'

The children came running out into the garden, crying: 'Please give us a ride in your car!'

Vishnu and Sumi looked at one another; he was still holding her wrist. Then they turned and went running through the house out to the car, with the children chasing after them. 'Sumi!' cried Mrs Shankar, and Gautam too called 'Wait!' But they flung themselves into the car and as soon as the children were all piled in at the back, they started off. Round and round they went, through those streets of standard Government housing, past the rows of ill-kept and over-crowded clerks' quarters with grim, iron-barred windows.

'So you are going away,' Sumi said.

'And you.' They both laughed, and Vishnu stepped suddenly on the accelerator so that the car hurtled forward and the children fell all over each other and shrieked with joy.

'Do you wish I was coming with you?' Sumi said.

'Of course.' And he did wish it – he thought suddenly how nice it would be to have her with him in Chandnipat, the two of them living in some shabby little place behind the bazaar.

'Play the radio!' cried the children, and he turned it on and a lot of very gay music came out. They arrived for the second time by the cinema poster at which they should have turned back to the house; but again they took the opposite turning.

'You know what I wish?' said Sumi.

'What?'

But she clasped her hands before her face and rocked herself to and fro in her seat. 'No, I feel ashamed.'

Vishnu stopped the car. 'Go on, say it.'

'Don't stop!' cried the children.

'Please go on driving,' Sumi said.

'Not before you – '

'All right, when you go on driving.' He started up again; now she was overcome with giggling. The children all leant out of the window and waved and hooted triumphantly at other children passed on the way.

'What I wish is that the boy my parents have chosen – '

'Yes?' They had come to the cinema poster again, and again Vishnu took the other turning.

'As if you don't know!'

'Know what?' Oh what fun, he thought, what fun the two of them could have had together in Chandnipat.

'All right,' she said. She composed herself and then she turned sideways and looked at him quite seriously: 'I hope my parents have chosen someone exactly like you.' She shut her eyes and, to her own and his surprise, when she opened them again tears came out.

'Oh no,' he said. 'He will be much nicer.'

She shook her head so vigorously that she splashed tears around.

'Oh yes he will,' said Vishnu. 'He will be very interesting. Remember he will have no arms – '

'Or legs,' said Sumi, wiping her eyes. They came to the cinema poster, and when Vishnu slowed down, the children pleaded 'Once more!' so he went once more by the other turning.

'Of course,' said Gulzari Lal, sounding somewhat pompous in his effort to show himself entirely impartial, 'if the boy wishes to start on his own, it is not my intention to hinder him in any way.'

Kusum applauded him with enthusiasm.

'On the other hand,' said Gulzari Lal, 'I see no reason for him to take his wife and child away with him. That is no place for them to live.' He took off his shoe and wriggled his toes to relax them. It was Sunday afternoon and they had lunched well. Now they were in his bedroom and he was looking forward to a long siesta.

'A wife's place is always by the side of her husband,' Kusum pointed out.

'If he goes into the jungle, he can't expect her to follow him.' He took off his other shoe, sitting on the side of his bed.

She turned on him: 'A good and loving wife will never hang back only on account of her own comfort! Even when there is danger to be faced, she will follow behind gladly.'

Gulzari Lal lay down on his bed. 'These are romantic ideas only. It is nice to dream about such things, but one must also be practical.'

'To be devoted to love and duty is not practical?' There was already a sharp note in her voice. But she checked it at once. She did not want a quarrel, she wanted to show herself all tender. She knelt by the side of the bed and laid her cheek against his hand. 'If you were to go into God knows what forsaken places, do you think I would stop to ask myself is it practical to go with him or not?'

'Come and lie down,' he said in a thick, moved voice.

She unwound herself from her sari and folded it with care. Then she lay beside him, plump and soft in her underskirt and short blouse.

He lovingly squeezed the folds of flesh on her bare midriff. 'Yes,' she said, submitting to this with gentle pleasure, 'love laughs at discomforts.' Her eyes, as she lay there, roved round the familiar room. It was very much a gentleman's room with solid, tall furniture and a smell of leather and after-shaving lotion; everything was scrupulously kept but there was nothing more personal than some silver-backed brushes laid out symmetrically on his dressing-table and a pile of men's magazines by his bedside. And in her thoughts – as she had done over so many years – she furnished it anew: with ruffled curtains blowing in a breeze and a lilac silk bedspread and little white and gold chairs matching a dressing-table that reflected an array of little bottles in its heart-shaped mirror. It was an enticing prospect and one that was now, she thought – with a little access of joy which made her kiss his well-shaved cheek in great affection – closer than it had ever been.

'Of course he will come and see them for weekends,' Gulzari Lal said.

'What sort of a marriage is that where the husband lives for five days in a week in one place and the wife and child in another? *We* would not care for such a marriage;' and she squeezed his hand as they lay there side by side.

He returned the pressure yet heaved a sad sigh.

But as far as she was concerned, the time for sighing and sadness was over. 'It will be soon now!' she cried. 'Only take a little courage!' And then she took it herself and leant across him, holding him with both her arms: 'Let them go,' she said. 'Then it will be only you and I, and what times we shall have together! Soon there will be your divorce – no no,' she cried as she saw a shadow fall, 'there is no going back now!' and she shook him a little by the shoulders. 'It must be so,' she said with such vehemence that he knew at once it really must.

But soon she grew gentle again and lay down by his side, nestling her face against him. 'It is true,' she said softly, 'we are both of us grandparents – yes, perhaps we are not so young any more as we would like to be, but there is still something left in the old bones,' and she giggled and touched him with an intimate gesture which thrilled and delighted him.

'Let them go,' she repeated. 'We shall be young again.' She laughed and he laughed with her. 'And they will come often to be with us, our darling Vishnu and Mala and Pritti, and my sweet children also will come – oh what love there will be in this house!' And she laughed out loud again and then kissed him, and he kissed her back without reserve; never had there been such accord between them.

At that moment they heard loud voices from another bedroom.

155

'They are quarrelling again,' said Kusum, not quite without satisfaction – for did not Mala and Vishnu's quarrelling only emphasize more strongly the perfect harmony that reigned between herself and Gulzari Lal?

Certainly, there was just then little harmony between Mala and Vishnu. Though they had started off well enough, only half an hour earlier. Vishnu, also heavy with his Sunday lunch, had lain down on the bed, quite naked under the fan. The room was dark and cool and he looked forward to a pleasantly restful hour. And Mala settled his pillows for him and lay across the bed, fanning her hand over him to keep away a drowsy fly that was buzzing round the room. She·felt inclined towards a little conversation and took up various topics with him, making remarks which he answered merely with deep sleepy grunts. At last she said, her hand fanning solicitously, 'What have you fixed up about our going away?' Full of food, heat and sleep, his eyes tight shut, his breathing regular, he appeared not to have heard. 'Please let me know as soon as you can,' she continued in a happy way, 'because there is so much to be arranged and also all our packing to do.' He aroused himself sufficiently to say: 'Who told you you are going?'

She stopped fanning. 'You *said* – ' she said in a still, shocked voice.

'Don't be silly.' And he settled back into his restful sleep.

'You *said*!' she wailed. 'You promised. We are going, you said, you and I and Pritti – '

'Let me sleep.'

There was a moment's silence which almost made him hope that he really might be allowed to sleep. But this did not last long.

'Let you sleep!' she screamed, digging her nails into his naked shoulder. 'You want to sleep!'

He sat up; his shoulder was hurting but he tried to be calm and reasonable. 'How can you come there? There is nothing there, no comforts, no house to live in even – '

'You promised.'

'That was only a joke.' He realized at once that it had been the wrong thing to say. Her eyes·opened wide, incredulous with fury. He went on talking rather quickly: 'And it was before I had seen the place. Now I know it won't be possible for you to live there, you would be very unhappy, and also Pritti . . . Of course, I shall come to see you often and perhaps sometimes you will come to visit me there. Papa will bring you in the car and we can all have a picnic – '

'I shall come with you!' she shouted at last, having collected herself

156

sufficiently to be able to speak – a process during which she had heard nothing of what he said.

'It is not possible, I told you – '

'I am coming!'

'I shall be too busy to take on such a burden.' His shoulder was still hurting and, squinting down at it, he saw that it was bleeding. 'My God,' he shouted, 'that is all I need – to have you there!'

'I shall never let you go without me!'

He attempted sarcastic laughter.

'I will throw myself under the wheels of your car when you set off! And Pritti also! You think I'm afraid? I'm not afraid!' And indeed, she did not look at that moment as if she could ever be afraid of anything.

'Stop shouting. Papa and Kusum will hear – '

'Let them hear! I want them to hear! I want everyone to know how you treat your wife!' She rushed to the door and wrenched it open. 'Where are you going?' he cried, but she was already outside. He dashed into the bathroom and seized a towel which he hastily wrapped round himself. He could hear her shouting through all the rooms and went running after her, tucking in his towel.

Kusum too had jumped up from Gulzari Lal's bed and was quickly winding her sari around her. Gulzari Lal was already outside, dressed only in his white leggings and a white undervest, his feet bare. Mala came like a whirlwind and threw herself against him, crying breathlessly: 'Now he says he won't take me!'

'Come back!' Vishnu was shouting, holding up his towel as he ran.

Kusum opened her arms wide for Mala who at once let herself be enfolded, sobbing: 'He won't take me!'

Pritti came running in from the veranda, with her ayah behind her. When she saw the state her mother was in, she too burst into tears.

Mala detached herself from Kusum and snatched up Pritti. She crushed her against herself and kissed her wildly. 'Even she knows, even this little child knows, that her father has no more use for her.' Pritti cried louder.

Vishnu, naked except for his towel and with his shoulder bleeding, felt reproachful eyes on him from all sides: Gulzari Lal, Kusum, even the ayah. For Mala – tall, dishevelled, her eyes brilliant with tears and anger, and holding a weeping child in her arms – presented an appeal which no one could resist: not even Vishnu.

He flung up his hands. He laughed. He said, 'All right, all right, I will take you' – and as soon as he had said it he found himself, to his surprise, not altogether displeased.

Brij Mohan was going to tea with Kusum. He sat on his veranda with a sheet tucked bib-wise round his neck, while a barber shaved him. 'Ah!' cried Brij Mohan when he saw Vishnu walking up the path. He looked at him and smiled under the lather. 'You have come to see the madwoman upstairs?'

Vishnu stopped and watched the barber. He saw that Brij Mohan had already had a haircut – the clippings lay around his chair, and the back of his neck and the space around his ears looked naked and fresh. 'Some lady's virtue must be in danger,' Vishnu said, 'you are making yourself so smart.'

Brij Mohan's shoulders heaved with laughter. 'One moment please, Sahibji,' pleaded the barber, bending forward anxiously with his large, curved razor.

'A young puppy like you still has many tricks to learn from an old dog like me,' Brij Mohan chuckled. The sheet was carefully unwound from his neck and a mirror held in front of his face. He looked into it, turning his jaw this side and that and running a critical hand over the shaved flesh. Then he shouted to his servant to run water for his bath.

'I can see this is going to be a very heavy onslaught,' Vishnu said as he went upstairs to his mother's room. Brij Mohan, in the best of humours, shouted after him: 'The old warrior marches into battle!' He smiled to himself, thinking of Kusum and the gay and cosy times he expected from her. Inside the room his servant was laying out clean clothes; he carried Brij Mohan's shirt, fresh from the washerman, on two carefully extended hands.

Sarla Devi was sitting on the mat in her room. She looked somewhat distraught and all the time Vishnu was telling her about how he was going away and what he was going to do, she kept silent and he could see she was not very interested. So he stopped talking and they sat in silence for a while. He realized then that what he had come for was her love and approval, and he was disappointed that she was showing him neither.

At last she roused herself and said, 'It will be good for you to go there', but it sounded as if she were making an effort to be polite and show interest.

'You have been telling me for so long that I must go away,' he said.

'That's true,' she said, but limply; so that he longed for her to be passionate again with him, the way she had been when she had told him to leave his father and engage in battle on his own. And 'Yes,' she roused herself some more, 'I am glad you are going.' But she did not say it the way he wanted her to.

She was failing him, but he knew that he had also failed her. He began to talk about Bundi Busti. He wanted to explain to her how it had not been his fault; he said how in future he would be on his own and it would be easier for him perhaps to help her over such matters. But she cut him short; she did not seem to be interested in Bundi Busti any more.

'You remember that girl – Tara?' The subject had evidently been on her mind and she went on talking rapidly, as if she expected it to have been on his mind too. 'How can we thrust such people away from us and say, now we have finished with you, go back where you have come from? No, we can't, we must not.'

'But what can you do?'

'Nothing,' she said and kept a sad silence.

'Of course not. Let her go, she has other customers. She doesn't want help from you.' What he really wanted to say was, why think of such people who are nothing to you? Think of me. But he felt too shy and proud; so instead he lowered his head and kicked at the edge of her mat.

'I feel so much for her. It is wrong to forget her.'

He got up to leave. When he was already half-way down the stone stairs, she came to the door and called after him: 'Why are you going so soon?' He did not answer. She leant over the parapet and called, 'It is good that you are going away to this place', in an effort to please him. But he did not look back. Downstairs Brij Mohan's barber was quarrelling with the servant over the sum he had been paid. The servant looked harried, dealing on the one hand with the barber and on the other calling reassuring words to Brij Mohan who, amid a splash of water, was roaring for his towel.

Once back in her room, Sarla Devi did not think long about Vishnu. Later she went out. She went to the red-light district, which was also a grain-market. One side of the street was blocked by a brick wall behind which was a railway line; on the other side were stores and warehouses with clerks inside them, sitting cross-legged on the floor behind big ledgers. On top of the warehouses were long lines of verandas partitioned into segments and with rooms behind them. Outside some of the rooms hung birdcages and flower-pots and others had washing strung up. Little groups of pimps with betel-stained mouths and gold ear-rings stood against the brick wall of the railway line.

Sarla Devi walked through the street, which was not easy for there was a lot of traffic to be avoided. Coolies carrying sacks shouted confused instructions at one another and huge lorries, painted green and yellow, noisily backed towards the warehouses. A cycle rickshaw stopped by the side of the road where she was walking; at the back sat a fat man in a yellow turban, singing drunkenly and waving his hands in the air. A pimp detached himself from his group by the brick wall and approached, cautious and smiling while the others watched.

Sarla Devi looked up, and above the street – remote but seemingly attainable – she saw a sky huge and soft with evening. There was a last, lingering, fading, orange streak on the horizon and flung out against it a flight of silhouetted birds with outstretched wings. She looked down again. She went on walking; she hoped she would be able to find Tara. She knew that, even if she did, Tara and her old woman would be angry with her and probably drive her away. But she had to go to them, she thought, looking up again at the sky, she had to engage – and then perhaps in the end, one day, when she had engaged enough then she could be free.